D0341148

snipe hunt

also by sarah r. shaber

Simon Said

sarah r. shaber

snipe hunt

Thomas Dunne Books

New York

This book is fiction. Names, characters, places, and incidents are imaginary or are used fictitiously. Any resemblance to actual events, locales, or persons, living or dead, is coincidental.

THOMAS DUNNE BOOKS.
An imprint of St. Martin's Press.

ISBN 0-312-25337-0

First Edition: March 2000

10 9 8 7 6 5 4 3 2 1

In Memory of

Elizabeth C. Norfleet

1908–1997

acknowledgments

I want to acknowledge the invaluable assistance of Jerry L. Wilson, Chief of Police of Holden Beach, North Carolina, who graciously allowed me to interview him about police work on the barrier islands. I shamelessly mined the memoirs of John F. Holden, *Holden Beach History,* for background. Betty Cogswell's memories of her life on the coast of South Carolina during World War II suggested a critical plot point. My neighbor Judy Crowell suggested the book's title, which inspired more plot ideas. I first learned about "Franklin's Prophecy" from an article in *The New Republic,* "Prophet and Loss," by Claude-Anne Lopez (January 27, 1997). My heartfelt thanks go to Carolina Crime Writers and the Cameron Park Book Club for their support and encouragement. Of course, I can't forget to thank my family. They are awesome.

snipe hunt

1

"I'M NOT LOOKING AT THE BODY," SIMON SAID.

"You don't have to," Morgan said. "Besides, we don't know if it is a body."

Morgan steered his black Ford F-150 pickup truck onto the high-rise bridge that linked Pearlie Beach to the mainland. The truck camper creaked over Simon's head as they crossed the sound, while a line of brown pelicans flew across the horizon, fishing for breakfast. Docks projected into the sound from both its banks. They were nearly empty; many of the pleasure craft had been taken out of the water for the winter, and the fishing boats had left at dawn, making the most of the last week of fishing season. Later today the fishermen would unload their catch at the wharf at Captain Nance's seafood market, and about four o'clock everyone on the island would wander over and select dinner from the day's catch. Tonight Simon and Morgan would fry up whatever they bought at Captain Nance's on the deck in a cast-iron skillet over a propane stove. Morgan's luscious homemade hushpuppies would cook in hot peanut oil first, seasoning the pan for the fish that would follow. Fortunately the food police were not permitted past Benson, where the barbecue and seafood joints sprang up along NC 421 and lined the road all the way to Wilmington. Simon wished he was back at the beach house wrapped in a blanket on the porch reading and anticipating his dinner right now, instead of setting off on this gruesome errand.

Thanksgiving week was not the most popular time to visit Pearlie Beach, but there was never a bad time. Just driving over the bridge onto the island would lower anyone's blood pressure ten points, any time of year. When Simon's friend and colleague in the History Department of Kenan College, Marcus Clegg, had invited Simon to go with his family to their beach house for Thanksgiving break, Simon had accepted instantly. Then David Morgan, Simon's close friend and an archaeologist for the state of North Carolina, asked him for help with an archaeological impact report nearby. Simon arranged for the two of them to stay in the Clegg cottage while they worked on their project. Marcus, his wife, and their young daughters would join them Wednesday. Thanksgiving Day they would eat an enormous meal and spend the rest of the weekend watching football games, walking on the beach, and reading. Marcus had a fabled paperback book collection that occupied an entire interior wall of the beach house. Simon planned to delve into several Nero Wolfe mysteries he hadn't read yet.

Unfortunately right now Simon and Morgan were driving away from the Clegg cottage. Morgan drove his truck off the bridge onto the mainland and turned onto a side road paved with crushed oyster shells. Ahead of them was a low white cinder-block building with a green roof.

Painted on the side of the building in faded red letters was the legend COASTAL REFRIGERATED TRUCKING, INC. A half dozen cars were parked outside. One was a blue Jeep Cherokee with the seal of the town of Pearlie Beach on both front doors and a blue light on the roof. Morgan pulled into the space next to it.

"I want to finish my cigarette," Morgan said.

"Don't hurry on my account," Simon said.

Morgan took a long drag on his Lucky Strike and flicked the butt out the open truck door.

"Have another," Simon said.

"I'd rather get this over with," Morgan said.

The receptionist inside the building didn't even look up at them as she spoke. She was too busy with a sausage biscuit and the Wilmington newspaper.

"You're early," she said, "but your load's ready to go. It's mostly shrimp. You'll unload at the State Farmer's Market in Raleigh."

"We're not truckers," Simon said. "We're supposed to meet Dale Pearlie and—"

"Oh! You're the guys to look at that thing!" She shuddered. "It's in the back icebox, down the hallway, last door to the left. Just knock. There should be some parkas hanging next to the door. Make sure you wear one. It's cold in there."

In sympathy, or maybe in apprehension, she drew her white cardigan tighter around her body.

"I wish they hadn't brought it here," she said.

"Not much point in sending it anywhere until we figure out just what it is," Simon said. "And this is the closest walk-in refrigerator—"

"Okay, okay," she said. She pointed down the hall. "Down there," she said again, and went back to her newspaper.

Morgan and Simon walked down the narrow hall and stopped in front of a large stainless steel door. They couldn't see anything through the small window fogged up with ice crystals. Several beat-up down parkas hung on hooks next to the door. Each man selected one and put it on. Simon chose the smallest, but still he had to push the sleeves up on his arms. Morgan had some difficulty zipping his over his beer belly.

"Let's do it," Simon said.

Morgan rotated the large wheeled latch on the icebox door, opened it, and the two men went inside.

THE DAY BEFORE, SIMON and Morgan had been sorting happily through the debris scooped up by a dredge belonging to the U.S. Army Corps of Engineers on the sound side of Pearlie Beach. The dredge was a huge ugly monster that looked like a Quonset hut mounted on a barge. It whined like a fire siren and vibrated oddly on the surface of the water. A wide orange flexible pipe exited its engine room and snaked under the water to vacuum up sand and debris from the floor of the sound. The sand was discharged onto the beach to replenish it, but the rest was hauled to the mainland for disposal. Morgan hoped to rescue some evidence from the trash that a large Tuscarora village had once thrived on the shore. He was concerned that most of the village had eroded into the sound and that large-scale dredging would scatter artifacts. So Morgan and Simon sorted and sifted. After hours they only had one Late Woodland period spear point.

"Disappointed?" Simon asked.

"Yes and no. It's true we haven't found my village, but it's good that the dredge isn't destroying a significant site."

Simon had a stabbing pain in his back from bending over and a headache from the bright sun. He stretched, bending backward and twisting to work out the kinks. Looking out across the water, he saw that seamen on the dredge had a log-shaped object caught in their equipment. They were disentangling it on the deck of the ship. Simon pointed it out to Morgan, and for a few minutes the two men were excited, thinking perhaps it was a prehistoric Indian canoe. They stood on the shore, with their hands shading their eyes, watching the crew loading the object onto a dinghy. As the dinghy crossed the short distance from the dredge to the dock where Simon and Morgan stood, the seamen on board the dredge were unusually quiet, and their captain stood watching their progress with his cap in his hand like a mourner in a churchyard. Somehow Simon didn't think the object was a canoe.

The boat tied up at the pier, and a sergeant climbed out.

"We have recovered the damnedest thing," he said. "I have never seen anything like it."

"Let's take a look," Morgan had said.

The object was completely covered with barnacles: tiny, hard, volcano-shaped growths that cement themselves to anything underwater. A colony of black mussels and clumps of lettucelike seaweed clung to it. Despite this the object seemed obviously and distressingly human. Simon and the sergeant watched as Morgan used a small mallet and chisel to chip away the concretions at what appeared to be the head. He carefully exposed the eyehole of an old diving mask.

"Damn," Morgan said.

"You don't suppose there's a person . . ." the sergeant began, then stopped.

"We'd better call the police," Simon said.

SIMON AND MORGAN WENT into the icebox. Dale Pearlie, the mayor-for-life of Pearlie Beach, and the town police chief, Donnie Lee Keck, looked up from their work. They had spent all night chipping years of encrusted ocean growth off the old diving suit with the tools Morgan had lent them. Pearlie put down a dental pick and wiped the perspiration from his forehead. His skin was green in the bad light of the refrigerator. The fluorescent lights in the chilly room popped and buzzed.

"This is the nastiest thing I have ever had to do in my life," Pearlie said.

"You should have let the medical examiner do it," Simon said.

The police chief put down his tools and stretched. He was about forty-five, thin, muscled, and still neat and composed despite the wretched night's work.

"Sure," Keck said. "Just send a big chunk of barnacles and who-knows-what off to the medical examiner and say that we think there might be a human inside it and he, or she, is probably dead, and would he mind letting us know? I don't think that's in his job description. I think we have to find out what it is first, then figure out where to send it. Might be it ought to go to the county landfill, after all."

Simon walked completely around the human shape on the table. Pearlie and Keck had done a good job of peeling off the encrusted layers of barnacles. The old rubber diving suit had a thick mask that enclosed the head like a balaclava. Two round eyeholes were opaque with algae. A circular metal snout covered the nose and mouth area. Two heavy rubber tubes hooked into the mask below the snout and led to a rusted metal and rubber box about the size of a shoe box fastened around the waist. A metal gauge with two knobs intersected with the box and one of the hoses. The feet were shod in weighted shoes. The diver had walked on the bottom, not swum. When Simon poked at the suit, it gave a little, like a flat bicycle tire.

"The equipment's a rebreather," Simon said. "World War II at the latest. Sometimes frogmen used rebreathers instead of those old heavy diving suits with air hoses that led to the surface. Navy divers used them to inspect the hulls of ships and check for mines in harbors. Pressurized air tanks weren't invented yet."

Rebreathers were extremely dangerous. Developed for wartime use, they eliminated the need for divers to stay in contact with an air pump above the surface by circulating pure oxygen through a closed system inside the diver's suit. Unfortunately, at depths greater than thirty-five feet, water pressure forced too much pure oxygen into the bloodstream, causing convulsions, drowning, or arterial embolism. Without knowing another thing about this corpse, Simon though it was likely the diver drowned when he strayed too deep underwater.

Morgan tugged at an object fused to the suit's right side. Then he used what looked like a putty knife to peel it away from the diving suit. He took the object to a sink and cleaned it off, prying its sides apart while he washed it. He shoved his fist inside the opening he had made, expanding the object to its original cylindrical shape.

"It's a rubber bucket," Morgan said. "For collecting stuff underwater."

"Poor bastard," Keck said.

"So," Pearlie said. "Who wants to take off the mask?"

"I'll do it," Keck said.

"I don't mind," Morgan said.

"I mind a lot," Pearlie said. "I'll wait outside."

"I'll keep you company," Simon said.

Outside the icebox door the two men shed their coats, tossed them on the floor, and sat on them with their backs up against the wall.

"I am so damn tired," Pearlie said.

Pearlie was a compact, balding, tanned man pushing sixty who managed Pearlie Beach Realty with his elderly mother, Inez. They either owned, or acted as leasing agents for, most of the resort property on the island. They were wealthy, but they were working people first, spending long days and weekends managing the business. Over many years their investment had weathered bad roads, ferry breakdowns, collapsed bridges, fires, wars, and hurricanes. Simon guessed from Pearlie's demeanor that this was his first corpse.

"You've had a rough night," Simon said.

"You said this guy, if there is a guy, was a navy diver from World War II?" Pearlie said.

"No," Simon said. "I said he could be."

"I had a cousin who was a navy frogman, stationed in Wilmington. He vanished in 1942. I never knew him—I was a toddler at the time. My family assumed he had gone AWOL until the navy told them his gear was missing, too. They never heard from him again, assumed he drowned. None of us have thought of him in years," Pearlie said.

Morgan and Keck came out of the icebox.

"We just slit enough of the suit, right where the mask met it, to see what we could see," Morgan said. "There's a skeleton inside, all right."

Pearlie groaned. "What now?" he asked.

"Call the medical examiner's office," Keck said. "We've done all we can here."

Simon and Morgan drove silently back to the beach house. It was a muggy, hazy morning, but the weather forecast for the rest of the week predicted clear skies and sunny, warm afternoons. Marcus's girls would be able to run barefoot on the beach and chase ghost crabs and dig for tiny multicolored coquina clams.

Pearlie Beach was a small island south and west of Wilmington on the North Carolina coast. It had a town hall, a police department with one chief and two officers, a chapel, a seafood market, a convenience store, a fishing pier, a small apartment building, and about three hundred beach cottages. Every single structure had been built since 1954, when Hurricane Hazel devastated eastern North Carolina, leaving nothing standing on the island. Across the bridge on the mainland, out of the jurisdiction of the conservative Pearlie Beach town council, were a dozen or so restaurants, a water slide, tourist shops, a miniature golf course, a bookstore, an A.B.C. liquor store, two large marinas, and a campground, all of which lined Pearlie Beach Road on both sides until it intersected with NC Highway 17. A few more businesses hugged the banks of the sound, including the

Do Drop Inn, a bar housed in the old ferry building, converted when a drawbridge was built to the mainland in 1956.

The Pearlie Beach Sound was so narrow a strong swimmer could cross it easily. As they drove across the bridge onto the island, Simon could see the huge ugly dredge spewing sand onto the beach. Beach renourishment had its critics, but Simon selfishly supported whatever preserved the barrier islands of North Carolina, even if it was expensive and postponed the inevitable for just another generation or two.

"How about breakfast?" Morgan asked.

"I don't think my stomach's up to it," Simon said. "A Coke would be good, though."

They turned off the street into the parking lot of the Pearlie Beach Grocery Store and Beach Emporium. It was a small white concrete block building with a bright blue metal roof. A white sign with blue lettering that matched the color of the roof advertised, NOVELTIES AND GIFTS, DIP ICE CREAM, T-SHIRTS, BAIT AND TACKLE. The outside walls on either side of the door were lined with drink machines, three newspaper racks, a phone booth, a rack of propane gas bottles, an air pump for inner tubes and bicycle tires, and two ice dispensers. Leland Pearlie, Dale's brother and the proprietor, was plugging one of the two ice dispensers into the outside wall socket. He was taller and heavier than his older brother and combed long side hairs over his bald spot.

"Got a shipment of ice coming in tomorrow," he said to Simon and Morgan. "Last one of the season. Hope it gets us through the weekend."

He followed them into the store. Leland's watchful

wife Darlene was at her usual post at the cash register. Gray roots showed through her bouffant hairdo. She wore no makeup, unfashionable glasses, and a blue polyester pantsuit. Simon's Aunt Rae, the materfamilias of his North Carolina mountain relatives, would say that Darlene looked like she had been "rode hard and put up wet." She was one of a vanishing race of southern women who worked themselves to the bone taking care of home, business, and family while trying to make their menfolks "do right." Since doing right meant staying away from cars, beer, and hunting and fishing, and included going to church and leaving enough money in the till to pay the bills before buying a new shotgun, they weren't often successful. Darlene never left Leland alone with the store receipts.

"Dale called me," Leland said. "He tells me you-all think that the corpse might be a navy frogman. He's wondering if he could be our cousin."

"Might be, I guess," Simon said. He picked up a twelve-pack of Coke.

"Any way to find out?" Leland said.

"The medical examiner can tell you, if he's got your cousin's dental records."

"But didn't you do something like this recently? I read about it in the newspaper. Aren't you the history professor who figured out who killed that woman in Raleigh? The one that disappeared so many years ago?"

Damn, Simon thought.

"Yeah, that's him," Morgan said. "You probably saw the big article the *News and Observer* did. They called him a 'forensic historian.' A couple of national papers picked the story up off the wires and ran it, too."

"It was a slow news day," Simon said.

Morgan selected a twelve-pack of Miller draft and a jumbo bag of potato chips and took them to the cash register, chuckling.

"Next thing you know, *Newsweek*'s got a whole page on him and *People* wanted to do a profile—"

"That's enough," Simon said. He handed Morgan the Coke and a box of Goody's headache powders.

"If you're going to embarrass me, you can pay," Simon said.

He turned to Leland Pearlie. "There's no foul play in this case," he said. "The man drowned. Rebreathers circulated pure oxygen, and at depths over thirty-five feet the water pressure caused oxygen poisoning. That's why Jacques Cousteau invented the aqualung."

Stunned by this excess of information, Leland rang up the two men's purchases without another word.

"Cut it out," Simon said to Morgan later, in the truck. "I'm tired of this forensic historian stuff."

Simon opened one of the Cokes and dumped two Goody's powders into it. He chugged half the can. The quality of the truck's audio was so poor Simon turned the radio off, even though Beach 106 was playing Aretha Franklin singing "Who's Zoomin' Who." He could not understand how Morgan could invest in fog lights, a frame-mounted tow bar, four-wheel drive, and heavy-duty shock absorbers and not buy a decent audio package for his truck. He wished he had driven his Thunderbird from Raleigh instead of hitching a ride with Morgan.

"Excuse me," Morgan said. "You weren't so sensitive a few months ago. Remember that talk you gave at the Museum of History? You hung around for hours afterwards. I personally saw you signing autographs. You loved it."

"That was before I started to get wild phone calls from all over the country. One guy called from California and wanted me to help him prove he was Ava Gardner's illegitimate son. He figured since I lived so close to Smithfield, it would be a breeze for me to do the research. Said he'd share his inheritance with me."

"Sounds like a good deal to me."

"The publicity has worn me out," Simon said. "And the department's short a person, I'm teaching an extra class, and chairing a search committee. I don't need phone calls at two o'clock in the morning asking me to consult on some old unsolved murder case. I've already got a full-time job."

Simon finished his Coke. He was more tired than he wanted to admit, even to Morgan, his best friend. It was indicative of his exhaustion that Simon, a compulsive teacher, had canceled two days' worth of classes to get to the beach early. Helping Morgan was just an excuse. Mostly he just wanted to get away from Raleigh before the crunch began. Simon calculated that he would have approximately sixty term papers, thirty book reports, and ninety exams to grade in the three weeks before the end of the semester. Then he'd spend Christmas break reading résumés and fielding phone calls from applicants for the position of Instructor in Civil War History at Kenan College, a two-year appointment that hadn't even been advertised yet. There were dozens of qualified, unemployed Ph.D.s in history out there, and Simon expected to hear from every last one of them.

Morgan picked up a paper bag from the floor of the

truck. With exaggerated gestures he placed it on the seat between himself and Simon.

"All right," Simon said, "I'll bite. What's that?"

"It's the collecting bucket I took off the corpse."

"What's in it?"

Simon reached for the bag, but Morgan clapped his hand on it.

"I don't want to add to your stress," he said. "You just rest up from all that celebrity stuff and let me handle this."

"Give it here."

Morgan grinned and withdrew his hand. Simon took the water-soaked rubber bucket out of the paper bag. He forced his hand into it and pulled out a small mound of black discs, fused together into a solid mass.

"Coins!" he said. "What kind are they?"

"Don't know yet. I thought you weren't interested."

"Did you just commandeer these, or did someone give you permission to take them?"

"Chief Keck let me have the bucket," Morgan said. "I gave him a receipt and everything."

Simon hefted the small mass of coins in his hand. "These are heavy," he said. "Gold?"

"Don't know. Could be."

"What do we do?"

"Scrub them good with dishwashing detergent and then use a reagent to dissolve the concretions. I've got some ten percent ferric chloride solution and two percent hydrochloric acid in the camper."

"So our dead diver discovered some old coins," Simon said. "Maybe he got distracted and went beyond his depth and drowned."

"Maybe so," Morgan said. "Even more interesting to

me, are there more where these came from?"

The two men pulled up to the Clegg beach house. The single-story clapboard cottage was painted a faded Wedgwood blue with white shutters and doors. Like all the beach houses on the island, it stood on pilings a story high so that storm wash could sweep under the house, and so residents could see the ocean over the dunes. A big parking area, a storage room, and an outdoor shower occupied the space under the house. The two men went up a flight of wooden stairs to the back door, which faced the street, and entered the house through the galley kitchen. A wide counter with half a dozen stools divided the kitchen from a dining area that held a picnic table and benches. To the right was a large living room furnished with mismatched bookshelves, a propane furnace, and three worn sofas upholstered in green Naugahyde scattered with quilts and knitted throws. A screened-in porch facing the ocean opened off the living area and extended the length of the cottage. It was furnished with weathered rocking chairs and metal gliders. The porch was fronted with a narrow deck, from which a wooden catwalk led out over the dunes. From there stairs dropped down to the beach. On the right side of the cottage were two bedrooms and a bath, and on the left, behind the living area, was a master bedroom and bath.

Simon made a real effort to ignore Morgan and the lump of coins. He popped the tab top of another Coke. He adjusted the thermostat on the furnace lower, since the day was warming up. He opened the blinds and let the morning light stream into the cottage. He turned on the CD player and jacked up the volume on the greatest hits of Ben E. King and the Drifters. He took the outdoor cushions out onto the porch and put them on the rocking chairs and gliders. He hung the hammock on the deck. All the while he could hear water running in the kitchen as Morgan washed the coins. Finally Simon's curiosity got the better of him and he went back inside. Morgan was intently scrubbing the coins with a wire brush. Grinning, he held the mass up for Simon to see. A few flecks of gold glinted through the concretions.

"It is gold," Simon said. "Dollars or sovereigns?"

"I can't tell yet. And I've got to stop using this wire brush. I might damage the surface of the coins. Hang on to them while I go down to the camper and get some reagent."

Simon took the lump of coins outside onto the front stoop to look at it in the sunlight. Gold was valuable under any circumstances, but gold coins were very rare and very valuable indeed. They were illegal to own in the United States from 1934 to 1975, so countless coins had been melted down by their owners. A twenty-dollar gold piece in good condition was easily worth a thousand dollars.

Morgan came back up the stairs with a metal can in his hands.

"Let's soak those suckers in this stuff overnight and then see what we've got," he said.

Morgan found a quart-sized Mason canning jar in a kitchen cabinet, plopped the chunk of coins in the jar, and filled it with a liquid from the can. Simon stared at the little mound. The detritus caked on it began to bubble.

"Watching it won't make it dissolve faster," Morgan said. "Let's leave it until morning."

Simon selected *The Doorbell Rang* from the bookshelf

and picked up a worn quilt from a sofa and went outside onto the porch. He wrapped up against the autumn ocean breeze and had just started reading when a dog barked right next to him. He jumped. The Cleggs' next-door neighbor, Col. Timothy Watkins, a retired army officer and a year-round resident of Pearlie Beach, was standing on the deck outside the screened door of the porch.

"Sorry I startled you," Colonel Watkins said, pulling at the leash of his elderly German shepherd. "Wolfie doesn't see real well anymore, and he'll bark at just about anything."

Simon reluctantly put down his book, stood up, and reached for the latch of the door.

"Come on in," Simon said.

"I won't disturb you," the colonel said. "I saw some activity over here and I was just checking things out."

"We're guests of the Cleggs," Simon said. "I met you last summer, I believe. I'm Simon Shaw. I teach history at Kenan College in Raleigh."

"I remember you now," the colonel said.

The colonel lingered, absently petting his dog. He had a full head of white hair, and his face had taken the brunt of the sun and the sea for many years. It was scattered with blotches and broken veins. He was neatly dressed in a blue Ralph Lauren polo shirt tucked into his khaki slacks. His dark leather belt matched his new Docksiders, and his blue socks matched his shirt. He was wearing a Rolex watch with lots of dials and gizmos. He and his wife lived next door in one of the nicest homes on the beach, a three-story glass and stained-wood dream with a widow's walk on the roof.

"I just got back from an errand at Leland's store," the colonel said. "He told me about that diver's corpse the Army Corps of Engineers found."

"Yes," Simon said. "I think Dale Pearlie believes it's his cousin."

"Will they be able to identify him?" the colonel asked.

"I should think so," Simon said. "Especially if he was in the military."

"Well," the colonel said. "After all this time. I knew him, you know. We were both stationed at Camp Davis in Wilmington during the war. I heard then that he had deserted. Everyone thought he had stolen his diving apparatus. He talked constantly about looking for sunken treasure." The colonel rolled his eyes skyward. "The damn fool," he said.

Simon thought it would be wise not to mention the coins.

"We really don't know anything about what happened to the guy, whoever he is," Simon said.

"You're right, of course. Nothing substitutes for the facts."

"Were you a frogman, too?"

"The official term was *port clearance diver*. But no, my unit patrolled the beaches early every morning, on horseback, looking for bodies that washed up overnight. The government didn't want the locals to know how many of our ships were being sunk by German U-boats."

"But you retired here."

"There's no prettier spot anywhere."

The colonel nodded his head in a modified salute as he led his dog off the catwalk. Simon watched him march down the beach. He had a plastic bag with him and picked up trash as he walked.

Morgan came out on the porch with an armful of papers. "Who was that?" he asked.

"Colonel Watkins," Simon said. "The retired army officer from next door. His wife owns that tacky shell shop across the bridge. I met them last summer, when I was here writing an article on Anne Bloodworth's murder for the *North Carolina Historical Review.*"

Morgan sat down at the weathered picnic table and carefully arranged his work in two piles, laying a big conch shell on each to keep them from blowing away.

"What's happening with the coins?" Simon asked.

"Nothing yet."

"Colonel Watkins said that diver, Pearlie's cousin who disappeared, who maybe our diver is—"

"And who maybe our diver isn't."

"—constantly talked about looking for sunken treasure."

Morgan looked up, interested. "I hope you didn't tell him about the coins," he said.

"I know better than that," Simon said.

"Once we identify the coins, with your reading speed, you could research this in no time. You wouldn't even have to go to the library. Marcus has got all the classic coastal history books, and the National Records and Archives Administration is on the Internet now. There's even a Cape Fear shipwreck map pinned to the wall over the sofa in the house."

Simon had already noticed the books and studied the map, but he didn't want Morgan to know that. He was fighting the urge to get interested. He needed some rest, not another problem to solve.

"No," Simon said. "Once you identify the coins, we turn them over to the authorities, and that's that. I don't have the time or the energy to get involved in any treasure hunt."

Simon heard the knock at the kitchen door first. When he opened it he found Dale Pearlie and his mother, Inez, on the porch. Just the previous Saturday Inez Pearlie had been bustling gaily around the realty office dressed in green leggings and a sweater appliquéd with turkeys and pumpkins, handing out keys and welcoming guests. She looked terrible now, every long day of her eighty-odd years. She was dressed in a wrinkled old jogging outfit and hadn't bothered to apply makeup over a swollen and tear-stained face. Pink scalp showed through her disheveled gray hair.

Simon shook both their hands.

"I am sorry to come here in such a state," Inez Pearlie said. Her eyes welled up, and she couldn't continue.

"My mother is terribly upset," Dale Pearlie said. "We want to ask a favor of you."

"Of course," Simon said. "Come in."

Simon seated the two visitors on the sofa closest to the propane stove. Dale held his mother's hand and patted it. Without saying a word, Morgan went into the kitchen to make coffee, leaving Simon to talk to the Pearlies.

"I told you that I had a cousin who was a navy frogman who disappeared during the war," Dale said. "His name was Carl Chavis. He was my mother's nephew, her sister's son."

Inez blew her nose before speaking.

"My sister is in a nursing home in Wilmington. She's ninety-two years old. I just dread . . . well, what if the papers find out about the corpse, or maybe the TV stations, and we don't know if it's Carl yet, and she hears about the body?"

"What we're hoping is for a very early identification," Dale said. "So we can prepare everyone."

"I'm due to pick my sister up Thursday morning to spend Thanksgiving with us," Inez said. "I don't know what to do or what to say to her."

Morgan brought everyone a mug of coffee on a tray with a milk pitcher and a sugar bowl. Spooning and stirring gave Inez a chance to collect herself.

"I understand," Simon said. "But what can we do?"

"Dr. Morgan here tells me you know the medical examiner personally," Dale said.

Simon glared at Morgan.

"Sorry," Morgan said. "I told them before I realized how jaded you were by the demands of celebrity."

"I know that this is a big favor," Dale said, "but I was wondering if perhaps you could call his office. The body has already been picked up. If we could just know if it's Carl."

Pearlie handed Simon a worn brown envelope-sized accordion file tied closed with an old shoelace.

"I've got some of Carl's records here. When I cleaned out my dad's file cabinet years ago I almost threw them away. Thank God I didn't."

"Of course I'll contact him," Simon said. "Is there a fax machine anywhere in town?"

"In the realty office," Dale answered.

"Let's go there right now," Simon said.

"Thank you so much," Inez said. "You don't know how much better I feel."

AT THE REALTY OFFICE Simon wrote a short note to Dr. Philip Boyette, the state medical examiner. He asked Boyette to compare Carl Chavis's dental records with the dentition of the unusual corpse his office would receive that afternoon. It would be compassionate of him, Simon said; there were elderly relatives and the holidays to consider.

Leland Pearlie's daughter Dee Anna Frink, who worked in the realty office with her uncle and her grandmother, fed Simon's note and the other documents into the fax machine. She was a small blonde with a Talbots wardrobe and an Estée Lauder makeup job. Her red fingernails were so long she had to press the buttons on the fax machine by patting them with the pads of her fingers.

"Do you think he'll do it?" Dee Anna asked.

"He will if he can," Simon said. "All he's got to do is look at the teeth. The rest can wait."

"Family holidays are so damn complicated, even without corpses showing up," Dee Anna said. "My husband and I always have to eat two dinners. We have to be with both sets of parents or our lives aren't worth living, although I think my husband may stay in Miami this year. His business isn't finished and he won't think it's worth coming home if he has to turn around and go back."

Dee Anna cocked a hip and looked at him to see how he responded to this news. When he didn't make the appropriate comments, she sighed grumpily and went back to her cubicle.

Dale Pearlie came out of the back of the realty office.

"I can't find any more information about Carl," he said. "It was a hell of a long time ago."

Simon handed Carl Chavis's file back to Pearlie, but Pearlie grasped his hand with both of his.

"Would you keep it? Please? Perhaps you might have time to read through it and let me know if you find anything unusual."

Simon didn't want to keep the file, but he couldn't think of a kind way to say no.

"Okay," Simon said. "I'll take a few minutes and look through it."

SIMON SAT ON A wobbly barstool and rested his elbows on the cracked Formica counter while he waited for his lunch. Henry Pearlie took hot dog buns out of a steamer and put them on paper plates. Henry, Dale's "uncle," really his father's cousin, ran the grill exactly as he pleased, which was the way it had been run for fifty years. He cooked hot dogs in grease on the grill, made real milkshakes, and cut up fresh potatoes for french fries. He flatly refused to sell diet drinks despite constant complaints from his customers.

Henry picked four fat hot dogs off the grill with tongs and placed them on the steamed buns. He scooped fries out of a fryer basket and dumped them on the plates.

Simon started to lift the plates off the counter, but Henry stopped him.

"Hold your horses, I ain't done with them plates yet," he said.

"Hey, Viola," he called out to his helper, a heavy, elderly African-American woman wearing a pink flowered housedress and purple bedroom slippers. "Get me the slaw."

"Get it yourself," Viola answered. "I'm fixing the milk-shakes." Viola ladled vanilla ice cream into an antique commercial blender, added milk and chocolate syrup, and turned it on. The noise drowned out anything Henry might have said. Silently he got a plastic bucket of coleslaw out of a refrigerator.

Simon watched the Confederate battle flag tattooed on Henry's scrawny right arm wave as he dished up the slaw. Henry was a skinny old man who had passed more buoys in his lifetime than Simon had telephone poles. He had run a fish camp for years, until the inlet where it was located silted up. He skin-dived, spearhunted, fished, and farmed his tobacco allotment until age shut him down, He hadn't contributed a dime to Social Security. As a Pearlie, though, he was guaranteed lifetime employment at Pearlie Beach as long as he wanted it. So now he cooked breakfast and lunch at the pier six days a week. He had long gray hair pulled back into a ponytail and wore jeans and a white T-shirt. He was missing all his bicuspids and had a small gold earring in his left earlobe.

Henry treated the grill as his private museum. He had souvenirs of his favorite wars displayed everywhere. Most of it was Confederate junk—raggedy flags, buttons and stirrups, rotted leather straps, and pictures of Civil War scenes that had been cut out of magazines and tacked to the wall. On the counter next to a black rotary telephone was a lidless cigar box full of white oxidized lead bullets. A collection of Confederate scrip was tacked onto a bulletin board next to the menu board. It was worthless when it was printed and it was worthless still.

Contrasting with the decrepit war souvenirs was a rack of beautifully maintained fishing rods and two shiny spear guns. The rods were rigged, so Simon supposed he must still use them.

Viola finished making the milkshakes and Simon toted the food over to a table. Morgan sat at the rickety table looking at some of Henry's war memorabilia mounted on the wall next to the door of the grill. It wasn't exactly a door, though, and not much of a wall, either. The interior of the building was unfinished, and the three main sections were separated by stud walls covered with chicken wire. The largest section was the grill. Another section contained a pool table, pinball machines, and some beat-up easy chairs. The third functioned as a bait and tackle shop. In the back wall was the door to the fishing pier itself. In the center of all this activity was a cash register presided over by Viola when she wasn't making milkshakes.

Simon set their food down on the table.

"Has he got anything good?" Simon asked, referring to Henry's collection.

"Junk. A couple of Civil War muskets beaten to driftwood by the surf and a rusty German deck gun off a submarine. Stuff like this used to wash up on the beach by the ton."

The two men ate half their lunches before they spoke again.

"These are damn good hot dogs," Morgan said.

While they ate, they watched an elderly couple rolling a child's red wagon through thc building to the door of the pier. The wagon was piled with fishing equipment, including poles, bait buckets, and tackle boxes. The couple didn't say a word, just paid Viola and rolled through the door out to the pier. They didn't look like tourists. They were dressed in Walls outdoor work clothing, not L. L. Bean. Simon figured that the couple relied on their catch to provide supper several nights a week.

Simon couldn't finish his second hot dog and passed it over to Morgan. He pulled out the battered accordion file Dale Pearlie had pressed on him and flipped through the slots unenthusiastically.

"Anything interesting?" Morgan asked.

"Not really," Simon answered.

The file held a birth certificate, a high school senior picture, military identification, a newspaper clipping alluding to Chavis's disappearance, and a brief report from the military police. Carl Chavis had been born on March 8, 1920, in Wilmington, North Carolina. Chavis was an old North Carolina Indian name, and Carl's dark hair and high cheekbones suggested his racial heritage. Otherwise he was just another skinny teenager with a crewcut. The clipping mentioned his disappearance on a Monday, May 11, 1942, with the detail that his military diving suit was also missing. He wasn't on duty when he disappeared, and the military police concluded that he had drowned while engaged in unauthorized diving. The clipping was exactly seven sentences long. Chavis's disappearance didn't merit much attention while the country was preparing for war.

The file contained a second photograph. Simon inspected it curiously. It was a black and white picture of a group of five young men sitting on the porch of a large Victorian-style house. They were a happy, relaxed bunch, with cigarettes in hand and feet up on the railing. Two of the men were in uniform, two were wearing overalls and rubber boots, and the last one was dressed in pleated jodhpurs and a leather jacket. Simon compared Carl Chavis's senior picture to the faces in the photograph and easily picked him out of the group. He showed the picture to Morgan before putting it back in the file.

"I wonder who the rest of those guys were," Simon said.

The two men were interrupted by Viola, who came to the table to clear their dishes. Simon noticed she had a reddish tint to her hair and a few freckles in her dark brown face.

"That was the best milkshake I have had in a long time," Morgan said to her.

"Thank you, honey," she said. "I been making them the same way for years."

"How much does it cost to go out on the pier?" Simon asked.

"Six dollars if you're fishing, fifty cents if you're looking," Viola said.

Morgan and Simon paid for their lunch at the cash register. Simon handed Viola an additional fifty cents.

"I'm going to walk the pier before I go back to the cottage," Simon said.

"I've got to make some phone calls," Morgan said. "I'll see you later."

THE PEARLIE BEACH FISHING pier stretched five hundred feet out from the shore and rose thirty feet from the surface of the ocean. Waves crashed against thick wooden pilings below. Screaming seagulls circled overhead, scanning the deck for scraps of bait or bits of cleaned fish. Simon walked all the way to the end of the pier with his hands in his pockets. When he got to the end, he turned around, leaned on the rail, and looked back toward the shore. It was a beautiful day. The morning haze had burned off and the sun shone brightly. The ocean was the same soft blue as the sky. Pure white dunes, fuzzy with sea oats and beach grass, edged the strip of sand that divided the ocean from the sky. Pastel-painted or weathered board beach houses lined the shore behind the dunes. There were a few people strolling on the beach, occasionally leaning over to pick up something interesting, maybe an olive shell or a skate ray case. Simon let his head hang back so the sun could shine full on his face. The sea wind was chilly, though, so soon he started back down the pier. He passed about twenty silent anglers, including the couple with the child's red wagon, staring at their fishing lines as if concentration alone could make fish strike bait.

On a wooden bench at the back door of the pier he found Henry Pearlie cleaning a customer's catch. His knife flashed as he expertly severed heads and scooped out fish guts. He seemed oblivious to the sun and the breeze; he wasn't wearing either a hat or a jacket.

"What's the catch?" Simon asked.

"Mostly spot, a couple of mackerel," Henry said.

A brown pelican stood a few feet away from the two men, patiently eyeing the bucket of fish scraps at Henry's feet. Simon was taken by the big bird; he had never seen one so close. Pelicans cruised in flocks over the waves looking for food, diving into the ocean and scooping fish into their bills. Sometimes one would be fifty feet high in the sky when it tucked its wings into its body and plunged sharply downward. Diving pelicans hit the water headfirst, making a big splash, expanding their leathery beaks to suck up water and food. In the air one might have a wingspan of eight feet, evoking, in Simon's imagination, a pterodactyl.

This bird was tame, and Simon soon realized why. A sharp noise made the pelican start and stretch his wings. He was missing half a wing.

"He's crippled," Simon said.

"He got fishing line wrapped around his wing, it cut off the circulation, and he lost it," Henry said, still cleaning fish.

The large bird waited patiently for Henry's fish scraps. But Henry casually picked up the scrap bucket and tossed the contents over the pier railing into the water, where the big bird couldn't follow. The pelican stretched his long neck out toward the railing, then waddled over to a bench. With difficulty he hopped onto it. His webbed feet gripped the edge of the bench. The raised tendons looked like the fingers of a human hand.

Seething, Simon went inside the pier and bought a plastic zip-bag full of small bait mullet. He came back outside and emptied the bag near the pelican. The bird hopped off his perch and began to eat, tipping his long neck up to swallow the fish. Simon could swear the pelican watched Henry cautiously out of one eye while he ate.

Henry was swabbing off the cleaning station.

"That's a waste of good money," Henry said.

Simon didn't answer him. Henry shrugged and went inside. Simon watched the big bird finish eating, then waddle down the pier looking for another handout.

SIMON WENT BACK TO the realty office to give Carl Chavis's file to Dale Pearlie. He showed the group picture to him.

"I'll be damned," Dale said. "This photo was taken on the porch at the old Pavilion. My grandfather built it as a combination bathhouse, restaurant, and dance hall. Before any of the cottages were built, day-trippers came here from all over the state. The Pavilion was destroyed by Hurricane Hazel in 1954, and my dad didn't rebuild it. Built the fishing pier instead."

"Do you know any of these people?" Simon asked.

"Sure," Dale answered. "There's Carl, and here's my dad, and Uncle Henry." The elder Pearlies were the two men in overalls and rubber boots.

"They must have just come from work," Dale said. "Dad had a cannery farther down the beach then. When Dad decided to build rental cottages, he closed it down. I don't recognize the other men. Mama might, but she's not here right now."

"Heard from the medical examiner yet?" Simon asked.

"Not yet," Pearlie said. "But I feel it in my gut. We've found Carl's corpse."

"Explain your relationship again. I'm confused."

"Henry and my father were first cousins. Their fathers were brothers. Henry's father was a farmer; not a successful one, I'm afraid. Carl was my first cousin, but on my mother's side. He was a lot older than me. All these guys hung together since they were kids."

"Got any idea when this photo was taken?"

"Well, during the war, obviously, because of their ages and the uniforms and everything. And Carl's in it, and he disappeared in the spring of 1942."

"So it was taken sometime between January and the spring of 1942," Simon said.

Simon asked Dee Anna to scan the documents and

photos from Carl Chavis's file and print them out for him to keep. She enlarged and touched up the photo of the group on the porch. When it was printed, Simon was able to see more detail. The five men lounging on the porch of the Pavilion weren't posing for the camera. They were absorbed with each other, laughing and talking and completely relaxed, as people are who have known each other for years. Someone they knew well must have taken the photo, or the men wouldn't have been so unself-conscious. In the background an African-American girl in a maid's uniform cleared plates and silverware off a table. Her back was to the camera. Overhead a heavy fan hung down from the porch ceiling. The arms of the fan were blurred, so they must have been turning when the picture was taken.

Morgan was just hanging up the phone when Simon got back to the cottage.

"I called a friend of mine at the Maritime Archaeology Department at East Carolina," Morgan said. "Caught him just before he left for the holiday."

"And?" Simon said.

"I didn't tell him about the coins, but I asked him whether there might be a big cache of undiscovered gold around here," Morgan said, "at a depth of less than forty feet, say."

"What did he say?"

"He said, 'Sure, and people in hell are drowning in ice water.' Any wreck so close to shore would have been picked clean by now."

"That doesn't mean Carl Chavis didn't find gold in 1942," Simon said.

"No, it doesn't. But what I'm saying is, it's not still there."

Simon tended to agree with him.

"Oh, by the way," Morgan said. "Marcus called, they'll be here tomorrow, by ten probably. They're going to bring fixings for Thanksgiving dinner, and I said we'd take care of dinner tomorrow night."

"We can handle that," Simon said.

"They're only bringing the three youngest kids; the oldest is in some kind of preadolescent snit and is staying in Raleigh with a friend. And Marcus's wife, what's her name?"

"Marianne."

"Yeah, she's bringing a girlfriend. Since otherwise she'd be the only woman down here. Marcus wanted to know if you and I would mind sleeping in my camper."

"Have you washed your extra sleeping bag lately?"

"You know her, by the way."

"Who?"

"Marianne's friend. She's Julia McGloughlin, that redheaded woman you were so hot for last summer. The police attorney."

"Her hair's not red. It's auburn."

"They were worried you might mind. I said you wouldn't. You don't, do you?"

"No, of course not."

Simon wished he had gotten a haircut before he'd left home, and that he had brought something to wear other than jeans and sweatshirts. But Julia had already decided that he wasn't the man for her. Her background was "old" southern. Dating him would have been complicated for her. He was shorter than she, divorced, and had little ambition other than to influence the thinking of a few thousand college students and write a book or two. Besides, half of his family wasn't from "around here," and it showed.

Although his father's relations had lived in western North Carolina for generations and Simon was raised in Boone, where his father taught at Appalachian State University, Simon resembled his small dark Jewish mother. She had grown up in Queens, New York, and was working as a Vista public health nurse in the Appalachian Mountains when she met and married his father. She had never regretted her decision. The couple lived happily the rest of their lives in the mountains of North Carolina. Simon was their only child. They died in a car accident when Simon was in college.

Simon was a brilliant student. He blazed through college and graduate school, receiving his undergraduate degree in history from Duke and his Ph.D. from the University of North Carolina at Chapel Hill. Then he shocked his advisers and colleagues when he refused assistant professorships at both Duke and Yale. He settled in at Kenan College in Raleigh, where he could teach undergraduates. His first book won the Pulitzer Prize for history, and he became the youngest tenured Professor Kenan had ever had.

Simon and Julia met soon after Simon's divorce, and they connected immediately, but she declined an intimate relationship. Simon gathered that Julia expected to marry someone who wore a suit to work every day and made a couple hundred thousand dollars a year in law or business. Simon didn't blame her for this. It was difficult for anyone to challenge family expectations. Julia had tested her limits already by becoming a police attorney instead of joining a prestigious law firm.

"What happened to you two, anyway?" Morgan said.

"She said she didn't want to get involved with anyone so soon after breaking off her engagement."

"What's that got to do with anything?"

"Nothing. I expect she just changed her mind about dating me. I don't think I'm her type."

2

A COLD BREEZE BLEW ACROSS SIMON'S BACK FROM THE WINdow he had left ajar so he could hear the surf and smell the salty air. The sun slanted through the miniblinds at a late afternoon angle, and the sky was tinted rose and peach, hinting at sunset. He rolled over and looked at the clock. It was four o'clock in the afternoon. He must have fallen asleep reading.

In the bathroom he splashed cold water on his face and rubbed at the imprint of chenille bedspread on his cheek. He could hear the staccato clicks of Morgan typing on his laptop in the other room.

Simon went into the kitchen to get a Coke from the refrigerator. He made a concentrated effort not to inspect the jar of coins sitting on the kitchen counter. When he finally gave in and picked up the jar, the fluid was so foggy with dissolved gunk he couldn't see anything anyway.

Morgan didn't look up from his work at the dining room table when Simon popped the tab top of his drink.

"Writing your report?" Simon asked. Morgan didn't

answer, so Simon went behind him to look at his computer screen.

"National Registry of Shipwrecks," Simon read. "And how exactly does this relate to your missing Tuscarora village?"

"Not at all," Morgan said. "I'm just curious as hell about those coins. I want to know where they came from."

"They came from the bottom of the ocean," Simon said. "You know the Carolina coast is carpeted with shipwrecks; there are thousands of them."

"But we're not concerned with the whole North Carolina coast. You said yourself that the frogman's breathing apparatus would only work at less than forty feet. And the corpse was intact. At least, the diving suit with the skeleton inside it was. It couldn't have been bouncing around the ocean for years or it would have been beaten to pieces. It must have gotten hung up somewhere, right where Chavis, or whoever he is, drowned, until the dredge dislodged it here at Pearlie Beach. He found those coins right here."

Morgan took a red pencil and circled Pearlie Beach on the map. "Work with me," he said. "You're the historian. I don't deal in recorded time. Help me out."

Simon sat down next to him. He carefully inspected the shipwreck map Morgan had spread across the table.

"Okay," he said. "Most of the shipwrecks around Pearlie Beach were nineteenth-century shipping bound for the mouth of the Cape Fear River and Wilmington."

"Not the Spanish plate fleet?"

"Definitely not. They'd ride the Gulf Stream north from the Caribbean. They wouldn't come so close to the Carolina shore."

"Blockade runners, then?"

"And Yankee gunboats, rice and indigo barges, and passenger steamships. All of which could have had at least some gold on them, even if it was just in the pockets of the passengers."

Morgan shut down his computer. He went over to the kitchen counter, picked up the jar of coins soaking in reagent, and peered into it. Sighing, he put it down again.

"By tomorrow morning, maybe we'll be able to get a date off at least one of these coins. Let's go buy dinner."

After closing the porch door, Morgan turned to see Simon standing on the top of the stairs looking off toward the Pearlie Beach Sound, both hands shading his eyes.

"I wonder where he went into the water," Simon said.

"Who? Chavis?"

"I wonder if anyone around here remembers where he liked to dive."

CAPTAIN NANCE PEARLIE'S SEAFOOD market was a red tin-roofed building that sat right at the water's edge under the bridge on the sound side of Pearlie Beach. Most of the fishing boats that operated out of Pearlie Beach unloaded their catch at Captain Nance's. A trawler was tied to a weathered piling now, rocking gently up against the old tires that cushioned the docks, with its nets and lines drawn up drying in the sun. Two fishermen leaned on the trawler's boathouse, drinking Nehi orange drinks and sharing a bag of pork rinds.

Inside the cool, low-ceilinged building sawdust covered the floor, and tubs of the day's catch lined a counter on one side of the room. Thirty years' worth of calendars from local businesses like the Pearlie Beach Gas Company, the Intercoastal Marina, and Captain Willie's Restaurant wallpapered the other three walls. Through a plate-glass window behind the counter two elderly African-American men with thick callused fingers patiently picked crab. Nobody had yet invented a machine that could pick crab. That was why crabmeat cost fourteen dollars a pound on a good day.

Captain Nance and his wife Ruth minded their seafood market themselves, working seven days a week during the season, which extended from March until after Thanksgiving weekend. During the winter they relaxed at a condominium in Florida not far from Orlando. Captain Nance was Leland Pearlie's son. He looked like his father, except he had a full head of red hair with a touch of gray at the temples. Ruth was a pretty, plump woman, with curly brown hair and deep laugh lines around her eyes and mouth. Both of them wore heavy rubber aprons and rubber gloves.

Simon and Morgan inspected the tubs of seafood resting on ice.

"The shrimp look good," Simon said, eyeing a tray full of fresh jumbos.

"We're having shrimp tomorrow night," Morgan reminded him.

"Some big blues came in just an hour ago," Captain Nance said, wiping his hands on a towel tucked into his apron. "They were bled and iced down right away."

Bluefish were evil-looking game fish with rows of pointy teeth. They ran in packs, killing anything when they were in a feeding frenzy, often more than they could eat. Fishermen taking blues off a hook had been known to get deep cuts on their hands from the hungry fish. They were good enough eating to be worth the struggle to land them.

"Let's take that one," Simon said, pointing to a long shiny silver specimen.

"Want it cleaned?" Nance asked.

"Yes, please," Simon said.

Simon watched Nance expertly clean his fish with a special knife designed for the job. It had a sharp flat edge for slicing open the fish and severing the head from the body, a double point for scraping out guts or removing hooks, and a serrated edge for scaling. It was identical to the knife Henry Pearlie had used at the pier. Probably half the people within a hundred miles of the coast owned one.

Morgan scanned the contents of a commercial refrigerator kept stocked with homemade food prepared by local women.

"You should get some of Viola Munn's coleslaw," Ruth said. "She brought it in fresh today. That woman can cook. She's wasted at the pier."

"Did Dale find you boys?" Nance asked. "He was here a little while ago and said he was on his way to your place."

"No," Morgan said, "we walked here by way of the beach."

Ruth wrapped the cleaned bluefish tightly in an old edition of the *Brunswick Beacon,* like a baby in swaddling clothes.

"What did he want?" Simon asked

"I don't suppose he'd mind if I tell you," Nance said. "The medical examiner called him. That diver was Carl Chavis."

"Well," Simon said.

"My family appreciates you helping to get that identification made," Nance said. "Grandma Inez was real upset."

"It's okay," Simon said. "I was glad to help."

Ruth gave the bluefish to Morgan, who added it to an armful of other groceries: a pint of Viola's coleslaw, a Mason jar of homemade tartar sauce, cornmeal, and a Vidalia onion.

"Let me ask you a question," Nance said to Simon. "Someone told me you won the Pulitzer Prize."

"Yeah," Simon said.

"You look awful young to win a big award like that. What was your book about?"

"The South between the world wars," Simon said.

"I like to read," Nance said. "I've read every one of Tom Clancy's books."

"Me, too," Simon said.

"Danielle Steele rented a house here one summer," Ruth said, ringing up their purchases. "She paid for everything with hundred-dollar bills."

Simon handed Ruth a twenty.

OUT ON THE DECK of the Clegg cottage, Simon lit the propane-fed fire under the heavy iron tripod and set a big cast-iron skillet half filled with peanut oil on it. It was a little breezy, so he moved a chair to protect the flame from the wind. It would take about five minutes for the oil to get sizzling hot.

Inside, Morgan finished mincing a Vidalia onion. He mixed it with a little sugar, buttermilk, and cornmeal to make the hush puppy batter. Then he unwrapped the bluefish and shook Old Bay seasoning over the fillets before dredging them in flour. He and Simon took everything out on the deck. The sun was setting toward the mainland, throwing the marine forest on the sound into black relief against the dark blue sky. Already a few stars shone overhead.

Morgan scooped up tablespoonfuls of hushpuppy batter and dropped them into the hot oil, where they quickly began to bubble. He stirred the hushpuppies gently to make sure they browned evenly, then dished them out into a serving bowl lined with paper towels. When the hushpuppies were all cooked, Morgan dropped the bluefish fillets into the oil, timing them for exactly seven minutes. Simon laid out plates, cutlery, coleslaw, butter, tartar sauce, and four bottles of beer on the table. He weighted the paper plates and napkins with the bottles of beer to keep them from blowing away.

The two men ate every bite, only stopping to ask each other to pass the butter or the tartar sauce. When they were finished, Morgan lit a Lucky Strike, cupping his hand to keep the match from blowing out in the breeze. It was dark enough now that Simon couldn't see the ocean, but he could hear it. The tide was in, and the roar of the waves crashing drowned out other night noises.

"So," Morgan said, "the corpse was Carl Chavis."

"Doesn't seem to surprise anyone," Simon said.

Morgan tipped the ashes of his cigarette into his empty beer bottle. "My curiosity is about to eat me alive," he said. "If those coins can't be identified in the morning, you may need to put me in a straitjacket. Where do you think Chavis found that gold?"

"I've been thinking," Simon said. "Here's how I see it. Chavis was a twenty-two-year-old kid, in the navy, stationed at Wilmington during World War II. He's a frogman. It's his job to check the harbor and the river for mines."

"And?"

"Diving is a brand-new technology—the equipment to make it safe hasn't been invented yet. But Carl's excited. He thinks he can use this new skill of his to get rich. There are dozens of shipwrecks off this coast, and he figures some must have valuables on them. So he sneaks his equipment out on his time off and goes exploring. Sure enough, he finds some gold coins. But he drowns in the process. We think all this happened not too far from here because his corpse isn't beat up and his equipment won't let him go deeper than thirty-five feet. If he died because he went too deep, it would take just seconds. We find his corpse, and the coins, fifty-seven years later."

"And we wonder if there's any more gold where that came from," Morgan said.

"Since Carl Chavis died, diving has become a relatively safe sport. The wrecks close to shore have been picked clean by now. You said so yourself."

"Blackbeard's ship, the *Queen Anne's Revenge,* was found just a couple of years ago right in Beaufort Harbor. You can stand on the beach and throw a rock out to it."

"I'm talking about probabilities, not possibilities. Be realistic."

"It's okay for you to be relaxed about this. You're already famous. I've never been on TV before."

"First we have to identify the coins. Once we know their provenance we can do some research and see if any known wrecks match."

"Thank you."

"I'll help. But you realize that even if we can tie this

gold to a particular wreck, that doesn't mean there's any left."

WHEN THEY GOT TO the pier that night the pool table was already occupied by Henry Pearlie; Joe Pearlie, Dale's twenty-three-year-old son; and Woody Watkins, Colonel Watkins's son. Morgan joined them to make a foursome, and Simon hoisted himself up on the counter to watch. Carl Perkins singing "Honey, Don't" blasted out of an aged jukebox stocked with classic 45s. The only light in the great dark space was the one that hung over the pool table.

Henry handled his cue with the expertness of someone who had learned to play as soon as he was tall enough. He had changed clothes since Simon had seen him cooking in the grill. A belt with big CSA buckle circled his skinny body. The long-sleeved white shirt he wore had been washed so many times it was translucent in places. He had buttoned the shirt collar tightly over his prominent Adam's apple. Woody Watkins was a good pool player, too. When he leaned over his cue his blond hair dangled over his tanned face. He wore khaki cargo pants, a souvenir T-shirt from the Wrightsville Beach King Marlin Fishing Tournament, a windbreaker, and canvas deck shoes with no socks.

Joe Pearlie was a chubby young man with pink cheeks, fair hair, and thick lips. Simon's Aunt Rae would have said Joe had a weak chin and was an unsuitable candidate for most things, certainly employment or marriage. Joe had worked for the Pearlie Beach Police Department for less than a year.

Henry Pearlie broke with a loud crack. The balls scattered in all directions. While Henry considered his options, the men resumed the conversation that Simon and Morgan had interrupted.

"The medical examiner called Chief Keck first, then he called Daddy. There was no doubt at all, apparently," Joe said.

Henry sank two balls before speaking. "It's too bad. Course we knew Carl had to be dead. He was a nice kid, too. His family was real broke up," Henry said.

"What happens now?" Morgan asked.

"The medical examiner will do a complete postmortem," Joe said. "Since it was an unattended death. Don't know what else he could possibly find out. Then we'll bury him. All the Pearlies are laid to rest at the Jerusalem Baptist Church in Supply."

"He wasn't a Pearlie," Henry said.

"He was a close relation," Joe said.

"By marriage," Henry said.

"Are we going to play pool, or what?" Woody asked.

Joe leaned over to judge his shot. He took a long time.

"Hurry up," Woody said.

"Give him time," Henry answered. "This ain't the Charlotte Speedway."

Joe snapped his cue and missed his ball. Woody made a slight noise of annoyance. Joe flushed, his pink face getting pinker. He retreated from the pool table and sat with Simon, who started a conversation to distract the young man from his embarrassment.

"You like working in the police department here?" Simon asked.

"It's okay." Joe shrugged. "It's the best job I could get just out of rookie school. I'd rather work for the Brunswick

County Sheriff's Department. There's a lot more going on in the county than on this beach."

Simon wondered how many job offers the overweight, self-conscious young man had. Good thing his name was Pearlie.

"I would think you'd be busy during tourist season," Simon said.

"Yeah," Joe said, "busy helping people who've locked themselves out of their cars, or checking on old people no one's seen for a while, or patrolling the beach waking up teenagers who've fallen asleep in the sun and are burning themselves to a crisp. That kind of busy."

Woody leaned on his cue and grinned maliciously at Joe. "You had some excitement last summer, didn't you?" Woody asked.

Joe flushed again. Simon knew he must hate it.

"I didn't overreact," Joe said. "I followed the book all the way."

"Early one morning some folks on the pier noticed a guy burying a box on the beach," Woody said to Simon.

"He was wearing a camouflage jacket," Joe said, "and it was right after those bombings in Atlanta."

"So Joe comes zooming out to the pier with his siren going and arrests the guy, and the State Bureau of Investigation bomb squad drives over from Wilmington, and everyone in the cottages nearby has to evacuate," Woody said, grinning broadly. Simon noticed that even Henry was smiling as he leaned over the pool table.

"Then this SBI guy in a space suit digs up the box, and he puts it in an explosive chamber, and he blows it up," Woody said. "You know what it was? Candy! The guy was burying candy for a kid's treasure hunt! He had told everyone that, of course, but Joe here didn't listen. Called the cavalry anyway."

"You wouldn't be laughing if it had been a bomb," Joe said.

Woody, still snickering, took his turn at the pool table and coolly sank every shot. When he was done, he put his cue up, yawned, stretched, and drained his beer.

"Time to go home," Woody said. He peeled a ten-dollar bill off a wad in his pocket and handed it to Henry. When he left he slammed the screen door behind him.

"Don't be so sensitive, boy," Henry said to Joe. "We all know you did the right thing. And it's a funny story. Laugh at yourself a little."

"I wouldn't mind so much if he weren't such a jerk," Joe said.

"What does he do?" Morgan asked, racking up the balls.

"Surfs, dives, works at his momma's shop, takes care of chores around the house. Lives off his folks, basically."

"They can afford it," Henry said.

Morgan handed Simon a cue. He chalked it unenthusiastically. He didn't really want to play. He was tired of the exclusive company of men. The glare of the naked light bulb that hung in the cheap metal lamp over the pool table made whatever it illuminated ugly. Every surface in the room was either dusty or scarred by the rings of countless wet beer bottles and drink cans. The floor was sticky under his feet. He was here because he had nothing better to do to pass the time before going to bed, when he probably wouldn't sleep much anyway.

Simon was no stranger to depression. He liked nothing at all about being single. His wife had broken his heart when she left him, and Julia had declined his attentions. He succeeded in not feeling sorry for himself and enjoying his life most of the time, but this evening was just not one of those times.

THE NEXT MORNING SIMON groggily poured a cup of coffee in the kitchen of the cottage. He couldn't get used to sleeping alone. At home his cat Maybelline and her daughter Cecilia kept him company, curling up next to him in bed. He had no such companionship here and was beginning to feel sleep-deprived.

Morgan sat at the dining room table surrounded by books and papers. He leaned back in his chair, stretched, and smiled knowingly at Simon.

"What are you smirking about?" Simon asked.

Morgan waved a small blue book at him; it was the *Handbook of United States Coins.* Simon spit out a mouthful of coffee all over his sweatshirt.

"Damn," he said, "I forgot!"

Morgan tipped out the contents of a small brown envelope into Simon's outstretched cupped hands. A tiny pile of bright coins tumbled out. "Old son," he said, "we've got Confederate gold."

"No way," Simon said.

"Way," Morgan said. "There's no doubt." Simon closely inspected the coins in his hands. The seven dollars were about the size of a dime; the three half-eagles, or five-dollar gold pieces, were quarter-sized. The little mound of gold produced a solid, prosperous feeling in him.

"Real money," Simon said. "Not paper, not tin, not nickel." The coins were heavy in his hand.

"Feels good, doesn't it?" Morgan asked.

"Just out of curiosity, if this is Confederate money, why does it have 'United States of America' stamped on it?" Simon said.

"The *D* on the coins refers to the Dahlonega Mint in Georgia. It was a federal mint captured by the Confederate soldiers in April of 1861. They used up all the gold bullion there to print as many coins as they could."

"I remember now," Simon said. "They had to use Federal dies. They didn't have Confederate ones."

Simon inspected the coins with Morgan's magnifying glass. Without a doubt they had been minted by amateurs, the soldiers who had captured the mint. The surface of the coins was pitted and frosty, not smooth and shiny. Lady Liberty's image on all the coins was blurred, and the *U* in UNITED STATES was barely visible. The coins weren't at all pretty; their value was historic.

"How much are they worth?"

"Confederate coins minted at Dahlonega are extremely rare. Until now there were only sixty in existence. The price range quoted in this book is from two thousand to fourteen thousand dollars each," Morgan said.

"So this little pile of gold is worth a hundred fifty thousand dollars!"

"That's on the high side. You can give them back to me now."

Simon tipped the handful of coins back into the envelope Morgan held out to him.

"You certainly are calm," Simon said.

"I worked off most of my excitement this morning pacing up and down the beach while you were still asleep," Morgan said. "But I am thrilled, believe me."

"We need to stow this gold someplace safe," Simon said.

"I agree completely. Get dressed, I'll fix us some breakfast, then we'll take the coins to the police department."

"They belong in a bank safe."

"Chief Keck has my receipt for Chavis's bucket and its contents. I have to take the coins back to him. I'm sure he'll deal with them responsibly. We can take some pictures of them first so we'll have them in case we're in the mood to do a little research on where they could have come from."

" 'Little' is the operative word," Simon said. "The Cleggs and Julia should get here later this morning. You've met the Clegg children, haven't you?"

"Yeah," Morgan said. "But if I hadn't, it wouldn't matter. Children are fungible; they're all noisy and demanding and, these days, ignorant. At least these kids are girls. They're less trouble than boys, I would think."

Simon needed every muscle in his face to suppress his glee.

"This will be an interesting weekend," he said.

Simon took his shower, shaved, and dressed in jeans and a navy blue Kenan College sweatshirt. His hair was still wet when he sat down at the kitchen counter to watch Morgan prepare his breakfast specialty, which Simon referred to affectionately as "Death by Frying Pan."

"Might as well have something decent to eat before the women arrive and start telling us what to do," Morgan said.

He diced four strips of bacon and cooked it in a cast-iron frying pan with a minced head of garlic and a handful of chopped green onion. When the mixture was cooked to his satisfaction, he dumped a bag of frozen hash-brown potatoes into the pan. A few minutes later the potatoes were nicely crisped. He made two wells in the potatoes and cracked an egg into each, then sprinkled a cup of grated cheese over the lot and covered the pan until the eggs set, fairly hard, because after all they didn't want to get salmonella. The two men ate the food right out of the skillet, washing it down with a big glass of orange juice each.

Later they took two sets of photographs with Morgan's new digital camera. The first met professional archaeological standards. They carefully arranged the coins on black felt, next to a small ruler for scale. Simon trained a flashlight on the coins according to Morgan's instructions so that every tiny detail would appear in the pictures. The second set of photographs, taken with the camera on a timer, showed Morgan and Simon holding the coins and grinning like fools. Simon was optimistic that one day he'd have children and grandchildren to show them to, although his prospects did not seem too promising right now. "I can print these out right away, if I can get the computer program to work," Morgan said. "So far I've just figured out how to operate the camera." He put the envelope of coins into his pocket.

"Guess we'd better take them to Chief Keck," he said.

"Be strong," Simon said. "They're going to a good home."

Simon was relieved that they were taking the coins to Keck. Even waiting to take photos had made him anxious. He didn't at all like being responsible for someone else's property worth maybe a hundred thousand dollars. Especially if that person, or people, didn't even know the property existed. It wasn't professional.

"You know," Simon said, as they got into Morgan's truck to drive the mile and a half to the Pearlie Beach police station, "it's probably a good thing if not too many people know about this."

"I agree," Morgan said. "Every treasure nut with diving gear or a shovel could show up here. I suppose the only people who need to know are Chief Keck and Dale Pearlie. Dale's the mayor, after all."

WHEN THE BLACK PICKUP turned onto the graveled street that led to the police station, Simon and Morgan stumbled into the annual Pearlie Beach Chapel Bake Sale in full swing. The modest A-frame chapel and the nondescript brick Town Hall faced each other across the street, which then dead-ended almost immediately at the sound. Tables covered with pies, cakes, bread, and cookies crowded onto the bright lawn edged with aucuba and impatiens, still green, pink, and white in the mild autumn weather. White tablecloths on the tables, anchored by plates heaped with baked goods, fluttered in the breeze from the sound. Locals and tourists packed the lawn and spilled onto the street in front of the Town Hall. The clashing odors of yeast, sugar, and salty sea air struck them as soon as Simon and Morgan got out of the truck.

The Pearlie Beach Chapel was an interdenominational church that didn't have a regular pastor. It was a simple A-frame, probably built from a kit, with a driftwood cross mounted over the door. Clergy from all over North Carolina serviced the island's religious needs, spending a week at the beach free in one of the Pearlies' apartments in return for leading services. It was a coveted break for the lucky clergy who were asked to come, and a blessing for islanders and tourists alike, who didn't have to search the mainland for a church on Sunday. Simon easily picked out this week's pastor in the throng. She was a thin, pleasant-looking woman, dressed in a blue blazer and skirt, a black shirt, and a clerical collar. Although she was an Anglican among Baptists, she seemed at ease, listening to a gaggle of Pearlie women—Inez, Ruth, and Dee Anna—who surrounded her, chattering, while she ate a piece of chocolate cake.

Inez Pearlie looked out from the group and spotted Simon and Morgan. She certainly seemed to have recovered from the shock of finding her nephew's body. Her hair was coifed and her makeup was perfect. She was dressed in a lavender knit pantsuit with seashells embroidered on the tunic.

Inez hurried over to them and took Simon by the arm.

"You look well," Simon said.

"I am so relieved," she said. "I got up the nerve to speak to my sister about Carl. Do you know what? She didn't know who I was talking about! She has forgotten him completely! Old age has some blessings, I suppose."

Simon imagined a mother forgetting her child. It made him feel sick.

"Anyway, you two have been so good to us, come over and get a plate of food. On us."

"Actually, we need to talk to Chief Keck," Morgan said. "It's important."

"He's around here somewhere," Inez said, leading them into the cluster of tables.

They found Dale Pearlie at the first table.

"There's some of Viola's fudge left," he said. "You'd better get some before it's gone. She won a blue ribbon for it three years in a row at the State Fair."

Inez took two paper plates off the table and put a dark chunk of fudge on each.

"You let me fill these up for you," she said. "I know what's good." She set off down the aisles of food, stopping at each table to judge its offerings.

"Listen, Dale," Simon said. "We came here for a reason. It has to do with Carl Chavis's death, and we need to see Chief Keck."

"What's it about?" Dale asked.

"You remember the bucket I took away the morning we examined the body?" Morgan said. "It contained some valuables. We've cleaned them up and identified them, and I think Chief Keck needs to take charge of them now."

"Valuables, huh?" Dale said. "What kind of valuables?"

"Eleven gold Confederate coins," Simon said.

"Gold coins! Good Lord!" Dale said, too loudly. He turned toward the crowd, cupped his hands, and shouted, "Donnie Lee! We need you over here. Momma, you, too! It's about Carl!"

At the sound of Dale's voice everyone in the crowd looked at them for a second, causing a little gap in the hum of conversation. Chief Keck came toward them. He had a wedge of pecan pie in one hand and a cup of coffee in the other. Inez Pearlie came with him. She handed Simon and

Morgan each a plate piled with fudge, a piece of pecan pie, a hunk of pound cake, and a cup of coffee. Rather than ask for sugar and cream, Simon just dunked his pound cake in the coffee. First he'd take a bite of the coffee-soaked cake, then a sip of the coffee sweetened by cake crumbs.

"Well," Keck said, licking the last morsels of pecan and custard off his fingers. "What's this all about?"

"Can we go inside?" Morgan asked.

INSIDE THE TINY POLICE station Joe Pearlie was relieving a young African-American policewoman, Gaye Galloway, the third member of the Pearlie Beach police force, at the end of her shift. Gaye was a thinner, lighter version of her mother, Viola Munn. Freckles, obvious on her light brown skin, scattered across her face, and her hair, cut short, was definitely red. She was businesslike and efficient as she briefed Joe; he was stuffing down a plate of baked goods as fast as he could while he listened. When he saw the group enter, Joe hastily crammed his paper plate and napkin into a trash can. He stood up and tucked his shirt into his trousers. Dale looked away from his son.

"Anything happening?" Keck asked.

"Not a thing," Gaye said. "Everyone on the island's across the street, I believe."

"Show us what you've got," Dale said to Morgan.

Simon was uncomfortable. Several people had followed them into the police office. Their audience consisted of Dale and Inez; Chief Keck, Joe, and Gaye; and Leland Pearlie, Woody Watkins, and Dee Anna Frink. The tiny reception area barely contained them all. Simon saw no hope of keeping the coins a secret. He caught Morgan's eye. Morgan shrugged helplessly. He took the small brown envelope out of his shirt pocket and tipped the coins out on the counter. There was silence in the room for a few seconds before anyone spoke.

"Carl was looking for gold," Inez said. "He told me and Dale Senior so many times."

"Looks like he found it," Woody said.

Dee Anna edged her way to the counter and picked up one of the dollar coins. "It's so small," she said. "I've got more gold than this in my earrings."

"It's not the gold itself," Morgan said. "It's the history and the rarity of the coins that make them valuable."

"How much?" Inez asked. "I guess my sister's Carl's heir."

"It's not that simple," Simon said. "We won't know how much the coins are worth until an expert appraises them. I don't know how the legalities of ownership will work. Carl had them in his personal possession, but they were found inside the three-mile limit. The state of North Carolina may have some claim to them."

"The damn government," Leland snorted, "they've always got to get theirs."

Woody had picked up a coin, too. "I wonder where Chavis found these," he said.

"Do you think there's more?" Dee Anna asked.

"That's another question for the experts," Morgan said. "Personally I don't think there could be valuable artifacts left in this area, gold or otherwise. The Cape Fear River and the coast have been explored so thoroughly."

Simon didn't know if Morgan really believed this. He

did know that Morgan didn't want a horde of amateur treasure hunters to descend on the coast. Simon agreed with him.

"What do you think?" Dale asked Simon.

Simon had to swallow a mouthful of cake before he could answer. "You mean, is there a chest of Confederate gold lying around Pearlie Beach somewhere waiting for someone to find it and get rich? Anything's possible, but I doubt it."

The group clustered around the coins, touching them and murmuring.

Finally Keck shooed them away. "We're not going to find out anything more about this until after the holiday weekend, that's for sure. If you agree with me, Mayor, I'll take these over to the bank in Shallotte and lock them up in the town's safe-deposit box."

"That's a good idea," Dale said. "I'm sure Dr. Morgan here can tell us who to call on Monday about what to do next."

Keck placed the coins in the envelope and reached out a hand wordlessly toward Woody. Woody had closed his fist over the coin he had been handling. Reluctantly he gave the coin to Keck.

Simon was intensely relieved to see Chief Keck drive off with the coins. The folks who had crowded into the station with them went back to the bake sale. Simon figured that everyone in town would know about the gold within half an hour. Lots of them would react to the news without any common sense whatsoever.

Dale Pearlie lingered behind the others. "This is a family beach," he said. "The last thing we want is a bunch of ignorant treasure hunters showing up here to look for gold.

They'll trash up the beach and tear up the dunes in four-wheel-drive vehicles. Not to mention that some amateur diver might drown. Drowning's always terrible publicity for us. The only thing worse is a hurricane."

"Yeah," Simon said. "I can see that."

"And reporters," Dale said. "I hate those guys. Always looking for excitement. If they can't find it, they make it up. I know you are on vacation," Pearlie continued, "but you're the only historians I happen to know personally. Could I ask you to investigate whether or not there really could be gold here? Then we could answer people's questions."

"We were going to look into that very question anyway," Morgan said. "We'll let you know what we find out."

Simon and Morgan were getting into the truck when Viola scuffled up to them. She was carrying a bundle wrapped in aluminum foil and plastic wrap. A heavenly aroma of cinnamon, butter, and brown sugar wafted from it.

"I brought you some cinnamon rolls," she said, handing the package to Simon, "but don't you dare eat them now." She looked pointedly at Morgan as she spoke. "I want the Cleggs' little girls to get some. They are the sweetest babies."

Simon took the package from her. It was still warm. He remembered that Julia loved cinnamon rolls.

"Thanks," Simon said. "We'll save them until the rest of our crowd gets here."

3

JULIA WAS SITTING ON A LOWER STEP OF THE STAIRS AT THE Clegg cottage braiding Trina Clegg's hair when Simon and Morgan got back from the police station. She waved at them before finishing the hairdo with one last twist and an elastic band. She looked very good to Simon. She had lost a little weight, but not so much that it ruined her figure. Her hair, pulled back and braided, was longer, too. She was wearing a white shirt with the sleeves rolled up, a black denim skirt, silver earrings, and a silver chain with a tiny Celtic cross suspended from it. Simon delayed getting out of the truck for a few seconds to collect himself.

"Hey, there," he said.

"Hey, yourself," Julia answered. "We couldn't get in. We don't have a key."

Trina flew at him, threw herself into his arms, and hugged him with unself-conscious glee. She was a gawky ten-year-old with thick glasses and frizzy brown hair. Her skinny legs dangled.

"You've grown a foot," Simon said to her.

"Have not," Trina answered. "Just an inch and a half."

She twirled around, showing him the back of her head.

"Julia did my hair like hers," Trina said. "It's a French braid."

"Very elegant," Simon said.

"I'm the only one who got to ride with her," Trina said. "Isobel and Dolly had to go with Mom and Dad. They couldn't be trusted to behave."

"We had a great time, too," Julia said. "We bought a box of Krispy Kreme doughnuts before we left Raleigh, and we listened to the Spice Girls all the way here."

"Julia let me turn the volume up real loud," Trina said.

Morgan had acknowledged the two females with a nod and was leaning up against the banister of the staircase, smoking.

"Aren't you an archaeologist?" Trina asked him.

"Sure am," he said, shaking her hand formally. "I'm Dr. David Morgan. We met a while back. You've grown since then."

"I hope so. Otherwise there'd be something wrong with me. Did you bring any of your equipment with you?" she asked. "Can I see it?"

"Sure," Morgan said.

"Now?" she asked.

A little taken aback, but cooperative, Morgan took her by the hand and led her to his camper.

"You know," Trina said, her voice fading as the two of them walked under the house to the back of the parking area, "smoking isn't good for you. It causes cancer."

Simon and Julia were left standing alone next to her car, an aging black two-door BMW.

"Let me help you carry your stuff upstairs," Simon said.

"You don't mind me being here?" Julia asked.

"Of course not," he said.

Impulsively he stretched out his hand toward hers, and she took it.

"Thanks," she said. "No hard feelings, then?"

"No," he said. "Just warm ones. Specifically, lust."

"If I get my duffel and this bag of groceries, can you get Trina's stuff? That bag and her backpack?"

"You're changing the subject, but that's okay," Simon said. "I take correction very well."

"Hush," she said. "Try to behave. What have you and David been doing all week?"

"You would not believe," Simon said. "I'll tell you the whole story after Marcus and Marianne get here. It's too complicated to tell twice."

MARCUS AND MARIANNE CLEGG arrived a half hour later in an aging Dodge minivan with their two youngest daughters. The van was stuffed to the windows with two bikes, a tricycle, a couple of ice chests, and a jumble of duffel bags and toys. Marcus shushed Simon and Julia as he got out of the minivan.

"They're both asleep," he said. "For heaven's sake, don't wake them up. It's a mixed blessing," he said as he eased Isobel, age six, out of the car onto his shoulder. "We'll pay for it tonight."

Marianne had the three-year-old, Dolly, in her arms. "Let's put them in the bedroom," she said. "We can wake them up in half an hour, after we catch our breath."

Marcus and Marianne were grown-up flower children. They had retained some of the best traits of their youth and discarded the worst. Marcus was a brilliant scientist and historian, with dual appointments in the Psychology and History Departments at Kenan College. He was writing a book about the recantation of Galileo that Simon expected would make him famous. He wore his brown hair long, almost to his shoulders, John Lennon–style eyeglasses, blue jeans, and sandals. So did Marianne, for that matter. Her long, unstyled blond hair was gray at the temples, she used no makeup, and she wouldn't dream of exercising at a health club when she could be gardening or baking at home. When they got married they bought four acres studded with pines off a one-lane dirt road outside of Raleigh. It was unzoned; one neighbor bred and boarded dogs (the "Bed and Biscuit"); another was a shade-tree mechanic who kept up to five broken-down cars in his yard on any given day. They built a long, low, white concrete block ranch house with a green metal roof. The kids went to county schools. Marcus drove a Volkswagen Beetle with over two hundred thousand miles on the odometer and brought his lunch to work in a brown bag most days. Except for an excellent computer system, they had no remarkable possessions. "If you can't buy it at K-Mart," Marianne often said, "you don't need it." Simon guessed they lived on half their income at the most, putting the rest of it into their daughters' college funds and travel. They inherited the beach house from Marianne's aunt with the mortgage paid off, or they would never have kept it.

While they were unpacking and stowing groceries, Simon told Marcus, Marianne, and Julia the story of Carl

Chavis and his eleven pieces of Confederate gold.

"Has the press heard about this yet?" Marianne asked.

"They haven't had time," Simon said. "It just happened yesterday."

"Do you have any idea where the gold came from?" Julia asked.

"None at all," Simon said. "There's no historical record of a ship carrying a shipment of gold sinking in this area. Not even a rumor. Any large amount of gold would be listed on a ship's manifest, and Morgan has searched all the Internet archives and come up with nothing."

"So where did Chavis's gold come from?" Julia asked.

"Remember, it's just twenty-two dollars. A private citizen might have had that amount in a pocket or purse, and drowned, or thrown it overboard to keep it from the Yankees. It's a giant leap from eleven coins to a treasure."

"No one will believe that," Marcus said. "It's not romantic enough."

"The truth often isn't," Simon said.

Simon opened the ice chest he and Marcus had carried in from the van. Reposing amid plastic bags filled with ice was an enormous turkey.

"How big is this thing?" Simon asked. "Will it fit into the oven?"

"Thirty pounds," Marcus said proudly. "And we're going to smoke that sucker outside. It'll take all night."

Trina clattered up the back steps and came into the house from the porch, slamming the door behind her. Morgan followed her.

"He's got a portable X-ray machine," she said, breathlessly, to her parents "And he showed me X-ray pictures that he took of a skull. You can see everything! It was so cool! And then we printed out those pictures of the gold coins he and Simon found. Look," she said. She held out several letter-sized pictures of the coins. The prints highlighted the rich color and the imperfect casting of the coins.

"I thought you didn't know how to print these out," Simon said to Morgan.

"I did it," Trina said. "It was easy."

"Bright child," Morgan said to Simon.

Simon pinned the photos of the gold pieces on the bulletin board next to the copies of the newspaper clipping about Chavis's disappearance, the Cape Fear shipwreck map, and the photograph of Chavis and his buddies.

Dolly Clegg let out a bloodcurdling shriek from the bedroom. Everyone jumped except the Cleggs.

"Sorry," Marcus said. "She's a screamer."

Marianne went into the girls' bedroom.

Julia's pager sounded next.

"Since when do you carry a pager on vacation?" Simon asked.

"I don't trust those guys as far as I can throw them. I'd rather talk to them than go home on Monday and clean up some mess they've made because they couldn't get in touch with me."

"Six hundred adult policemen and policewomen, who've taken your course at the police academy, whom you bury in memos and seminars, can't get along without you for one weekend?"

Julia ignored him. Marcus pointed out her bedroom, and she went in to use the phone.

"If it's Otis, I want to speak to him!" Simon called out.

Otis Gates was a homicide detective with the Raleigh police. Simon and he had become friends on Simon's first and only excursion into crime investigation. They made quite a pair. Otis was a middle-aged African-American ex-football player twice Simon's size.

"Here he is," Julia called out to Simon, the phone receiver outstretched. Simon took it and closed the bedroom door after Julia, who left to join the Cleggs on their porch.

"I'm sure you had a real important question for her," Simon said.

Otis chuckled. Simon heard Aretha Franklin singing "I Knew You Were Waitin' for Me" softly in the background, accompanied by a rhythmic clicking. Simon recognized the sound of Otis beating time to the music with a pair of drumsticks he kept in his desk drawer.

"Julia would wither away if she didn't hear from us every day," Otis said. "I just called to make her feel needed."

"I suppose you're going to be in Raleigh all weekend?"

"My year to be on call for Thanksgiving," Otis said. "Alma and the boys went to her sister's. I'm going to catch up on my paperwork. Is Julia in the room with you?"

"No."

"She's still interested in you."

"Hogwash. She dumped me."

"Meaningless," Otis said. "Women never know what they want. I'm positive she accepted Marianne's invitation because of you."

"Thanks for telling me," Simon said. "It's not like I was getting any sleep anyhow."

DOLLY CLEGG SAT IN the sand with her short chubby legs stretched out in front of her, sifting beach sand the consistency of sugar through a kitchen colander into a heap between her legs. Nearby, Isobel played in a few inches of tepid water in a tidal pool warmed by the afternoon sun. She splashed from one end of it to the other, spooking the little flock of sanderlings that were feeding at the pool's edge. The birds skittered away, only to run into Dolly, who screamed at them. They took to the air, flashing white-striped wings, and alighted farther down the beach where they could feed on sand fleas in peace.

Simon and Julia lounged in beach chairs under an umbrella with their pale bare legs stretched out in the warm afternoon sun. They had one eye on the two youngest Clegg girls and the other on their books. Simon was reading *Shipwrecks of the Carolinas,* turning the pages rapidly.

"You can't be reading that quickly," Julia said.

"Just refreshing my memory," Simon said.

Julia had appropriated *The Doorbell Rang,* but she wasn't reading it. It lay on her lap, open to the first page, as she gazed out at the blue ocean crashing into the shore ten feet away from them.

"It is so beautiful," Julia said. "I wish we could go swimming. It feels warm enough."

"I dare you to try it. That water's freezing. It is late November, after all," Simon said. "And it's only seventy-four degrees out. It just seems warmer than that here in the sun."

Trina ran up and plopped down next to them, spattering sand into their laps. Her hair had come loose from her braid and her glasses were foggy with ocean spray. Simon thought he saw tears in her eyes.

"Are you okay?" he asked.

"They won't let me play with them," Trina said. "They keep calling me a geek."

A short distance away a band of preteens in bright bathing suits were building a complicated sand castle. Trina had been trying to join them all afternoon. One boy saw Simon glaring at them and stuck his tongue out at him.

"They are so immature," Trina said. "Who wants to play with them anyway?"

"Forget it," Julia said. "Let's go see if the water is as cold as Simon says it is."

They stopped ankle-deep in the foam at the spent end of the breakers. The water was frigid. Dolly danced from foot to foot once, then wordlessly lifted her arms to Simon, who hoisted her onto his shoulders.

"I'm convinced," Julia said, skipping back to dry sand. "You two had better come out, or you'll catch cold," she said to Trina and Isobel.

"I'll give you each five dollars if you can dunk your heads underwater," Simon said to them.

"Simon!" Julia said. "You shouldn't say that! It's freezing!"

Simon backed onto dry sand himself, with Dolly still on his shoulders. "Well, girls," he said. "Think you're brave enough?" Driven by greed, Isobel and Trina moved farther out into the surf, but stopped just below the waist, jumping as each swell moved into the shore to keep as much as their bodies out of water as possible. A larger than usual wave broke over them, sending Isobel running to shore, shivering. Julia met her with a towel and a sweatshirt. Trina, wet from the chest down, moved farther out.

"Honey," Simon called to her, "better come in. I was just teasing."

Trina looked past them, off to the right, and Simon followed her gaze to the group of kids who had rejected her. They had stopped playing and were watching Trina.

Another wave broke over Trina, soaking her from the neck down. She was visibly trembling, but began to bob up and down, holding her nose, in preparation to duck underwater. Simon handed Dolly to Julia and moved quickly out into the surf.

"Are you going in after her?" Julia asked.

"I don't want to embarrass her if I don't have to," Simon said. "She's a good swimmer."

"You don't think the cold will affect her?"

"Trina," Simon called out to her, "I was just kidding. Come on in. You've earned your five dollars."

"Come in, Trina," Isobel called. "The cold water will paralyze you and you'll drown. I saw it on TV!"

"I can do it," Trina shouted. "Watch me!"

Trina sank under the water just as a wave broke over her. Simon instantly dived under the wave, and the two of them came up together, coughing and spitting. They struggled through the surf toward the beach, laughing and hanging on to each other. One more wave broke over them before they got back to shore.

Trina shook violently while Simon and Julia toweled her off and rubbed her arms and legs. She was proud of herself.

"You owe me five dollars," she said to Simon.

"I do. But tell me," he said, "if I dared you to jump off a cliff, would you do it?"

"Maybe," she said. "Depends. Would I have a parachute?"

After going inside to change into warm clothes, Trina made boats out of bits of wood and sailed them across the tidal pool to her sisters. Simon, who had put on jeans and a sweatshirt, and Julia were just settling back into their lounge chairs when Colonel Watkins's wife Anita came across the sand toward them, holding a pink straw hat over her hair, which was a little too blond to be believable. She was much younger than her husband—fifty-five to his nearly eighty years. The defining moment of her entire life was her coronation as Miss Brunswick County in 1962, and she continued to dress and act the part of the pageant queen. Simon introduced her to Julia.

"The Cleggs told me you were out here," Anita said.

"We're watching the girls while they get the cottage organized," Julia said.

Anita noticed the shipwreck book Simon was reading.

"I just think it's so interesting about that gold," Anita said. "Woody has told us all about it. I was wondering if you-all would like to come over to our place for drinks later this afternoon. The Cleggs can't come because of the children, but I've already asked Dr. Morgan and he accepted. Woody will be there, of course, and Dee Anna, her husband leaves her alone so much, and the preacher for the chapel this week. You know we don't have a regular preacher, don't you? We have a different one every week—it's a vacation for them. A week at the beach in exchange for leading services."

"Certainly," Simon said. "We'd be glad to come."

"Do you think," Anita said, "that you could bring those photos of the gold coins? The ones I saw on the wall of the house when I went inside? My husband would be so interested."

"I don't see why not," Simon said.

"Wonderful," she said. "We'll look forward to it."

She fluttered away across the sand, protecting her hat from the wind with both hands.

"Why did you do that?" Julia said. "They just want to pump you about the coins."

"I know that," Simon said. "But I've got questions, too. Colonel Watkins knew Carl Chavis. Maybe he knows something about Carl's treasure-hunting."

COL. TIMOTHY WATKINS AND his family lived well. When his house was built, it was the grandest on the island. Three stories tall, all glass and stained wood, topped with a widow's walk, it dwarfed the Cleggs' cottage next door. The American flag and the official white-and-gold-bordered flag of the U.S. Army flew from the widow's walk at all appropriate times. Watkins owned the vacant lot on the other side of his place, too, refusing to sell it despite receiving several financially breathtaking offers for it.

Watkins met them at the door dressed in matching Alexander Julian slacks and shirt, putting Simon's jeans and navy blue Kenan College sweatshirt to shame.

"Glad you-all could come," Watkins said, leading them into a living room decorated by someone who did it for a living. "Let me fix you a drink."

A large fireplace faced with marble with several pieces of Oriental porcelain on the mantel dominated the off-white living room, furnished with overstuffed sofas and chairs covered in neutral fabrics. An original Bob Timberlake oil painting of the Hatteras lighthouse hung over the fireplace, and Simon recognized a Kyle Highsmith among the other paintings on the wall. A mahogany sideboard held a jade carving of an Oriental temple at least twenty inches tall.

Watkins opened the cabinet door of a fully stocked bar with its own refrigerator.

"What can I get you?" he asked.

"A beer would be fine," Morgan replied.

"The same for me," Simon said.

"And me," Julia said.

Simon loved a woman who drank beer.

Watkins poured three Michelobs into pilsner glasses. His hands were gnarled and age-spotted, and he opened the beer bottles with some difficulty. Arthritis, Simon supposed.

The rest of the party was already on the large deck that led off the living room. It was higher than the porch at the Cleggs', and Simon could see over the dunes and all the way out to the surf breaking on the beach.

Once seated, Simon found himself speculating that Dee Anna was a younger clone of Anita. Her dyed hair was a shade lighter than Anita's and although her clothes were not quite as expensive, they were cut out of the same mold. It would be a while before Dee Anna caught up to Anita in the gold jewelry category, though. A heavy charm dangled from every link of Anita's gold bracelet. Simon was surprised she could lift her arm.

Woody was relaxed, lounging with one leg thrown over the arm of his chair. But then, Woody was always relaxed. He leaned so close to Dee Anna, and her chair was so close to his, that Simon guessed their relationship was intimate.

The chapel "preacher" was wearing a blue-striped shirtwaist dress and a blue beaded sweater.

"I'm Clare Monahan," the young clergywoman said. She shook hands with each of them in turn. "My home church is in Durham. I'm serving here this week."

"Oh, dear," Anita said. "I forgot to introduce you."

Clare was in her late thirties, Simon guessed, and had short brown hair, little makeup, and a firm handshake.

"Clare is almost home folks," Watkins said. "I knew her grandparents years ago."

"My grandfather died during the war," Clare said. "He was a coastwatcher. When my grandmother remarried, the family moved to Baltimore. This is my first visit."

"You must be happy to be here," Julia said.

"I'm thrilled," Clare said. "Usually the rector of my church has this week, but he was busy this year, so he let me come instead. I do have two services, one Thanksgiving and one Sunday, but I'll still have time to do some diving."

"Woody will guide you to the best spots, won't you, dear?" Anita said to her son.

"Sure," Woody said. "This coast is littered with wrecks. Which these guys," he said, nodding at Simon and Morgan, "would be in a better position to know about than us amateurs."

Dee Anna was more direct. "Woody tells me that you once solved a really old murder," she said to Simon. "That sounds so exciting! Do you think there might be more gold where Chavis got those coins? Are you going to try to find it?"

"I'd put six months' pay on the lottery before I'd look for a significant amount of gold around here. And no one's been murdered."

"Why do you think there's no gold?"

"There's no objective historical evidence to support it."

Colonel Watkins silently stirred his drink with his index finger. Woody drank his beer without taking his eyes off Simon. "What about the *Phantom*?" he asked.

"It's miles from here, on the other side of Cape Fear, closer to Cape Lookout."

"He could have driven there."

"In 1942? During the war? That makes no sense. Where did he get the car? And the gasoline? All that was rationed. If he found gold on the *Phantom*, why was his corpse found in Pearlie Beach Sound?"

"He's right about the rationing," Colonel Watkins said. "You couldn't get gas or tire coupons unless you were a doctor or something."

"He could have traveled by boat," Woody said.

"Boats need gasoline, too," Simon said. "Besides, there were German submarines right offshore. Lots of them. Not conducive to boating."

"So," Woody said, waving the photos of the gold coins, which the guests were passing around, "where did these come from?"

"It's just twenty-two dollars. Some poor Confederate drowned with that much money on him, or threw it overboard, and Chavis lucked on it. Besides, even if there was more gold, sport divers have been crawling all over these wrecks for years."

"That's right, dear," Anita said. "You must have dived on the *Phantom* at least a dozen times yourself."

"I never heard of anyone finding gold before," Woody said.

"If someone did, he might have kept it secret. Anything inside the three-mile limit would be state property," Morgan said.

Colonel Watkins had the pictures of the gold coins in his hands. He took out his reading glasses to look at them carefully.

"What did you find on the *Phantom*?" Clare asked Woody.

"Lead ingots, gun stocks, forks and knives, padlocks, buttons, all kinds of stuff," Woody said.

"So sensible to wage war when you can't even make your own buttons," Simon said.

Julia instantly propelled a cracker spread with cream cheese and pepper jelly toward Simon's mouth. The last thing they needed was to shock their hosts with Simon's opinions on the Civil War, which were unorthodox for a southerner, to say the least. He usually had the sense to keep his mouth shut among people he didn't know. All Simon's close friends were alert to the need to muzzle him if he slipped up, hence Julia's stuffing him with crackers and cheese at a crucial moment.

"Let's not go there," she said.

Simon obediently abandoned the subject and ate his cracker.

"You knew Carl Chavis, didn't you?" Morgan asked Colonel Watkins.

"A little," Watkins said. "We were stationed on the same base in Wilmington."

"Would you look at this photograph we found in Chavis's file?" Simon said. "Do you recognize these men?"

Simon showed the photograph to Watkins. He scrutinized the picture of the group of men just as carefully as he had looked at the photos of the gold, tilting it into the fading daylight.

"This brings back memories," Watkins said. "It was

taken on the porch of the Pavilion." He tapped the image of one of the uniformed men in the photo. "This is me. As to the other men in the picture, the two who look so much alike are Dale and Henry Pearlie. And Carl is the other man in uniform. I don't recognize the man in the leather jacket at all. I was in Wilmington for just a few months, from January to May of 1942. I went off to Officer Candidate School a couple of weeks after Carl vanished."

Watkins handed the photograph back to Simon.

"You don't remember anything about Chavis's disappearance?" Simon asked.

"No," Watkins said. "I'm sure the military police investigated it thoroughly and found out everything worth knowing. Come see my collection, why don't you?"

Viewing personal collections has always been the lot of historians and archaeologists, so Morgan and Simon accepted their fate and followed Watkins into his study. Clare and Julia went with them.

Watkins's study was large and comfortable, furnished with floor-to-ceiling bookshelves and a large desk. The shelves were crowded with pictures and memorabilia but few books. Simon was surprised at the depth of Watkins's collection of World War II memorabilia. It was not junk. Watkins proudly showed them displays of Nazi insignia, SS epaulets, buckles, firearms, old photographs, and German medals, including two Iron Crosses.

"This isn't everything I've got," Watkins said. "I have the two biggest safe-deposit boxes at my bank. I like to rotate my collection."

"All this stuff gives me the shivers," Julia said.

"That's because it's just plain scary," Morgan said. "The Nazi movement was evil and came close to conquering most of the civilized world. We don't want that to happen again, or even to think about it, so when we see reminders of it, we naturally feel anxious."

"I especially hate the swastika. It evokes such horrors," Clare said. "I was reading an old book, published in the twenties, in the church library the other day and the swastika was used as a decorative element on the cover and endpapers. It shocked me so. You know, the swastika was originally a Christian symbol, a Greek cross, but it will never mean anything other than Nazism ever again."

"Where did you get all this?" Simon asked.

"I was in Germany at the end," Watkins said. "The German officers, especially the Gestapo, stripped off their uniforms and abandoned everything in hopes they wouldn't be identified. They dressed in rags and hid in the refugee camps. You'd find this stuff lying just off the roads. I brought lots of souvenirs home with me."

Watkins pointed out another shelf of artifacts.

"These are Civil War items Woody found on his dives," Watkins said. "All of them came off blockade runners."

Arranged on a shelf was a collection of objects eroded and pitted by a century under the sea: silverware, ladles, padlocks, and a mass of something that proved to be tiny brass tailor's pins.

"What's this hard black stuff gluing everything into clumps?" asked Julia. "It's like cement."

"Ashes," Morgan said. "When ships burned, the ashes mixed with water and hardened."

Morgan nodded toward a rifle mounted on the wall of the study. "That Enfield is in amazing condition," he said.

"Woody didn't find that," Watkins said. "I bought it from a dealer. A diver brought up a sealed barrel from the

Phantom years ago. It was filled with linseed oil and a dozen British Enfield rifles. That's what the Confederacy used. The Yankees carried Winchesters and Remingtons."

When the group got back to the deck, Dee Anna and Woody were sipping their drinks and talking. Anita must have been in the kitchen, because Simon could smell dinner cooking.

At his door Watkins shook their hands good-bye.

"One more thing," Watkins said. "Would you ask the Cleggs to keep the outside lights of their cottage off at night this weekend? It's a new moon, and I've got a telescope up on the widow's walk on my roof. I want to use it tonight."

"Sure," Simon said.

Outside the Watkins home, Morgan opened the door of Clare's green Mustang for her. "So," he said, "what time is the service on Thanksgiving?"

"Don't feel that you have to come to church just because we've met," Clare said. "Although I do preach an excellent service on thankfulness, if I say so myself. Ten A.M."

THE SKY OVER THE ocean slowly darkened from turquoise to cobalt as the sun set. The Cleggs' deck was chilly, but the entire party sat outside, bundled up in sweatshirts and jeans, watching Simon and Morgan cook. Water bubbled in the large stockpot set over the flame of the gas cooker. Morgan had just tossed in a package of Old Bay crab boil. Simon added two pounds of smoked link sausage cut into pieces. Precisely five minutes later they added twelve ears of husked corn broken into halves. Exactly five minutes after that they dropped in four pounds of fresh shrimp.

Three minutes later the Frogmore stew was ready. They dished it into bowls and sat down at the picnic table with plenty of beer and a stack of napkins. Marcus and Marianne peeled the shrimp and scraped the kernels off the corn for Isobel and Dolly, who happily slurped the stew with spoons, their short legs swinging from their chairs. The rest of them ate with their fingers, first peeling the shrimp and salting the corn.

After the shrimp shells and corn cobs were thrown away and the bowls put in the dishwasher, they sat inside in front of the propane fire. Dolly and Isobel slowly drifted into sleep in their parents' laps.

"I'm confused about the Pearlies," Julia said. "Explain all these relationships to me again."

"It's not that complicated," Marcus said. "Henry and Dale Pearlie Senior, who is deceased, were first cousins. Dale and Inez's children are Dale Junior and Leland. Nance and Dee Anna Frink are Leland's kids; Joe is Dale Junior's son. They all call Henry 'Uncle Henry.' "

"So how was Carl Chavis related to the family?"

"He was Inez's nephew, her sister's son," Simon said.

"And Colonel Watkins was stationed here during the war and retired here. Okay, I think I've got it. Now, what on earth is the *Phantom*?"

"It was a blockade runner that ran aground and was destroyed by Yankee gunboats in 1863," Simon said. "It's always been rumored to have had a strongbox full of Confederate gold on it. It probably didn't. It was on its way to Wilmington with supplies for the army. A shipment of gold would have been outward bound from Wilmington, to pay for those supplies in Europe. In fact the Confederacy didn't have much gold. Their money was raw cotton."

"It's possible, though?"

"Sure, anything's possible. If you stretch your imagination just as far as you can, you can just barely conceive that Carl Chavis found gold on the *Phantom*, or some other wreck, in 1942. He placed some of the coins in his bucket, then got beyond a safe depth and drowned. Then years later one of the first sport divers on the wreck, say in the early fifties, found the rest of the gold and kept it without reporting it. But the wreck of the *Phantom* is miles and miles away from Pearlie Beach, around Cape Fear and to the north of Topsail Island. If Chavis died there, how on earth did his body get into the Pearlie Beach Sound? It just doesn't make sense."

"The *Lynx* had a shipment of Confederate gold. It was outbound from Wilmington when the Yankees attacked it," Morgan said. "But the gold was salvaged by the Confederates after the ship went aground."

"If we assume that Chavis died very close to Pearlie Beach, which I think is reasonable considering the condition of the corpse, there are only a few blockade runners he could have been diving on: the *Ranger*, the *Elizabeth*, and the *Iron Age*. And there are more off Holden Beach and Long Beach. But they're very close to shore, and there's no gold on them now, if there ever was, which I doubt."

"Can you still see the wrecks?" Trina asked.

"Sure," Simon said. "We'll go on a field trip and look at them this weekend, if you like."

"So your conclusion is that Carl Chavis found a very small cache of gold," Julia said, "and that there never was any bigger treasure?"

"That's it," Simon said. "I wrote up my thinking on the subject and took it to Sheriff Keck and Dale Pearlie before we went next door."

"Not very exciting," Marcus said. "There are going to be plenty of people who won't believe it."

"That's their problem," Simon said. "Tomorrow I'm going back to my study of the works of Rex Stout. I want *The Doorbell Rang* back, please," Simon said to Julia.

LATER THAT EVENING SIMON and Morgan sat under the Clegg house, among the pilings, on a couple of lawn chairs that Morgan kept strapped to the roof of his camper. Now that the sun was completely down and the warmth had left the ground, it was cold. Morgan smoked a cigarette while Simon picked sandspurs off his socks and shoes. A patch of the nasty little burrs grew between the Clegg cottage and the Watkins's property. Sandspurs concentrated more pain potential in their tiny needlelike prickles than anything else Simon knew of, relative to size, which was about a quarter of an inch. Sandspurs had arrived on Pearlie Beach with Hurricane Hazel, and nothing could eradicate them. They were as impervious to extermination as cockroaches.

Chief Keck's official Jeep Cherokee pulled into the cottage driveway. His headlights illuminated the two men sitting under the cottage. Keck got out, felt the cold air, and reached inside the car for his jacket.

"Might I ask what the two of you are doing out here in the cold and the dark when you have a perfectly good cottage to go into?" he asked.

"Not enough bedrooms inside," Simon said. "We're sleeping in the camper."

"Let me get you a chair," Morgan said.

"Thanks," Keck said. He sat down and crossed his legs. He had a large manila envelope in his hand.

"Just dropping by for a chat?" Simon asked.

"Not exactly," Keck said. "I got your report. It made a lot of sense. Until I heard from your medical examiner friend."

Simon and Morgan looked at each other apprehensively.

"Well you might look nervous," Keck said. "It's not pretty. Apparently Chavis's corpse interested him and he had a few hours to spare before the holiday."

"Oh, no," Simon said.

"Oh, yes," Keck said.

"What did he find?" Morgan asked.

"Chavis was murdered," Keck said.

Morgan sucked hard on his cigarette, the red tip glowed brightly, and he coughed.

"Explain, please," Simon said.

"Well," Keck said, "first of all, after checking Chavis's dental work, and confirming his identity, Dr. Boyette found his dog tags hung up on a rib. So there's really no question it's him."

"Okay, and then what?" Simon said.

"He got the diving suit and mask off, I didn't ask how," Keck said. "Don't want to know, and the skeleton was fairly intact. The four-inch blade of a fish-cleaning knife was found in Chavis's chest cavity. The fourth and fifth ribs were scarred. Boyette thinks that the serrated edge of the knife got hung up on Chavis's ribs and the murderer couldn't dislodge it. The hilt's missing; either it broke off or the murderer broke it off. Anyway, Chavis's heart or lungs or both were pierced. Maybe he died right away, or maybe he drowned after the injury. No way to know. But it was murder."

Keck held the manila envelope out to Simon. Simon didn't take it, and after a few seconds Keck let his hand drop into his lap.

"The medical examiner said you might be interested in this case, and the Pearlies gave their permission for you to have a copy of his report," Keck said.

Morgan took the envelope from Keck. Simon didn't say anything.

"Well," Keck said. "My working assumption is that someone killed Carl Chavis for the gold he found. There must have been more than what he had already stashed in that bucket. What do you think?"

Simon didn't answer. He was looking toward the widow's walk on top of Watkins's house, where he saw a reflection from the lens of Watkins's telescope.

"Simon?" Morgan asked.

"Oh," Simon said. "I'm sorry. What were you saying?"

"I was speculating about Carl's murder. I think it must have been related to the gold."

"Sure," Simon said. "That seems to be the most likely explanation."

Keck was disappointed. The medical examiner had told him that Simon would be intrigued by Chavis's murder. Instead Simon seemed uninterested to the point of lethargy.

"Are you going to look at the report?" Keck asked.

"Certainly he will," Morgan answered.

"We're on vacation," Simon said. "I doubt that we have anything to contribute anyway. Fifty-some years is a long time. There are almost no primary documents to examine and there's no historical record of any gold around here. I don't see what we can do."

Keck was disappointed, but he didn't say anything. He got up to leave.

"Say hello to the Cleggs for me," Keck said. "Have a good day tomorrow."

The Cherokee backed out of the driveway.

"What's wrong with you?" Morgan said to Simon.

"I hate this," Simon said. "That Chavis kid was murdered, and I don't think there's anything anyone can do about it."

SIMON HAD FORGOTTEN HOW seriously Morgan snored. His grunts and snorts reverberated off the metal walls of the tiny camper. Simon didn't understand how Morgan could stand to spend so much of his life in his camper, although he certainly grasped the reasoning behind it. The state of North Carolina's travel allowance for employees was pathetically inadequate. Morgan's work required him to travel to and live near whatever dig site he was supervising, so the camper was a godsend. He could avoid cheap motels and cheap food. He could smoke. He could take his dogs with him. He never had to unpack. And traveling to conferences out of state with the camper was wonderful publicity for North Carolina's stinginess. He would park the camper at whatever hotel was hosting a prestigious convention, like the annual meeting of the American Association of Archaeology, and stay right there. He especially liked to set up a few lawn chairs next to his camper in the parking lot and invite colleagues for drinks and handfuls of North Carolina peanuts.

Simon stretched out on the dinette bunk comfortably, an advantage of being small, but his sleeping bag smelled of cigarettes and Morgan's dogs. And Simon couldn't get Chavis's murder out of his mind. Of course murder happened. What he hated was that someone got away with it, and maybe got away rich. Murderers were supposed to be caught and punished, if possible. It was a requisite of a civilized society, and he was a civilized man.

The inside of the truck camper closed in on him. He might as well have been sealed up in an empty tuna fish can. He sat up on his bunk. Morgan was lying on his back with his knees in the air, snoring away.

Simon went outside, taking the sleeping bag with him. He inhaled a lungful of cold, salty air mixed with the subtle aroma of the Thanksgiving turkey smoking on the deck. He found a depression in the dune free of sandspurs and rolled out the sleeping bag. He crawled into it and was quickly very warm. He listened to the surf roll in and out, inexorably, guided by the moon, if not eternally, then for as many millions of years as he cared to contemplate. The noise was like the quiet breathing of a soundly sleeping bedmate, whom he preferred to think of as female. Or perhaps it reminded his subconscious of the rhythmic sounds of his mother's heart in the womb. Within a few minutes Simon was sound asleep, breathing in unison with the surf.

SIMON WAS NAKED IN the hold of the ship except for a ragged pair of canvas breeches. It was hot as Hades so close to the boiler. He stoked the steam furnace with shovelfuls of coal that he threw into the eighteen-inch opening of the firebox. His bare feet, legs, chest, face, and arms were filthy with coal dust except where sweat striped his body. He could hear the wind blowing at near gale force and the guns of the Yankee cruiser firing. Only with a full head of steam could the blockade runner avoid wrecking on the shoals and escape into the Cape Fear River. So he shoveled furiously while his muscles seized in protest.

The ship was designed just for the job of smuggling supplies to the Confederacy. Built in Liverpool, it was a newfangled ironclad steamer, powered by a screw propeller instead of a paddle wheel. It was painted light gray and burned smokeless anthracite coal. Its shallow draft allowed it to navigate in shallow waters. Almost invisible at more than two hundred yards, especially at dusk or in bad weather, the ship had made this trip successfully before now. But somehow the cursed Yankees had seen them hugging the shore, slinking toward Wilmington, and opened fire.

A Yankee shell hit the ship, killing the steersman and knocking it off course. Shortly the ship collided with the shoals at eighteen knots, throwing Simon across the hold. He was half buried in coal. Water began to pour into the hold. When he heard the fire in the firebox begin to sizzle, he abandoned his post. When the fire went out, the water pumps would stop working, and the boat would sink very quickly. Terrified of drowning belowdecks, he clambered up the narrow wooden ladder to the deck of the ship. A couple of red-eyed rats scampered up with him. When he got out on deck, fires burned fore and aft. Crewmen were running back and forth, shouting and lowering the lifeboats. The captain, a disheveled man with a straggly beard and a big belly protrud-

ing from his blue jacket, paced back and forth on the bridge, calmly delivering his orders.

Of course Simon couldn't swim. Few people in the nineteenth century could. His choices were to stay on board and burn to death, try to force his way onto a dinghy, jump overboard and hope he landed in shallow water, or stay on board and pray the captain could beach the ship safely.

A beautiful redheaded woman, a passenger who had embarked in Bermuda, came out of the passenger cabin onto the deck. She was dressed in elegant green velvet. Her slave, wearing a pink flowered housecoat and purple bedroom slippers, was by her side. The woman and her slave struggled with a small, heavy strongbox. They labored to get it to the side of the ship, where they tipped it over the rails as the ship listed severely to starboard. Simon decided to try his luck in a dinghy. Shaking with cold and fear, he slid overhand down a rope into the boat. Just as the boat lowered into the black, surging water and the ropes were thrown over the side, a German U-boat surfaced soundlessly beside the blockade runner. Its deck gun opened fire, dashing whatever hope the ship had of staying afloat. Its job done, silently the submarine submerged. The last thing Simon saw of it was the tip of its conning tower dipping under the surface of the sea.

4

A SMALL FOOT NUDGED SIMON. HE GRABBED IT AND OPENED his eyes. The sky was high, clear, and blue, foretelling a warm Thanksgiving Day. The foot squirmed and its owner giggled. Simon released it, disentangling himself from the sleeping bag.

"You'd better get up," Isobel Clegg said. "Or all the cinnamon buns will be gone."

The little girl standing next to him on the dune wore a turquoise blue adult-sized sweatshirt that hung down to her knees. Her bare legs and feet terminated in tiny toenails painted hot pink. The morning sun shone behind her, blurring her short curls into a blond aura. She held a half-eaten bun in one hand and an apple juice box in the other. Her mouth was smeared with icing.

"Did you sleep out here all night?" she asked. "Wasn't it cold? Did the crabs try to bite you? Julia says you have to come in now or she's going to eat your breakfast." This was the most conversation Simon had ever heard out of this particular Clegg daughter. Usually Isobel couldn't get a word in edgewise between Dolly demanding attention and Trina expounding on something or other.

Isobel took a big bite of her roll and slurped up the last of her juice.

"Tell everyone I'll be right there," Simon said.

Simon washed his face, showered, and shaved in the tiny space that passed for a bathroom in Morgan's camper. He felt good. He had slept better outside on the dune than he had in several days.

On the deck of the cottage David Morgan stretched out on a chaise lounge, drinking coffee and smoking a cigarette. A clamshell resting on his belly served as his ashtray. On a corner of the deck the turkey was still cooking in the smoker, suspended over smoldering charcoal, damp hickory chips, and a drip pan full of garlic, aromatic vegetables, and white wine. The aroma was indescribable.

"Did I snore?" Morgan said.

"Does a frog bump its butt?" Simon said, and went inside.

Marianne and Julia meant business. They hadn't even changed out of their nightclothes before tackling Thanksgiving dinner. Marianne wore a red-checked apron over a long flannel nightgown. She was viciously beating something in a large pottery bowl with a whisk. Julia was barefoot, dressed in plaid pajama pants and a long-sleeved Duke T-shirt. Her hair was pulled back with a scrunchee she must have borrowed from one of the girls. It was hot pink with purple polka dots. She sat on a stool at the counter, reading a recipe in an old *Gourmet* cookbook. Simon thought she looked immensely desirable.

"Julia and I are doing all the cooking," Marianne said. "You guys are cleaning up."

"Sounds fair to me," Simon said.

"You got up just in time," Julia said. "There's one cinnamon roll left, and half a pot of coffee. Did you sleep outside all night?"

"Yeah," Simon said. "And I feel great." He perched on a stool at the counter while he ate. Viola's roll melted in his mouth. He paused halfway through eating so he could anticipate finishing it. Marianne's coffee tasted much better than Morgan's.

"I did have this one wild dream," Simon said to Julia. "I think you were in it."

"Uh-oh," Marianne said.

"It wasn't like that, unfortunately," Simon said. "I was a boiler stoker on a blockade runner, Julia was a southern lady, Viola was her slave—"

"How politically incorrect," Julia said.

"—and David Morgan was the captain," Simon said to her. "You were dressed like Vivien Leigh in her green velvet curtains in *Gone With the Wind.*"

"What happened?" Julia asked.

"A German submarine shot at us and we sank."

"Dear boy," Marianne said, "I'm not trying to run you off, but I need this counter space to chop onions."

Simon took his coffee into the living area, where Marcus sprawled on a sofa with his daughters watching the Macy's Thanksgiving Day Parade.

"I want to see Santa Claus," Dolly said.

"He'll be at the end of the parade," Trina said. "Everybody knows that."

"Thanksgiving was once the perfect holiday," Marcus said. "Four days of eating, watching football in front of a nice fire, jumping in piles of leaves, walking off leftovers.

Now Christmas arrives instantly after Thanksgiving dinner. Everyone runs out and exhausts themselves shopping and decorating. I hate it. That's one reason we come here. Limits our exposure to the insanity."

Mindlessly and happily Simon watched floats and bands and giant balloons pass by on the small screen, cheering with the girls when Raleigh's Broughton High School band marched by the camera, resplendent in new purple and gold uniforms. During a commercial Simon got up to refresh his cup of coffee, emptying the pot, and he glanced through the door to the deck. Morgan was no longer in his lounge chair. He found out why when the man entered the cottage a few minutes later.

For an instant Simon didn't recognize him. Morgan had pulled his hair back into a short ponytail and trimmed his beard. His khaki pants actually fit. They were pressed, neatly belted, and circled his body at his waist rather than under his belly. He wore a clean white polo shirt and a blue blazer. There was a brief moment of shock in the cottage. Marianne stopped chopping onions with her knife poised in midair. Then everyone quickly resumed whatever they had been doing.

"Well," Marianne said, pretending nonchalance, "what's the occasion?"

"I thought I'd go to church," Morgan said.

This time it took longer for them to recover from the shock. Morgan ignored them, maintaining his dignity.

"After all, we did meet that lady priest yesterday," he said, "and it seems to me that it would be rude for at least one of us not to go to the service."

"Oh," Simon said, "definitely. Rude."

"Have a nice time," Julia said. "Pray for us. We need it."

"Oh, yes, I will," Morgan said. "Do I need to get anything while I'm out? Bread? Toilet paper?"

"I think we're okay," Marcus said.

Morgan left and no one spoke until they heard his truck leaving.

"Well," Marianne said. "How about that?

"I am astounded," Simon said.

Over the next two hours Thanksgiving dinner took shape. Marianne assembled pan stuffing from crumbled fresh cornbread, chopped onions and celery, pecan pieces, and melted butter and chicken broth. Julia made salad, vinaigrette dressing, and a green bean casserole. Acorn squash stuffed with apples baked in the oven with a mince pie and a pumpkin pie. Dinner rolls rose in a covered bowl on top of the stove. Apple cider and cinnamon sticks simmered in a crock pot. Simon loaded the dishwasher with the first installment of dirty dishes. The girls, supervised by Marcus, set the table. They all nibbled on cheese and crackers to alleviate their hunger pains until dinner. The adults added applejack brandy to their mugs of hot cider. The drink made Simon just woozy enough to induce complete relaxation.

At twelve-thirty they heard Morgan's truck pull into the parking area under the cottage. Simon had prepared suitable insulting remarks in anticipation of his arrival, but he bit his tongue when Morgan came into the cottage. The Reverend Clare Monahan was with him. She was still in her working clothes, a black blazer, black shirt, clerical collar, Black Watch plaid flannel skirt, and black pumps.

"I thought perhaps Clare could have something to drink with us before she goes to the Pearlies' home for dinner," Morgan said.

"Of course," Marcus said. He jumped up to find a mug and refresh the cheese and cracker tray.

"I'm not intruding?" Clare said.

"Of course not," Marianne said, moving Dolly to her lap so Clare could sit on the sofa.

"I love the Macy's parade," Clare said. "At home I videotape it so I can see it when I get back from church."

Morgan drew up a chair from the table and sat next to the arm of the sofa. He took the mug of hot cider from Marcus and handed it to Clare.

Simon finally found his voice.

"So," he said to Clare, "you're going to the Pearlies' for Thanksgiving dinner?"

"It's traditional," she said. "They always have the visiting clergy for dinner. I couldn't say no. But I can't eat too much—I want to go diving this afternoon."

"Where?" Julia asked.

"I don't know yet," Clare said. "This morning early I walked out through the surf to the *Elizabeth,* with just a snorkel. It was very disappointing. The wreck was a jumble of wood with some rusty iron bits scattered about. Sand swirled everywhere. The visibility was terrible. And I think I saw a sand shark."

"The surf has been beating up on those wrecks for decades," Morgan said. "It's surprising there's anything left of any of them."

Later, on her way out of the cottage, Clare stopped to

look at Simon's exhibits tacked to the bulletin board; the photos of the Dahlonega gold coins found with Carl Chavis's corpse, the Cape Fear shipwreck map, the newspaper clipping about Chavis's disappearance, and the photograph of the five men taken on the porch of the Pearlie Beach Pavilion in 1942. She started, one hand across her mouth and the other pointed to the picture.

"Oh," she said. "That's my grandfather!"

Simon quickly went over to her. She indicated the as-yet-unidentified man in the photograph.

"Nick Monahan was his name," she said. "He died in the spring of 1942. He was in the civil air patrol. He flew off on a scouting mission one morning and didn't make it home."

Simon knew that the civil air patrol was vital to defending the American coast during the first year of the war. As soon as Germany declared war on the United States, the Nazis dispatched submarines to disrupt American shipping to Great Britain. Their commanders were supplied with six torpedoes, two deck guns, and American tourist maps of the coast. They created havoc among the cargo ships supplying Great Britain. Until more ships and airplanes could be built, the army and navy enlisted the help of civilians to track the enemy submarines. Anyone with an airplane or a private boat big enough to patrol the coast volunteered. Even Ernest Hemingway sallied forth from Cuba on the *Pilar* to patrol the Florida coast. The government didn't want Americans to know how vulnerable their coast was, so very little leaked into the newspapers at the time.

"Are you sure that's him?" Simon asked.

"Of course," she said. "Look here. I have some pictures

of him I took over to the Watkins's house last night. My grandfather and the colonel were good friends."

Clare drew several old black and white pictures out of her handbag. One of Clare's pictures showed Monahan quite clearly, wearing jodhpurs, leather jacket, and a jaunty white pilot's scarf, standing on a dock next to his seaplane. The plane itself seemed impossibly primitive. It looked like a wooden coffin, with wings and floats attached to the body of the plane with broomsticks and baling wire. The double cockpit and the big Pratt and Whitney engine were exposed to the elements. Simon wouldn't care to fly once in a circle around an airport in it, much less carry freight and passengers in the unpredictable weather of the coast, or search for submarines out over the open ocean. Monahan must have been fearless, and he was certainly the same person sitting with Chavis, the Pearlies, and Colonel Watkins on the Pavilion porch in 1942. He was even wearing similar clothing in both photographs.

"You see," Clare said, "I know very little about my grandfather. My grandmother remarried, and I never even saw a picture of him before. When my father died last year, my mother sent me a box of my grandfather's stuff, and it included pictures, letters, and maps. And Colonel Watkins was so kind to me when I contacted him. I was at his house for an hour before you got there last night and we talked and talked about my grandfather and the war."

"Did you show Colonel Watkins these pictures?"

"Yes, of course. That's why I have them with me. I haven't changed pocketbooks since last night."

"But Colonel Watkins looked at the photograph I took to his house and said he couldn't identify this man," Simon said.

Clare shrugged. "I can't imagine why he would have done that," she said. "It's clearly my grandfather."

THE PERFECTLY SMOKED TURKEY sat in the center of the table. Steaming side dishes surrounded it, as if paying homage. The table was set with the cottage's collection of mismatched cutlery, plastic plates, and jelly glasses. Some of the serving pieces were Tupperware containers. Everyone stood around the table, slavering, until Marianne finished making gravy from the contents of the smoker's drip pan, and they finally sat down to eat. While his daughters complained of desperate hunger, Marcus offered a quick, interdenominational blessing in deference to Simon's familial connection to Judaism. Simon wouldn't have minded if Marcus had invoked Krishna, but he appreciated the gesture.

No one even attempted conversation until they had cleaned their plates for the first time and reloaded. Simon was glad to see that Julia took seconds. He disliked it when people dieted on holidays. It spoiled the occasion for everyone.

The turkey didn't taste quite like a traditional roast bird, but it was wonderfully tender, its familiar turkey flavor enhanced by hickory smoke and ocean air. And even though the cornbread stuffing had been baked in the oven, rather than roasted inside the turkey, Marianne's gravy moistened it to perfection.

"When I drove Clare to the Pearlies', she told me a little more about her grandfather," Morgan said, intently buttering every surface of a hot yeast dinner roll. "He docked his plane on the mainland right across from Pearlie Beach. He ran a delivery service, basically, airlifting letters, packages, medicine, and visitors to the barrier islands. This area didn't have the roads and bridges it does now, and the ferries were slow. He could land his seaplane on the Intercoastal Waterway and tie up at a customer's dock just about anywhere. When World War II started he went to work at the army air base at Wilmington as a mechanic. In his spare time he used his seaplane to patrol for German submarines. He got to be friends with Colonel Watkins at the air base."

"It's odd that Colonel Watkins didn't recognize Monahan in that picture last night, with Clare sitting right there," Julia said. "Kind of suspicious, actually."

"I've been wondering about that myself," Simon said. "He is elderly and he did have to get his reading glasses. Maybe he really couldn't see well enough to recognize Monahan. And of course Claire didn't look at our picture last night. If she hadn't noticed it today, we still wouldn't know who the guy was."

"You don't think this has anything to do with, you know, the event?" Marianne asked. Earlier, out of earshot of the girls, Simon had told the adults about Chavis's murder.

"Who knows?" Simon said.

"What event?" Trina asked.

Marcus knew better than to underestimate the perspicacity of this particular daughter.

"Carl Chavis's death," Marcus said to her. "Everyone wonders if it had something to do with the Confederate gold coins that Simon and Dr. Morgan found on his body."

"How could you tell?" Trina said. "It was so long ago."

"Before any of us were born," Marianne said.

Trina's eyes widened. "Wow," she said. "That was the olden days!"

"Did Clare tell you where her grandfather kept his seaplane?" Simon asked Morgan.

"Yeah," he said. "On the sound just east of Lockwood's Folly Inlet, off a dirt road, State Road 1112, I think she said. She visited it a couple of days ago. The dock and hangar are still there, falling down, of course."

BY TWO O'CLOCK THAT afternoon Simon was the only person in the house who was conscious. Julia and Trina had gone for a walk. Marcus snoozed on a living room sofa with Dolly stretched out on his chest, snoring. Marianne and Isobel napped in their respective bedrooms. Morgan was in his camper, smoking and reading a stack of academic journals. A long afternoon of tryptophan-laced lethargy stretched ahead. Simon took advantage of the opportunity to read the medical examiner's report on Carl Chavis's corpse. He had retrieved it from Morgan after dinner.

"I thought you weren't interested in this," Morgan had said.

"I can't help myself," Simon said. "Fortunately there's not enough evidence here to obsess me too long. It'll pass the afternoon."

Besides, working up the "case" might distract him from Julia.

Simon skipped all the photographs in the file and the most graphic details of the autopsy report. He had seen enough of the corpse at the icebox at Coastal Refrigerated Trucking, thank you very much. It was enough for him that

Dr. Boyette had identified Chavis and concluded that he had been murdered.

And there was no doubt in Boyette's mind that Chavis had been murdered. A four-inch-long fishing knife, the common type with a two-pronged tip and a double-edged blade, one side standard and one serrated, was still hung on one of Chavis's ribs, minus the handle. Knives like it were common on the coast. Simon had seen Henry Pearlie and Captain Nance Pearlie each use one to clean fish already this weekend. The rib involved showed scarring from what must have been several attempts to withdraw the knife. The knife would have punctured a lung and perhaps Chavis's heart. Boyette further speculated that the skeleton could have stayed intact inside the old diving suit for all these years only if it had been "secured." In other words, Simon thought, hidden, weighted, or tied down underwater, until finally dislodged by the dredge. This convinced him that Chavis had died near where his corpse was found. He set aside the medical report and unfolded his map of Cape Fear.

The southernmost part of the North Carolina coast assumed the shape of a backward L. The point of the L was Cape Fear, where the Cape Fear River emptied into the sea. Frying-Pan Shoals, a treacherous range of hidden shallows and reefs, stretched south of the cape. Shipping from the north or from Bermunda bound to the port of Wilmington, thirty miles up the Cape Fear River, sailed far to the south and around the shoals, then along the leg of the L, which was lined with barrier islands, among them Pearlie Beach, to slip into Wilmington. There were plenty that didn't make it. Wilmington was a critical eastern port during every American war, from the Revolution to World War II, and was patrolled by English frigates in the eighteenth century, Yankee gunboats in the nineteenth, and German U-boats during World Wars I and II. While wrecks from every era lined the shore, fully ninety percent of them were Civil War blockade runners. Wilmington was the last port of the Confederacy to remain open, and for months the Confederate army depended on it to sustain their lost cause. Two weeks after Wilmington fell, Lee surrendered at Appomattox.

When Julia and Trina came back from their walk, carrying a toy bucket full of seashells between them, they found Simon marking up his map with a red felt-tipped pen.

"What are you doing?" Trina asked Simon.

"Working on our mystery," Simon said. "Take a look at this."

He turned the map so that Trina and Julia could see it.

"Look here," Simon said. "Lockwood's Folly Inlet cuts into the shore at the east end of Pearlie Beach, separating us from Holden Beach. It penetrates the mainland about, what, about three miles? Then, directly across from the inlet, off the beaches there are so many Civil War–era shipwrecks I don't have room to write them all on the map. There's the *Ranger,* the *Elizabeth,* the *Iron Age,* the *Enchantress*—and there are more nearby to the west and east."

"So?" Julia said.

"Nick Monahan's seaplane dock was on the sound, east of the inlet. Henry Pearlie's fish camp was across the inlet, on the west bank. The Pavilion and the cannery were here on Pearlie Beach. Chavis's body was found here, in the sound off the beach. Simon kept making little red X's on the map as he talked. They crowded closely together.

"It's a very small area," Simon said.

Trina used her fingers and the mile scale on the map to measure the area off.

"Fifteen square miles," she said.

"There are so many coincidences," Simon said. "You could invent quite a story around these guys and a lost shipment of Confederate gold."

"I already have," Julia said. "I figure Carl Chavis found gold, told his buddies about it, and one of them, or maybe all of them, killed him, becoming rich and keeping the murder secret for years. They didn't think his body would ever be found, and didn't know that he still had a few coins on him."

"Unfortunately, that's all it is, a story. It's romantic and thrilling, but has no basis in fact."

"Do you think you can figure out what happened?" Trina said.

"I don't know, honey," Simon said. "It was a long time ago."

"Is everybody dead who lived then?"

"Not everybody," Simon said.

INEZ PEARLIE ANSWERED HER door in an apron and wiped her hands on a dish towel stuck in her pocket before she took Simon's and Julia's hands in her own to greet them. Julia was struck by the elderly woman's youthful looks and vitality. Her skin was so clear and unlined she must have worn a hat outside every day of her life. Inez was delighted to see them and bent over to kiss Trina on the top of her head.

"Thanks for letting us interrupt your Thanksgiving," Simon said.

"You're not interrupting," Inez said. "My crowd went home long ago. I just finished cleaning up, and Dale's driving my sister back to the nursing home. Clare Monahan's gone, too. She's such a nice young woman. I shall have to change my mind about women being clergy, though she shouldn't wear that black shirt and white collar all the time. It's very unbecoming. Washes out her complexion."

"We're on a field trip," Trina said. "We're going to drive around and look at wrecks and stuff. Everybody else at our house is asleep."

Inez led them into her living room. It was as well kept as she was. An out-of-fashion Colonial green paint covered every wall of the home that Simon could see from where he stood. The living room suite of furniture upholstered in an off-white brocade was protected by white lace doilies stretched over the backs and armrests of the sofa and chairs. Watercolors of coastal scenes covered the walls, except over the fireplace, where there hung a really bad portrait of a family group: a man, woman, and two teenage boys. Simon guessed that the family was the Pearlies; Dale Senior, Inez, Dale Junior, and Leland, about forty years ago.

Inez noticed Simon inspecting the portrait.

"My sister painted that," she said. "She did all the watercolors, too."

"Very nice," Simon said.

"How about a piece of pumpkin pie and some coffee?" Inez asked.

"No, please," Julia said. "We just ate. But coffee would be great."

Inez went into her kitchen and soon returned with coffee for the adults and hot chocolate for Trina.

"You want me to look at the photograph you found?" she asked.

"Please," Simon said. He handed it to her.

Inez moved a lamp closer so she could see the picture better. Simon thought he saw her eyes fill with tears.

"I'm sorry," he said. "This has upset you."

"No," she said. "It just brings back such memories. You know, I believe I took this picture, in the spring of 1942. Yes, I'm sure I did. It was Dale Senior's birthday. I invited his friends over for cake. I had to use an entire month's ration of flour and sugar and butter and chocolate to make it."

"These men were close friends?" Julia asked.

"Well, some closer than others," she said. "Dale, Henry, and Carl had known each other for their whole lives. And of course they knew Nick from doing business with him, and Carl and Nick brought Colonel Watkins around. He was just an enlisted man then."

Trina excused herself to find the bathroom. Inez waited for her to be out of earshot before she continued.

"It was so upsetting to hear that Carl had been murdered," she said. "All through Thanksgiving dinner I felt like his ghost was sitting at the table with us. And then we had my sister here, and knowing she had forgotten him, well, it was troubling."

"I can imagine," Julia said.

"I suppose there's no way we could find out what happened?" Inez said.

"Probably not," Simon said, "but I admit to a perverse interest in old unsolved murders. Would you mind if I poked around a little? I wouldn't want to do it if it bothered you."

"Not at all," Inez said. "We owe the poor boy that much."

The back door slammed and Dale Pearlie came into the room.

"She's safe and sound," Dale said. "I think she had completely forgotten where she'd been by the time she got back."

"That's not the point," Inez said. "She's my sister, she belongs at our table on Thanksgiving Day."

"Anything you say, Momma," Dale said.

Trina came back from the bathroom and sat down, legs dangling.

"I've told Professor Shaw that he can look into Carl's death," Inez said.

"Why not?" Dale said. "There's no harm in that. I don't want to be inhospitable, but would you excuse me? The football game's about to start."

Soon afterward they could hear the sounds of television coming from another room.

"Could you answer just a couple of questions for me?" Simon asked Inez.

"Of course," she said.

"Could you tell me how Nick Monahan and your husband died?"

"Nick was obsessed with scouting for German submarines. One day he just didn't come back from a patrol. It was very soon after Carl disappeared. My husband always said a sub shot him down. Nick used to buzz the subs he saw, you see, and his plane already had a couple of bullet holes from the Germans shooting at him. Dale Senior died in 1971. He was securing a boat at the marina as a storm came up and he fell and was crushed between the boat and the dock."

"How awful," Julia said.

"I've gotten over being furious with him," Inez said. "I think. It wasn't even his boat. He was doing it for one of our renters. Henry was so upset. He was supposed to meet him at the dock to help him, but he was too late. Found Dale there. Blamed himself for years."

"Did Henry run the fish camp during the war?" Simon asked.

"Technically, yes," Inez said. "But really there wasn't much fishing going on. The coast guard required every fisherman, amateur and professional, to get a permit to go out every single day. Our menhaden cannery barely stayed open. No, Henry worked for us some during the war, and did quite a bit of black-marketing on the side. About the only thing around here that wasn't rationed was the sand."

"Those must have been tough times," Julia said.

"Yes and no. Yes because of the war, but our lives improved a lot in other ways. Just like everyone else, we struggled during the Depression. We didn't have any cottages then, just the Pavilion, and no one could afford to come to the beach. When the war came, the economy improved, and the Pavilion made us real money. After the war we spent it on developing the island."

"But didn't Hurricane Hazel destroy Pearlie Beach in 1954?" Simon asked.

"Honey," Inez said, "*destroy* is a mild word for what that storm did. That hurricane was like a visit from hell. There wasn't a building left standing. I didn't know what we'd do. We had no insurance. But Dale Senior found the money to rebuild, somewhere. I think he got it from his parents. He wouldn't have borrowed it. His people were primitive Baptists. They thought usury was the devil's tool. Anyhow, Dale Senior was like a madman for six months, before the next summer season, driving back and forth to Raleigh to pressure the state to repair the roads and bridges, building twelve cottages, contracting for the pier. And now," Inez said, gesturing widely in her neat living room to encompass the entire beach outside, "look at it now. Of course, I have to credit Dale Junior, too. He took over after Dale Senior died."

Simon noticed that she didn't mention her second son, Leland.

"Anyway, during the war, Dale Senior and I worked ourselves just about to death. Henry helped us out by running the Pavilion on Sundays and Mondays so we could have some days off." Inez chuckled. "Henry used to make Dale Senior furious, letting folks brown-bag, playing poker with the GIs, and sometimes even flying the Confederate flag from the flagpole, but he was a good worker, and we needed him."

TRINA WAS THRILLED TO have the full attention of two adults. She skipped happily down the beach to the waterline between Julia and Simon, holding on to their hands. Simon lifted her to his shoulders, where she scanned the ocean with his binoculars, a powerful pair that had belonged to Simon's mother. She had been a passionate birdwatcher, and Simon had assumed her habit of taking the binoculars with him almost everywhere.

"I don't see it," Trina said.

"It's out there, honey," Simon said. "It's low tide now. You should be able to see it."

"There it is," Julia said, pointing west.

Trina swung the binoculars around.

"I see a pole sticking up out of the water," she said.

"That's the rudder post," Simon said, shifting one of her feet away from his ribs.

"It says in the guidebook that the *Ranger* sailed here from Bermuda with a shipment of Austrian rifles for the Confederacy," Julia said. "The Yankees had shot out the lightship on Frying-Pan Shoals, and the ship went aground here. Then they shot it up and set it on fire."

Simon lowered Trina from his shoulders to the ground. Together the three of them studied the photo of the *Ranger* in the guidebook.

"How come you can't see the wreck as clear as this picture?" Trina asked.

"That's an aerial photograph," Simon said, stretching the kinks out of his back. "You can see everything better from the air." Realizing the import of what he had said, he stopped midway through his stretch and looked at Julia.

"Nick Monahan?" she said.

"Yeah," Simon said.

Julia took the binoculars from Trina and searched the ocean for the *Ranger* again.

"Simon," she said. "There's somebody out there."

"What?" Simon said.

"There's a person—no, two people—out on the *Ranger*," she said.

Trina hopped from one foot to the other in excitement. "They're looking for the gold!" she shouted.

"No, they're not, honey," Simon said. "Divers go out to these wrecks all the time. And there's no gold on the *Ranger*. If it ever carried any gold, it went to pay for those rifles in Bermuda."

The two divers wearing black wetsuits and snorkels waded ashore toward them, struggling to stay upright in the surf. They both had black mesh bags secured to their diving belts. When they reached the beach, Clare Monahan stripped off her mask first, then Woody Watkins.

"Hello, there," Clare said.

Woody didn't speak, just raised his shoulders at them as he walked up the beach toward the weathered wooden stairs over the dune, where he sat on the bottom step to wait for Clare.

"Did you find anything cool?" Trina asked her.

"Not really," Clare said. "Any Civil War relics that were portable were recovered long ago, I'm afraid."

Clare emptied her bag to show the contents to Trina. A vintage Coke bottle black with barnacles, the plastic rings from a six-pack of beer wrapped around a conch shell deformed by the rings, and a perfect pink and purple scallop shell tumbled onto the sand.

"Ugh," Trina said. "Garbage."

"Except for this," Clare said, holding up the scallop shell. The shell was almost transparent. The sunlight shone right through it, making the pink and purple shell glow. "Would you like to keep it?" Clare asked her.

"Yes, please," Trina said, placing the shell carefully in her pants pocket.

"Isn't the water freezing?" Julia asked her.

"Not with a wet suit," Clare said. "What's hard is staying oriented and seeing anything so close to shore. I'm not sure it's worth the effort."

"Are you coming?" Woody called to her. "Tide's coming in. If you want to visit the *Lynx,* we should go now."

"Okay," Clare said. She walked up the beach, dumping the garbage in a trash can that sat at the foot of the steps that went up and over the dunes.

A few minutes later they heard a car engine start and its wheels spin in the sand as it drove away.

"I'm surprised she would hang out with Woody," Julia said. "He's such a loser."

"I expect that he's just showing her around," Simon said. "She did say that Colonel Watkins was a friend of her grandfather's."

"Let's go see some more shipwrecks," Trina asked.

They parked Julia's car at the western end of the island and walked out to the beach. A large green sign marked the area as a sea turtle sanctuary.

"Should we go out there?" Julia asked.

"All the nests have hatched out by now," Trina said, running down to the edge of the water. She shaded her eyes and looked out to sea.

"I don't see anything," she said.

Simon read from his guidebook, then pointed out toward a sandbar.

"There," he said, "the *Bendigo*."

"I see it," Julia said. "It's just a hulk." She pointed Trina in the right direction.

"I see it now, too," Trina said.

Simon handed her the binoculars.

"There," he said, "you can see the frames of the boilers. The *Iron Age* is out there, too, somewhere. It was a Yankee gunship, sunk by Confederate shore batteries. It's in around ten feet of water, so we can't see it."

"It's like a graveyard," Trina said. "Dead ships everywhere."

"That's what they call the North Carolina coast," Julia said. "The graveyard of the Atlantic."

SIMON, JULIA, AND TRINA stopped at the pier on their way back to the cottage. Henry's old pickup was parked outside, pasted over with colorful bumper stickers, most of which featured the Confederate battle flag. They expressed such popular sentiments as GUN CONTROL MEANS HITTING YOUR TARGET, and KEEP CRIMINALS AWAY, FLY A CONFEDERATE FLAG. Viola's little bright blue Ford Escort GT parked nearby sported a popular fish-shaped Christian symbol and a bumper sticker for the Hepzibah Baptist Church. Julia and Trina lingered outside the door to the grill, looking at photos of prize-winning fish caught from the pier. Simon went right inside.

He joined Viola, who sat at a table with her daughter, Gaye Galloway. Gaye was in uniform; Joe Pearlie, who was with them, wore plain clothes. Viola wasn't working today. She was still in her church clothes, royal blue from the tip of the ostrich feathers in her felt hat, to her brocade suit, to the embroidered satin dress bedroom slippers on her feet. Silently Henry came to their table and refilled coffee cups. Viola thanked him, and he nodded to her before going back behind the kitchen counter. Watching a scene like this, Simon could believe that the South had come a long way in the last thirty years.

"I don't see why," Viola said to Gaye, "you have to work on Thanksgiving while Joe here, who doesn't have a family, gets the day off."

"It's my turn, Momma," Gaye said.

"I would have been happy to trade," Joe said. "Then I

wouldn't have had to have dinner with my daddy and grandma. What an experience that was. Daddy's watching every bite I take, and Grandma's asking me why I don't bring a girlfriend with me. Then there was Grandma's sister. She's practically unconscious, except that she keeps asking Daddy where Momma was. And we all had to be careful what we said, because Reverend Monahan was with us. I have awful heartburn."

"Where is your momma these days?" Viola asked.

"In New Bern with her husband," Joe said. "Where else would she be?"

"You know Chief Keck wants us to do our assigned duty, and everyone has to take turns working holidays," Gaye told her mother. "And I don't mind, it's my job. We'll have dinner when I get off, Momma, you know that."

"And tomorrow you'll get in the car and drive off to Kinston to see Mack's family," Viola said. "Just deserting me."

"As if you'll notice," Gaye said. "You'll be cooking all weekend for the church picnic on Sunday, just like always."

Viola spotted Trina.

"Here's one of my babies!" she said. She grabbed Trina and hugged her. "I've watched this child and her sisters grow up," she said, pulling Trina onto her lap.

"I need to go back to work," Gaye said, wiping her mouth and getting up from the table.

"Isn't my girl something?" Viola said to Simon and Julia. "A police officer! If her daddy were alive, he'd be so proud. He was just a sharecropper, and now Gaye and her husband own most of the land he used to work for practically nothing. They grow all that green stuff that people pay a fortune for these days, I can't remember the names."

"Romaine," Joe said. "Parsley. Basil."

"Whatever," Viola said. "All I know is, I can pick collards and kale for nothing out of my backyard."

"That's the real reason Viola works here," Joe said, "so that she can annoy Uncle Henry. Her having riz so far, and him sunk so low."

"Not so," Viola said, hugging Trina. "It's so I can see all these babies."

Julia sat down in Gaye's chair, Trina snuggled up to Viola, and Simon went looking for the bathroom. Henry, washing dishes sullenly at the counter, showed him the way.

The entrance to the men's bathroom was outside the building. It was a box jutting out over the ocean, as if someone most of the way through building the pier remembered that even fishing didn't postpone bodily functions. Inside, all the pipes were corroded and the bowl of the toilet was brown with rust. The window was open to the outside, for ventilation, Simon supposed. The place must be freezing during the winter.

When Simon washed his hands his sleeve caught on a rusty nail protruding from the cheap paneling. As he carefully unhooked it from his sweatshirt, a section of the paneling pulled back, showing the interior of the wall stuffed with old magazines. Simon carefully pulled the paneling out farther and saw enough of a magazine cover to read the date, winter 1937, much older than the pier itself. At first he was elated. Magazines and newspapers were often used for insulation in old buildings. Sometimes they turned out to be rare sources of historical information. He pulled out a magazine to look at it. A few seconds later, his lips pressed tightly together and his hands shaking, he stuffed the magazine back into the wall, almost angrily. He took off a shoe to pound the nail as deep into the wall as he could.

Simon went back into the pier and sat down at the counter instead of returning to the table, where Viola, Julia, Trina, and Joe were still talking.

"Coffee, please, decaf," Simon said to Henry.

The old man sniffed. "I don't have decaf," he said. "God put caffeine in coffee."

"Okay, regular," Simon said. "And I'd like milk and sugar, please."

Henry sniffed again, but brought him the creamer and sugar bowl, and watched Simon doctor the mug of coffee.

"That ain't coffee, that's a milkshake," Henry said.

"Tell me something, Henry," Simon said.

"Sure."

"I know the pier was built in 1954."

"1955, actually."

"Who built it?"

"A pier contractor from Norfolk. Built nothing but piers. That's why we had to wait a year after Hurricane Hazel. His jobs was backed way up."

"Where did his crew come from?"

"He had his own crew."

"Nobody local?"

"Well, there was some local boys worked on it, I guess. I don't really remember. Why?"

"Just curious," Simon said.

TRINA WAS STILL ON Viola's lap being petted.

"And where is your big sister this year?" Viola said. "April is the prettiest girl."

Trina's smile faded.

"She's no fun anymore," Trina said. "All she does is mess with her hair and paint her fingernails and talk on the telephone."

"She told me last summer that she was going to try out for cheerleader," Viola said. "Did she make it? Gaye was a cheerleader and she loved it."

"Yeah," Trina said. She got out of Viola's lap completely and came around and sat on the edge of Julia's chair. She looked miserable.

The three of them went out on the pier. Trina walked down its length ahead of them, kicking an empty Coke can ahead of her.

"I know what's bothering Trina," Julia said. "She's got three blond sisters. But what's wrong with you? You look like your party just lost the White House, Congress, and the governor's office."

"I found some nasty literature in the men's room," Simon said. "It bothered me, that's all."

Trina moodily came back to them, still kicking the Coke can.

"I'll explain later," Simon said.

5

AS SOON AS THEY WALKED INTO THE CLEGG COTTAGE JULIA'S beeper sounded its nasty little buzz. She went into her bedroom to return the call.

"How come you don't have a beeper?" Trina asked Simon.

"My students can wait until Monday for my lecture on the Rural Electrification Act of 1935," Simon said.

"Oh," Trina said.

Julia had left her door open and Simon heard the conclusion of her conversation with Sergeant Otis Gates.

"You can do what you want," she said, "but I'm telling you, you won't win that case." She hung up the telephone and came back into the living room.

"Simon says he doesn't need a beeper because nobody's interested in anything he knows," Trina said.

"The rest of your family is out on the beach," Julia said to Trina. "Why don't you put on your bathing suit and go on out there? It's a gorgeous afternoon."

After Trina went into her bedroom to change, Julia put

an arm around Simon's neck and hugged him, kissing him affectionately on his forehead.

"Would you like a beeper of your own, sweetie? I'll get you one."

"Unless you could teach my cats how to use it, I don't see the point," Simon said. "No one else needs me that much."

He enclosed her waist with his arms and pulled her to him.

"I feel much better," he said, his voice muffled against her.

"I'm sure you do," Julia said.

They released each other as Trina came back into the room ready for the beach.

"I like your swimsuit, hon," Julia said.

"I don't, it's an old one of my sister's, and I despise pink," Trina said. "I like purple. But I never get any new clothes. It's not fair."

Simon and Julia followed Trina only as far as the deck. They pulled two rocking chairs together and sat rocking gently and holding hands.

"Look!" Simon said, pointing skyward. "Pelicans!"

Four of the big birds wheeled out of the sky and dropped to just a few feet over the ocean, skimming the water. As Simon and Julia watched, one after the other folded its wings and dived into the waves, big leathery beak open wide to scoop up fish.

"That's not all," Julia said. "I think I see dolphins."

She hurried inside and came back with Simon's binoculars. Simon leaned forward in his chair and shaded his eyes with his hands.

"There must be a big damn school of fish out there attracting them," he said.

Julia stood beside him and watched the view for a few seconds, then handed the binoculars to Simon. He observed one of the pelicans, which floated comfortably on the water and suddenly plunged its head into the ocean, indelicately raising its tailfeathers in the air. Then it surfaced, tilted its head up, and swallowed its catch whole. A dolphin broke the surface close by, startling the big bird into the air.

"My turn," Julia said.

He gave her the glasses, and she gasped with delight as she watched. Now all the birds floated on the water, intermittently diving and surfacing. Half a dozen dolphins leapt around them. Sunlight glinted off the drops of water they churned up, as if they had tossed diamonds into the air. Suddenly the pelicans took to the air again. The birds flying above the water and the dolphins swimming below moved south in tandem, parallel to the beach, following the invisible school of fish.

"That was outstanding," she said.

"This is outstanding," he said. He knelt at her feet and pulled her to him, nuzzling her where her jeans met her shirt.

"Don't," she said. "Not out here."

But she caressed his face as he pulled her shirt out of her jeans and kissed her stomach.

"I don't believe it," he said. "You've got a tattoo."

"A moment of weakness on my last birthday."

"I like it."

Simon kissed the tiny star gently, then slowly kissed

her all around it, systematically circumnavigating her navel. He inhaled her scent, still Giorgio.

"I've missed you," he said.

"I've missed you, too," she said.

Simon took that as encouragement, standing up, embracing her, and kissing her hard.

"Not out here," she said again, returning his kisses.

"Let's go inside, then," Simon said. "The bedroom door locks."

They were interrupted by a clatter on the steps up from the beach. Dolly's head appeared.

"I have to go to the bathroom," she said. "Can you take me?" she said to Julia.

"Mom told you not to ask her. You're a big girl, you can go by yourself," Isobel said, appearing beside her sister. She passed Dolly and ran into the cottage. Dolly climbed the rest of the steps slowly, hauling herself up with both hands on the rail. A toy bucket, suspended by its handle from one arm, bumped along the railings. A pink beach towel dragged behind her. By this time Simon and Julia were ten feet apart.

"The rest of them are on the way in," Julia said.

"Timing is everything," Simon said.

MARCUS KNEW SOMETHING HAD gone on between Simon and Julia the minute he stepped onto the deck and saw their faces.

"Quid fit?" ["What's happening?"] Marcus said to Simon.

"Nescio quid dicas," ["I don't know what you're talking about,"] Simon answered.

Inside the cottage Marianne and Marcus were making turkey sandwiches for their exhausted daughters. The three girls lay prone on a sofa, wrapped up in quilts and afghans, watching *Mary Poppins* on the Disney Channel. There was only one television set in the cottage. Much as Simon envied the Cleggs' family life, it looked like a long, boring evening lay ahead.

"There's no reason for you guys to stay here," Marianne said. "Go out if you like. The Do Drop Inn is always open."

"They have a big-screen TV," Marcus said. "You could catch the UNC game."

Simon and Julia stopped at Morgan's camper and invited him to go with them. The three of them took Julia's car.

THE SETTING SUN CAST its sunset glow over the Intercoastal Waterway, turning the surface of the sound a warm flame color beneath it. Boaters who had spent their Thanksgiving on the water were returning to their moorings for the night. Julia pulled her car off the main road and parked under the bridge at Captain Nance's so they could watch the slow, stately procession. In the growing dusk the boats' navigation lights shone white at the tip of mast or antenna, green on the starboard side, and red on the port side. The colors reflected off the water as they cruised by, so that the sound looked like a sheet of shimmering stained glass.

Simon gave his binoculars to Julia, who sat on the hood of her car and watched the boats. Simon leaned on the car fender next to her. Morgan walked a few feet away, closer to Captain Nance's dock, to smoke a cigarette.

A green-hulled sailboat had dropped anchor nearby for the night. In a net sling suspended from the crossbars of the mast, a toddler bounced happily around the deck. The sling had holes for his legs like a walker, and kept him from falling overboard. His mother set a portable table for dinner while his father cooked hamburgers on a charcoal grill suspended from the railing, hanging over the water to keep the hot coals away from the deck. The embers glowed, and the smell of the burgers drifted over the water toward them.

"Interesting," Simon said.

"What?" Julia said.

"There's a big motorboat leaving Captain Nance's dock."

Julia handed the binoculars to Simon, who focused on the boat, a thirty-five-footer with an enclosed cabin and two big diesel outboard engines. Two men, wearing rain slickers with hoods pulled up over their heads despite the clear sky, saw him and then quickly turned their backs on him.

"It's Captain Nance himself," Simon said. "And his father, Leland Pearlie. What on earth do you think they're doing?"

"Fishing, I suppose?" Julia said.

"They're not rigged for it," Simon said. "There's not a rod in sight. But something is going on. There's a tall two-by-four attached to the cabin with a couple of white metal boxes and some aerials and other gizmos bolted to it. And their navigation lights aren't lit. Very dangerous."

He handed the binoculars to Morgan, who had crushed his cigarette butt and joined them at the car.

"Do you know what apparatus is on that boat?" Simon asked him.

Morgan focused the glasses.

"It's an integrated marine mapping system," he said.

"Sounds wonderful," Simon asked, "What is that?"

"You know what the Global Positioning System is?" Morgan asked.

"It's a worldwide navigation system that uses satellites. Tells you your position in latitude and longitude anywhere in the world. You can even get it in cars now," Simon said.

"Lots of boats have it these days. Comes in handy when you get lost, and the ocean is easy to get lost in. Most of it looks pretty much the same. Anyway, integrate GPS with sonar, which shows you the bottom of the ocean, add some sophisticated software, and you can draw a map of the ocean floor."

"In layman's terms," Julia said, "if you find something in the ocean and want to be able to locate it again, you can do it with this system."

"Exactly. A colleague of mine used a rig just like this when he mapped the floor of the Cape Fear River looking for shipwrecks a few years ago."

"Shipwrecks!" Julia said. "They're looking for gold!"

"Don't jump to conclusions," Morgan said. "They could be doing anything."

"Like what?" Simon said. "Those guys have lived here their whole lives. What could they be doing out on the water Thanksgiving night? With a marine mapping system? When they saw us they turned away, like they didn't want to be recognized. And they're running without lights."

Julia had the binoculars again. "Its getting darker," she said, "and I can't see very well, but I think they're turning down that inlet you showed me on the map, where Henry's fish camp and Nick Monahan's seaplane dock was. I'll bet you anything they're looking for the rest of Carl Chavis's gold."

JULIA'S CAR WAS PARKED in Nance's seafood market lot near the two huge pilings that once docked the ferry on the Pearlie Beach side. They were only a hundred feet away from the Do Drop Inn across the sound, but to get to it by car was a three-mile trip. To get to the inn they crossed the bridge to the mainland, drove north a mile on Pearlie Beach Road, turned right, passed a couple of banks and a restaurant, turned right again at the Tri-Beach Volunteer Fire Department onto Old Ferry Road, and drove down it a mile, until they stopped at the edge of the sound, at the door of the Do Drop Inn.

They could hear the jukebox blaring before they got out of the car. Inside, the big-screen TV was tuned to the UNC-UCLA pregame show with the volume off, so as not to compete with Shania Twain on the jukebox. Simon was a rock and roll fan himself, but he could appreciate rockabilly in the right environment. He dropped some quarters in the jukebox and selected the only two Carl Perkins songs on the menu, "One More Shot (at Lovin' You)" and "Blue Suede Shoes."

The Do Drop Inn was low and dark inside. Its floorboards lay directly on packed dirt and moved slightly when you walked on them. Mismatched wooden tables and chairs furnished the big main room. Posters and pictures of tobacco farming and fishing scenes covered the walls. An autographed photo of Jim Graham, North Carolina's commissioner of agriculture since the Deluge, occupied an honored spot on the wall behind the bar.

Morgan ordered for the three of them—a peck of steamed oysters, saltine crackers, seafood sauce, melted butter, and a pitcher of Miller draft. Julia and Simon were amenable to this. After all, they'd eaten Thanksgiving dinner a few hours ago and didn't want anything heavy. Out a nearby window they could see the road leading down to the water's edge and the two pillars where the ferry once docked, identical to the ones across the sound next to Captain Nance's. A halogen lamp powerful as a streetlight, mounted on an exterior wall, lit the seafood market parking lot.

The bar was crowded with people of all ages, male and female. None of the patrons seemed depressed to be spending Thanksgiving evening in a bar. Simon suspected that not one would trade kids, a house in the suburbs, and a turkey sandwich for what they had right here at the Do Drop Inn: beer, country music, football, and casual companionship. Simon sometimes thought that the happiest individuals he knew were those who wanted the least out of life.

Henry Pearlie sat on a barstool, nursing a beer and eating boiled peanuts out of a can, intently watching the football game on television.

Woody Watkins and Dee Anna occupied a nearby table in the company of two young men Simon didn't know. Their companions were scuzzy-looking, to say the least. They both had dirty shoulder-length hair pulled back under baseball caps worn backward, blue jeans with holes in the knees, and rubber fishing boots. Dee Anna had exchanged her usual preppy look for jeans, cowboy boots, and an embroidered denim shirt with the top three buttons undone. Three empty beer pitchers sat on their table. Woody was pouring unsteadily from a fresh pitcher, but Dee Anna covered her glass with her hand.

The peck of oysters arrived.

"Want me to shuck these for you?" the waiter asked.

"Lord, no, we'll do it ourselves," Morgan said.

Julia was handy with an oyster knife. She gripped the round handle firmly, inserted the short blade into the tiny gap between the two halves of the oyster shell, and twisted expertly. She dunked the oyster into the melted butter, lay it over a saltine cracker, and ate it in two bites—without dripping juice or sprinkling cracker crumbs all over herself. This was a woman Simon could spend the rest of his life with. But then he already knew that.

"I won't need to eat for a month after we get home," Julia said.

"You can eat all you want at the beach," Simon said. "You work everything off. Walking."

"Walking? Walking where? To the end of the pier and back? Have you ever used one of those exercise bicycles at the YMCA and read the meter that tells you how many calories you've used? We'd have to walk to the moon and back to burn all this food off."

"I understand," Morgan said, "that oysters are getting scarce. I plan to eat all I can before someone declares them to be an endangered species."

Julia pushed her plate away. "I'm full," she said. She leaned back and pushed her hair from her face, untangling it from her earrings and combing through it with her fingers in a gesture Simon had memorized months ago.

Two beers and Carl Perkins's songs were affecting his mood. It was a good thing Morgan had come with them, Simon thought, or he might be tempted to say something serious to Julia and make a fool of himself.

Julia caught him watching her.

"Sorry," Simon said.

"Don't apologize."

Morgan finished the oysters. "Want some more?" he asked.

"No, please," Julia said.

"Me neither," Simon said.

"Just as well," Morgan said, patting his stomach. "We have to leave room for turkey sandwiches when we get home."

Dee Anna came over to their table and sat down, so close to Simon that she brushed up against him. She reeked of beer and heavy perfume. She showed him her cleavage when she leaned over him to use his empty plate as an ashtray. Simon moved to the far edge of his chair, uncomfortable with her behavior. Obviously Dee Anna had joined them to distract Woody from his drinking buddies, but it hadn't worked. Woody hadn't noticed; not yet, anyway. Dee Anna compulsively twisted her diamond and wedding bands. Apparently her husband hadn't come home for Thanksgiving.

Henry let out a whoop from his stool at the bar where he was watching the game. UNC must have scored. A heavy elderly woman with dyed red hair wearing an unfashionable ultrasuede pantsuit had joined him. The two of them were holding hands.

"Who's the lady with Henry?" Simon asked. "His girlfriend?"

"His wife," Dee Anna said. "They haven't lived together in, oh, forty years, but they never got divorced. About twenty years ago when they started getting old, she said he could move back in with her, but he couldn't meet her conditions."

"What conditions?" Julia said.

"She wanted him to go to church with her every Wednesday night, twice on Sunday, and to all her choir concerts. He couldn't do it. Mack and Gaye Galloway let him live in the old tenant house on their farm. Funny how things work out. That farm used to belong to Henry, and Gaye's daddy used to sharecrop for him. Gaye grew up in that very same tenant house."

Woody must have missed Dee Anna at last, because he appeared at their table, beer glass in hand.

"What are you doing over here?" he asked Dee Anna.

"Having an intelligent conversation with people who aren't drinking themselves blind."

"Oh, really? Well, come on back, we'll talk to you."

"I don't want to. You know how I feel about Darryl and Mike. If you moved those boys' dinner plates five inches, they'd starve. I wouldn't have come if I'd known the three of you were going to talk about fishing all night."

"They're the best flounder giggers on the island," Woody said. "But I forget. You went to college. Maybe I should join this group and learn something."

Woody pulled an empty chair away from another table and shoved it between Dee Anna and Julia. He leered at them both, one at a time.

"This is where I like to be, sandwiched between two beautiful women."

"I'm sorry," Dee Anna said to the three of them. "I didn't know he would come over here."

Like hell you didn't, Morgan thought.

"So what are you educated types talking about?" Woody said. "Carl Chavis? Shipwrecks? Gold?"

"Not at all," Morgan said.

"Uh-huh," Woody said. "Right." He peered at Simon. He was so drunk he was having trouble focusing his eyes.

"Don't you think there's gold on the *Phantom*?" he said.

"No, but you tell me," Simon said. "You're the one who's dived on it."

"You're a per-fessor of history, you know damn well there was a strongbox full of gold listed on the *Phantom*'s manifest," Woody said.

"The manifest lists 'one small box merchandise.' There's no indication in the historical record anywhere that it contained gold. That's just a rumor. Besides, the wreck of the *Phantom* is too far from here to be the source of Carl Chavis's coins."

"Another ship, then," Woody said. "The *Ranger,* or the *Lynx,* or one we don't know about."

"Doubtful," Simon said. "Not so close to shore."

"How do we know you're telling the truth? You could be lying to all of us and looking for it yourself. I saw you and her running all over the island with a map this afternoon." He pointed a finger aggressively at Julia.

"We were sightseeing," Julia said.

"Like hell," Woody said.

"You're drunk," Morgan said. "Do us all a favor and go away."

Woody turned his bleary eyes on Morgan. He slammed

down his drink so that the beer sloshed over the sides.

"You're in on it with the per-fessor," Woody said. He looked back at Julia.

"You, too," Woody said to her.

Woody had raised his voice to get the attention of everyone in the bar.

"And how would we know if you're lying or not? You could tell us any damn thing, and we would have to believe you," Woody said. "There's a whole lot of Confederate gold unaccounted for, and for all we know, you all may have figured out where it is and be looking for it behind our backs."

"That's just not so," Simon said.

The bartender, a muscled man with multiple Harley Davidson tattoos, moved to the end of the bar closest to their table and watched Woody carefully, his arms crossed. The conversation in the bar had almost completely stopped, and the patrons were watching them, not apprehensively, but attentively, as if they were viewing their favorite television show.

"Your kind are all alike," Woody said.

Simon carefully put down his beer glass and placed both hands flat on the table in front of him.

"What kind would that be?" he asked.

"Hey," Morgan said, "don't encourage him."

"Come on, honey," Dee Anna said to Woody. "Let's go back to our table."

"Shut up," Woody said.

Instantly, without saying a word, Dee Anna left the table. She made a beeline for the ladies' rest room, slamming the door behind her. Darryl and Mike turned their chairs around, watching Woody intently, like a couple of

Doberman pinschers waiting for their master's order to attack.

Julia sat quietly with one hand resting on Simon's forearm. She wasn't telling him what to do. Just like everyone else in the room, she was waiting to see what happened next.

"What kind is that?" Simon asked again. "Would that be small men, college professors, or Jews?"

"Good Lord, Simon," Morgan said. "Let it go."

"In your case, they're one and the same, ain't they?" Woody asked.

Simon took a deep breath and exhaled it. "Yeah," he said, "guess so." He leaned back in his chair, took out his wallet, selected a credit card, threw it on the table, and beckoned for the waiter to collect it.

Morgan relaxed, and he heard Julia exhale. There would be no fight. Simon was too civilized to take the bait. The bartender uncrossed his arms and resumed wiping down the counter, signaling the bar's customers to get back to drinking and talking.

But Simon was just tidying up, preparing to deal with Woody. Nothing made Simon angrier than ignorance. Not lack of intelligence or opportunity, but a spoiled arrogance that made light of both.

"And you're, what, big, ignorant, and unemployed?" Simon asked, after signing his credit card slip.

Woody's face burned dark red. Oh, no, Morgan thought. At their table Woody's pals were delighted at the prospect of a confrontation. Julia took her hand off Simon's arm and silently walked out of the bar.

Simon wasn't sorry that Julia had left the room. He really didn't want her to see him brawling. Violent behavior wasn't part of his personality, but he had lost his temper, and it was too late to back down now without losing face on Pearlie Beach forever. He hoped Morgan didn't plan to intervene. If he didn't, maybe Woody's so-called friends would stay on the sidelines. Perhaps the bartender would stop a fight, and perhaps not. If just he and Woody tangled, it probably wouldn't cause much damage and would be entertaining for the crowd. It was true that Woody was bigger and younger than Simon, but he was quite drunk. Simon was in fairly good shape and had taken tae kwon do last year at the Y. He had been quite good at it. His instructor had told him that the guy with the most brains and the lowest center of gravity was the guaranteed winner in almost any fight. He qualified on both counts.

"I've had zits bigger than you," Woody said.

"And that makes you right? If you beat me up, I'll still be right, and you'll still be a stupid jerk."

The crowd murmured in agreement, which infuriated Woody. He picked up a half-filled pitcher of beer off the table, raised it over his head, and threw it. It shattered against the wall. The crash of splintered glass set the whole room in motion. The customers left their tables and lined the walls of the tavern. Woody's pals immediately came to his side, the bartender vaulted over the counter, and Simon and Morgan reluctantly got to their feet, resigned to defending themselves. Woody, on his feet now, too, shoved the table aside. Simon made a mental calculation of the distance between himself and Woody's knees, while Morgan wondered if he had enough cash on him for his copayment at the emergency room. The bartender showed no signs of intervening, and the other customers settled in to watch. Henry turned around and leaned on the bar, drinking his beer and chewing on his peanuts as though he were at a ball game.

The volunteer fire station was only a mile away, so just a couple of minutes elapsed between the time they first faintly heard the sirens and when the earsplitting whine was right outside the building. The fire engine's rotating red lights shone through the building's windows, so brightly that Simon shielded his eyes with one hand. Someone opened the door to admit two firemen, one brandishing a fire axe and another wielding the business end of a fire hose.

"We got a call from your kitchen," one said. "There's a grease fire spreading."

Shocked, the bartender leapt back over the counter and raced through the swinging door behind the bar into the kitchen, followed by the firemen. Half the bar's customers were already outside, and the rest crowded between Woody and his pals and Simon and Morgan. Morgan grabbed Simon's arm.

"Let's get the hell out of here," he said.

Simon was with him. They were outside and into Julia's car in a New York minute. She was waiting for them right outside the door.

Simon got into the passenger seat next to her and Morgan squeezed into the back. Julia peeled away from the curb.

"Funny," Simon said, "I don't see any smoke."

Julia slowed down to join the line of cars heading north toward NC 17.

"Lucky break for Woody Watkins," Morgan said. "We would have kicked his butt for sure."

"Did I ever tell you I took tae kwon do?" Simon asked. "I got as far as a brown belt before I quit."

"I'm glad you left," he said to Julia. "It was getting ugly and I didn't want you to see—"

Julia abruptly turned the car into the empty parking lot of the Pearlie Beach Surf and Scuba Shop. She turned to Simon, hauled off, and punched him, hard, in the arm.

"Hey," he said, "what's that about?"

"You idiots," she said. "Why do you think I left? Do you think I had the vapors and had to get myself someplace safe where I wouldn't see blood? I was trying to think of a way to get you out of that mess before those goons mopped the floor with your worthless bodies!"

"Oh," Simon said, rubbing his arm.

"Do you think those fire trucks just came by luck? I called in a false fire alarm! I'll have you know that's a Class Two misdemeanor! And I'm an officer of the court!"

"Oh," Simon said.

"Damn it," she said, "did the two of you lose your minds in there?"

"We couldn't help it," Morgan said. "It's the testosterone, mixed with a little adrenaline. We're prisoners of our body chemistry."

"Make fun of me if you want, but if that call can be traced to my cell phone, I could be in a hell of a lot of trouble. Do you think it would be possible for the two of you to admit that I saved your skins?"

"What makes you think we needed rescuing? We're perfectly capable of thwarting a couple of drunks, thank you very much. We didn't need your help," Simon said.

Julia threw the car into gear and jerked out of the parking lot, much too fast. She missed the driveway and drove over the curb and dropped to the street below so hard that Morgan bumped his head on the roof of the car.

None of them spoke for a long time.

"Boy," Morgan said, "for two people who aren't dating, you guys sure do fight good."

AS SOON AS THEY pulled under the cottage Morgan vamoosed into his camper, wisely pulling down the shades as soon as he got inside.

Julia got out of her car, slammed the door, threw her pocketbook over her shoulder, and stalked up the back stairs to the deck of the cottage. Simon caught up with her just as she reached the last few steps, grabbing her by her shirttail, forcing her to turn around and face him.

"Hey," Simon said. "Don't stay angry. I'm sorry about all this."

"I didn't mean to suggest that you couldn't take care of yourself," Julia said. "I just didn't want you to fight at all. I see enough violence in my job."

Simon pulled her down to sit on a step with him.

"Tell me," Simon said. "What would you have had me do? Let a spoiled moron like Woody intimidate me?"

"You could have . . ."

"What? Walked away?"

"I don't know."

"Besides, I would have won that fight. The man was so drunk he could hardly see. But I'm glad I didn't have to find out."

"I'm glad, too."

"If someone traces your phone call and finds out that you turned in a false alarm, could you be charged with something?"

Julia smiled in spite of herself, shaking her head.

"Probably not, under the circumstances. Besides, the penalty for a first offense is only thirty days community service, but it would be embarrassing as hell. Otis would never let me forget it."

Simon put an arm around her neck and pulled her to him, kissing her with more sweetness than passion this time.

"One positive about this evening . . ." he said.

"What?"

"You must like me some, or you wouldn't have bothered to rescue me from myself."

"Don't read too much into it."

Simon kissed her again. Simultaneously they looked toward the cottage, where lights were still blazing in the living room.

"I guess I'd better get down to the camper and go to bed," Simon said. "You don't own any earplugs, by any remote chance?"

"I almost forgot," Julia said. "I told Marianne this morning it's unnecessary for me to have the guest bedroom, I can sleep with the girls. They have a queen-sized bed and a bunk bed in their room, and I can sleep with Isobel. I've already moved all my stuff."

MORGAN SMOKED AS HE watched Simon pack his gear.

"Sure you want to move upstairs?" he asked. "The odds against you are terrible. Five females, two guys."

"Throw me that sweatshirt, please."

"You'll be domesticated again before you know what's hit you."

Simon ignored Morgan's statement, especially the

"again" part of it. He slung his duffel bag over his shoulder and retrieved his briefcase from a kitchen cabinet.

"See you tomorrow," he said.

THAT NIGHT SIMON COULDN'T sleep, as usual. Between puzzling over Carl Chavis's murder, rehashing the incident at the Do Drop Inn, and pining over Julia, his brain was in overdrive. Even after getting up and drinking two fingers of bourbon mixed with the same amount of cold Coke, he couldn't relax.

He didn't think he was exaggerating the furtive activity going on in Pearlie Beach since he and Morgan had shared their discovery of the Confederate gold coins on Carl Chavis's body. Colonel Watkins didn't admit he recognized Nick Monahan in the photograph Simon showed him; Woody Watkins accused Simon, in public, of hiding information about a Confederate treasure; even Clare Monahan's arrival for the holiday seemed mysterious; and Nance and Leland Pearlie were skulking around the island in their boat at night without lights. What was going on? Who killed Carl Chavis? Was he murdered for a stash of Confederate gold he found? Was that stash the foundation of the Watkins and Pearlie family fortunes? If so, why were the second and third generations of those families out looking for it? Had some crucial information about its location died with Carl, with Nick, and then with Dale Senior? Or was the mere thought of Confederate gold making everyone crazy, including himself?

Then there was the Jewish thing. Simon had astounded himself when he let Woody identify him as Jewish. It wasn't just that he had let the comment slide; consciously he had accepted it. What did that mean? His parents had rejected their families' religions. He had lived his entire life in the skeptical atmosphere of universities and colleges. He respected both his traditional southern Baptist and Jewish origins, but was taught by his parents to consider them quaint and unenlightened. He had attended a couple dozen weddings, funerals, bar mitzvahs, and other family events at several churches and synagogues, but for him they were just opportunities to visit with his cousins and eat great food. He had just finished reading *The Gift of Asher Lev,* by Chaim Potok, which his cousin Leah Simon had sent him for his birthday. Reading anything by Potok encouraged him to reflect upon his half Jewishness for a time. Maybe that explained it.

Then there was Julia. It was unthinkable that she had cleared out the guest bedroom for him for any reason other than the one she gave. He knew her well enough to know that she was not going to open the connecting door between the bedrooms and slip into his bed. No way would anything sexual happen around the Cleggs and their children.

The bathroom light clicked on, followed by the sound of running water. Hope quickened in Simon's heart. The door to his room opened just as the bathroom light went off, and a small figure wearing a worn Carter's nightgown came into his room. Dolly's eyes were open, but her flat expression indicated that she was sleepwalking. She had a dilapidated teddy bear under one arm and her thumb in her mouth. Confidently she climbed into Simon's bed and wiggled into a comfortable position.

"Why aren't you twenty-five years old?" Simon asked her.

Dolly didn't answer him. Her eyes closed and she fell into deep baby-sleep.

"I envy you," Simon said. "I used to sleep like that."

She didn't stir when Simon picked her up and tucked her back into her own bed.

6

THE NEXT MORNING EARLY SIMON TOOK HIS COFFEE OUT ON the deck. Marianne was already up, stretched out on a lounge chair. It was a clear, bright day, accented by a brisk breeze that drove a few wispy clouds south. The rising sun scattered light in a path across the ocean from the horizon to the shore. It looked like a road paved with diamonds floating on the water.

"So," Marianne said. "You and Julia seem to be getting along very well."

Simon was not about to tell her about his macho meltdown at the Do Drop Inn, Julia's rescue effort, their subsequent argument, and their reconciliation.

"Sure," he said, "we're grown-ups. We know how to behave."

"In fact," Marianne said, "the two of you seem to have been pretty much joined at the hip the entire weekend."

"Don't get any ideas," Simon said. "We're just friends."

"There's no such thing," Marcus said, sliding open the porch door and joining them on the deck with a family-sized cup of coffee. "Between men and women, there's just sex."

"I always said you had an enlightened attitude," Simon said.

"I don't care how men and women rationalize or romanticize their relationships," Marcus said. "Successful reproduction is what it's all about."

"No wonder you're a failed therapist," Simon said.

Marcus pulled up a lounge chair next to Marianne and took her hand.

"Ah, but I am a great success at something much more important. I have four children to carry on my genes."

"What do you say to that?" Simon asked Marianne.

"I don't pay any attention to what he says," she said, "as long as he adores me."

"Of course I do," Marcus said. "I let nature take its course—result: love and family. To do anything else is to think too much."

"What was this about Marcus being a failed therapist?" Julia said, joining them on the deck.

"You know how teachers have to student-teach before they can be licensed?" Marcus said. "In order to get my Ph.D. I had to spend a semester counseling. We practiced on students who came to the campus mental health center. I got the lowest rating ever. I had to promise my adviser to stay away from human beings before he would pass me."

"So that's why your life's work is studying what rats will do for sex," Simon said.

"Anything," Marcus said. "They'll do anything their tiny minds can comprehend. But back to psychotherapy. I thought my advice to my patients was wonderful. Obey the ten commandments, ignore your parents after you're grown up, and don't read women's magazines or watch television. After fifteen minutes my subjects were cured, as far as I was concerned."

Julia had noticed that after she joined the group on the deck there had been a minute pause in the conversation before Marcus had answered her question. If they had been talking about her relationship with Simon, they were wasting their breath. She refused to be the object of matchmatching. She didn't know what he had told them about last night, and she didn't care.

She liked Simon very much, but she didn't intend to get involved romantically with him. She didn't understand where the obvious sexual chemistry between them came from, but she could deal with that. A woman had to think about more than attraction in a man. Simon was just all wrong for her. Besides, he couldn't be as sweet as he seemed, or his wife wouldn't have left him. Maybe she divorced him because he wasn't ambitious enough. Someone with his credentials surely could do better than Kenan College.

Marianne puzzled Julia, too. She sat calmly next to her husband, holding his hand, and listened to him make knuckle-dragging comments about men and women without flinching. Julia knew Marianne had a brain; they had met and become friends at a Jane Austen book club. But the woman had no career, no clothes, two too many children, and twenty extra pounds. Yet she seemed perfectly happy.

Next door Col. Timothy Watkins slammed the lid of his metal garbage can down, hard. The sound rang out harshly in the early morning quiet.

"You would think," he said, at the top of his voice, "that you could at least carry out the garbage."

"Calm down, Dad," Woody said. "I've got a bag, haven't I? What do you want from me?"

"You've got one damn bag, and I've got two. I'm eighty years old, for God's sake."

"Mine's leaking."

"Poor boy."

"Lay off me."

"I can't believe you asked your mother for money. If you want money, get a job. You shouldn't be dating that woman, anyway. She's married."

"That's none of your business."

"I swear I don't know where you came from. I regret the day that you were born more than I can say."

Woody must have kicked over the metal garbage can, because there was another loud metallic crash.

"Don't come back into the house until you clean that up," Watkins said. "You'd think I was talking to a ten-year-old."

The group on the deck heard Watkins go back into his house and close the door.

"I wish you were dead," Woody said.

They sat in absolute silence while Woody cleaned up the trash and slammed the lid on the garbage can, and until they heard him go into the house.

"Well," Marcus said. "Talk about your dysfunctional families."

"Let's go inside and make pancakes," Marianne said. "The girls should be getting up soon."

Simon couldn't get Carl Chavis's murder out of his mind. Despite Simon's professional conclusions that there was no substantial Confederate gold stash at Pearlie Beach in 1942 or today, the man died in his diving suit with eleven very rare Confederate gold coins in his possession. That was incontrovertible fact. Why did the murderer leave those coins behind? And was there even a remote chance that there was more gold out there somewhere? He couldn't dismiss that possibility just because the historical record didn't support it. He was investigating a murder, not writing an academic paper.

Simon knew just a few individuals left on Pearlie Beach who were alive in 1942. He wanted to talk to them all, and find more if he could. Beside, he was drawn to old people like a moth to flame. He chose twentieth-century American history as his specialty mostly so he could talk to its witnesses. As the century drew to a close he had realized they wouldn't be around forever. He left his friends right after breakfast and went to call on Inez Pearlie.

"I am so glad to see you!" she said, opening her door to him. "I've been thinking about you all morning."

Inez was perfectly turned out, as usual, this time in a sky-blue knit pantsuit with matching espadrilles and chunky silver earrings shaped like sand dollars. She took him by the arm and pulled him into her house before he had a chance to speak.

"Come see what I've found," she said.

An old battered metal file box sat on her dining room table. The lid hung open on its hinges, revealing a jumble of papers inside.

"I've been going through some of Dale Senior's papers," she said, "and I found this!"

She held up a yellowed newspaper only a few pages long. She opened it up to an interior page and showed it to him triumphantly. There was a small square section missing from the middle of the page.

"You know that clipping in the stuff we gave you?" she said. "This is the very newspaper it came from."

Simon took the fragile pages of the *Wilmington Star* dated Wednesday, May 13, 1942, two days after Carl Chavis disappeared. It would tell him exactly what was going on in the community at the time of the murder. Of course he could have found the newspaper at a university library, but there wasn't one handy right now. Holding it in his hands evoked in him a more personal feeling for the incident than reading it on microfiche ever could.

The kitchen door slammed, and Dale entered the dining room. He did not look happy to find Simon there.

"What are you doing here?" he demanded.

"I asked him in," Inez said. "To show him what I found in your father's papers."

"We discussed this," Dale said to his mother.

"No, you told me what you thought, and I didn't agree with you," she said.

Dale turned to Simon. "I don't want you looking into Carl's death anymore," Dale said.

"But—" Simon began.

Dale stopped him with a shake of his head. "Carl's murder happened over fifty years ago. It's not important now, and your investigation will just bring bad publicity to the island. This is a family beach, people come here to relax, I don't want reporters and treasure-hunters hanging around."

"It's important to me," Inez said.

"Whoever killed Carl is dead now, too. Killed him for a few gold coins Carl found by chance somewhere, I agree with Dr. Shaw about that. But there's no point in dredging the whole thing up. We've got a business to run here."

Inez and Simon were both silent.

"I'm going over to the office," Dale said. He gestured to the box of papers on the table. "I wish you would throw this stuff away. It's a fire hazard."

Inez and Simon waited until they heard his car start before they resumed their conversation.

"I don't understand," Simon said. "When I was here yesterday, Dale said he didn't mind me investigating Carl's death."

Inez shook her head in puzzlement herself.

"I know. But Leland and Nance came over last night and spent a lot of time talking in the den. Afterwards Dale told me the three of them agreed to discourage you."

"I don't want to cause trouble."

"You're not causing me trouble. Dale and Leland can't tell me what to do. I'm their mother. I changed their diapers. I'll do as I please, and I want you to continue as long as you're willing."

"Is there anything else in this box of papers I might be interested in?" Simon said.

"Just this," Inez said, handing him a folded pamphlet. Simon opened it up. It was an old tourist map of the island.

"Dale Senior had that drawn up just as the war was starting and Wilmington was booming and people started coming to the beach again," she said. "He wanted to make sure they could find us."

Simon gently folded both the map and newspaper and tucked them into the inside pocket of his jacket.

"I'd like to ask you some more questions," Simon said, "if you have the time."

"Go right ahead."

"Tell me about Nick Monahan."

"Let's see, let me think." She scrunched up her face. "He came from good people. He and his wife and family lived just up the road in Varnumtown. He ran a charter and freight service. Had a seaplane. But you know that."

"He disappeared about the same time that Carl did," Simon said.

"Yes, but I'm sure the two events weren't related. He monitored this part of the shore for the Civil Air Patrol and was out scouting for German submarines and just didn't come back."

"I wonder," Simon said, "if he didn't see something other than a submarine on one of his patrols."

"I never heard of anything like that."

"It's just a thought," Simon said.

"It's quite a coincidence, isn't it, that Nick's granddaughter would show up about the same time Carl's body was found, after all these years?"

"Yes," Simon said. "It is."

THERE WERE ONLY A few cars in the pier parking lot. It was too early for the lunch crowd and too choppy to fish. Simon pulled Julia's car into a space next to Henry Pearlie's old pickup. A gun rack mounted inside over the rear window held both a twenty-gauge shotgun and a hunting rifle with a scope. Simon checked the truck doors to make sure they were locked. Not that a locked door would stop anyone who really wanted one of those guns. As he walked around the front of Henry's truck he noticed a hand-lettered sign tacked to a post that read, CONFEDERATE PARKING ONLY, ALL OTHERS, GO UP NORTH. Two souvenir-sized Confederate flags were taped to either side of the message.

Simon was a loyal southerner. On his father's side he traced his lineage back five generations to an infant wrapped in a gray Confederate army blanket abandoned outside the Baptist church in Boone. He loved North Carolina and planned to live there the rest of his life. But he had no affection for the Confederate flag. It symbolized slavery to too many law-abiding, God-fearing African-American citizens, and was brandished by too many racist organizations, for him ever to be comfortable with it. He wished southerners would adopt some other symbol of their devotion.

Inside the pier Henry was alone, mopping the floor. Simon sat down on a stool at the counter.

"There ain't gonna be enough people here for me to fire up the grill today," Henry said, "so I can't cook you nothing. I could get you a drink, if you like, though."

"A Coke would be great," Simon said.

Henry reached up to his elbow into an old fashioned red Coca-Cola chest and brought up a six-and-a-half-ounce glass bottle of Coke, shaking the ice and water off it. The sight instantly transported Simon back to his childhood, when he would go into his grandfather's general store and reach into the cooler for a drink. Nothing else would ever taste as invigorating to him. He tilted the bottle back and swallowed half of it in one gulp. It was so cold it almost burned, and the sugar and caffeine jolted him immediately. He often wondered what a Coke jolt was like before 1903 when the cocaine was removed from the formula.

"You're up and out bright and early this morning," Henry said.

"I'm pestering people," Simon said. "I'm still interested in Carl Chavis's murder."

Henry shrugged. "It was a damn shame," he said. "But it's been so long ago now."

"It seems to me that if there was any Confederate gold around here at one time, you would know," Simon said.

"You mean with my connections?" Henry said, grinning. "Yeah, I've spent a lot of time on these waters. Bootlegging first, then working the black market during the war. I admit to that. And I remember Carl being crazy to find sunken treasure with that underwater getup he learned how to use in the navy. But I never, never heard tell of any gold around here. I think your idea about it is probably true."

"Which idea was that?"

"That the kid must have found, you know, a small amount of gold, a personal stash maybe, and when he showed it to someone, he got killed for it."

"They left eleven coins behind," Simon said.

"That they did," Henry said. "Got scared or something, maybe."

"I was talking to Inez Pearlie this morning," Simon said. "Asking her about Nick Monahan. Did you know him?"

"There was no one in the whole United States of America who hated the Nazis more than Nick did. He flew an old Vought Corsair seaplane. He wanted to buy a Grumman Duck, but he couldn't afford it. You know what he did once? Stole a bomb from the air base and took it up in the plane with him. Laid it right across his lap! When he saw a German submarine, he dropped it! He missed, but the U-boat submerged. He was fearless."

"What do you think happened to him?" Simon asked.

"Most likely he was buzzing a sub and got blown out of the sky," Henry said. "Those U-boats had two antiaircraft machine guns on deck. He already had a couple of bullet holes in the airplane from when they had shot at him.

"Hey," Henry said, changing the subject, "I got something interesting to show you. I don't keep it on display because I don't want everyone handling it."

Henry took a pair of rubber kitchen gloves out of a drawer and put them on. Then from a cabinet he removed an object in a plastic bag and carefully unwrapped it, tossing it to Simon.

It was an old leather European football, what Americans would call a soccer ball, embossed with the eagle of the Third Reich and a big black swastika. Simon wondered why even the most common objects from Nazi times sported the swastika. It was like having the American flag stamped on your toaster oven.

"Colonel Watkins found it patrolling the beach during the war and I got it from him," Henry said. "I figure some Germans were tossing it around on the deck of a sub and lost it overboard."

Simon didn't doubt it. A German submarine was a claustrophobic's nightmare. U-boats were war tubes, not cruise ships. The fifty-man crew shared twenty bunks and one head. Each man packed only one pair of spare knitted blue wool underwear. With the exception of a few areas warmed by space heaters, it was just as cold inside as the water outside. Lights stayed on around the clock. Fog from condensed breath filled the sub. Every square inch was stuffed with ammunition for the deck guns, torpedoes, fresh water, and food. At the beginning of each voyage, until some of the supplies were consumed, the crew would have to crawl to get around. The cook's first task before preparing any meal was to cut the mold off the sausages, cheese, and black bread that was the core of most meals on board.

Henry took the football back from him, carefully wrapped it up in the plastic bag again, and stowed it away in the cabinet.

Simon stopped at the pier bathroom before heading home. Using his pocketknife, he quietly pried the nail out of the wall, pulled the paneling loose, and retrieved one of the magazines he had discovered the day before. It was yellowed with age, but otherwise intact. He tucked it inside his jacket. He replaced the paneling and left the pier without saying anything to Henry.

Simon walked back to the cottage by way of the beach with his hands in his pockets, leaning slightly into the wind. He had mixed feelings about finding the magazine and its fellows jammed back in the wall of the bathroom. On the one hand that was where they belonged—in a toilet. On the other hand, he felt somewhat responsible for keeping anyone else from finding them.

"IS THIS SLOW ENOUGH, Mommy?" Dolly asked. With exaggerated, precise movements, the little girl pulled on the twine, hand over hand, that hung over the edge of the dock into the murky water. Next to her Isobel watched her own length of string for any sign of a quiver. Julia monitored her, while Marianne sat with Dolly, one arm tight around her to keep her from falling off the high dock.

"That's good," Marianne said. "You're doing great."

The little girl's brow furrowed as she concentrated. Finally the fish head, tied to the end of the twine, rose up out of the depths of the water and into view. Gripping it with its claws and chowing down was a large blue crab, its eyes rotating on stalks. It was a fearsome sight. Dolly shrieked, the crab let go of the bait, and it, the twine, and the bait sank into the water. Dolly sobbed while Marianne comforted her.

Julia and Isobel bent their heads together, away from Dolly, and tried not to laugh.

"You silly girl," Isobel said to her sister. "It's just a crab. You knew we were crabbing. What did you think you were going to catch?"

"Shush, she's just three years old," Julia said.

Marianne consoled Dolly until her sobs subsided, but she refused to crab again. She sat on her mother's lap and watched Isobel and Julia. Isobel's line jerked ever so slightly. She gently pulled it in, while Julia hovered with a fish net.

"Very, very slowly," Julia said.

Isobel carefully drew up the fish head. Another big crab was feeding, oblivious to his fate. Quickly Julia scooped him up.

"I got him!" Isobel shouted.

No one except Marianne wanted to untangle the crab from the net. She carefully reached into the net, grasped the crab behind his last pair of legs, drawing him out of the net, legs waving wildly.

"It's a big one," Julia said.

"Are we going to eat it?" Dolly asked, standing on stubby legs a safe distance away.

"No, honey, we're going to throw it back in a second," Marianne said. "Tell me, do you remember how to tell if it's a boy or a girl?"

"If it's a boy, underneath on the shell is the outline of the Washington Monument; if it's a girl, it's the outline of the Capitol," Isobel said. Her mother turned the crab over. "It's a boy," Isobel said.

Marianne threw the crab back into the water. "Why are we throwing it back?" Marianne asked rhetorically.

"Because we don't need to eat it, and we want to have lots of baby crabs," Isobel said, almost by rote. "Let's catch some more!"

Marianne and Julia picked out two more fish heads from the bag they had scrounged from Captain Nance's market and tied heavy twine around them. The girls—for Dolly had found some new courage—threw the heads over the dock and waited.

Dolly's line jerked, and she carefully pulled it up. The crab nibbling on the bait was just silver-dollar-sized, which didn't frighten her and gave Marianne the opportunity to talk about molting. Dolly even let the tiny crab scuttle around the dock at her feet before throwing it back into the water.

Bored with crabbing, the girls put on rubber boots and waded along the muddy shore of the inlet near the dock, scooping up minnows in the crab net and throwing them back. Julia and Marianne sat on two lawn chairs they had brought with them and watched.

"This is a nice spot," Julia said. "Very peaceful. No people."

"I like bringing the kids here. It gives them a good idea of what the coast is like when it's undeveloped. It's the Pearlies' property. Nance told me about it a couple of summers ago. In the spring and summer we bring binoculars and a picnic and bird-watch."

The little oasis was down a dirt road off NC 17. At the head of an inlet, a long dock reached into the water from a high bank. Fronting the dock was a green storage shed with a large lock on the door. Pine trees grew almost to the water's edge, and the undergrowth would have been impenetrable except for a short path that led to a small dirt parking area off a rutted road which led back to NC 17.

The women didn't hear the car.

"What the hell are you doing here? This is private property."

The harshness of the voice startled the two women, and when they turned around they saw a double-barreled shotgun pointed right at them. It was in the hands of Leland Pearlie. Marianne, with a sharp intake of breath, grabbed Julia's arm.

"Put that thing down," Julia said. "Right now. What do you think you're doing?"

"Oh, no," Pearlie said, embarrassed. "I didn't realize it was you, Mrs. Clegg. I am sorry."

"Put that gun down, now!" Julia repeated.

Dolly and Isobel were frightened by the harsh sound of Leland's voice and came in from wading to their mother. When she saw the shotgun, Dolly hid behind Marianne's back.

"I didn't mean to frighten you," Leland said. "It's just that, well, there's some valuable gear stored in that shed."

Marianne found her voice.

"Nance gave us permission to come here a couple of summers ago. We assumed it was still okay. Of course we'll leave now."

By this time Leland was ashen, trying to figure a way out of his embarrassing predicament.

"Please don't," he said. "I don't know what got into me. I wasn't thinking. . . . I mean, there was a break-in at a cottage down the road. Oh, hell," he said, giving up.

Julia thought he seemed truly distressed.

"It's okay," she said.

"It's just Mr. Pearlie," Marianne said to the girls. "He thought we were someone else. But I think we should leave now, anyway."

Dolly, sucking her thumb, ventured out from behind her mother and stared at Leland with big eyes.

The two women packed up their chairs and a plastic tote. Leland, still apologizing, helped them carry their stuff to the minivan.

"What was that about?" Marianne said, turning off the dirt road onto NC 17. "I have never known the Pearlies to be anything other than sweet as pie to everyone, and I have certainly never seen any of them with a gun before, except Joe, of course, and I would be surprised if he'd ever shot his outside a firing range."

TRINA KICKED THE SAND viciously. The wind blew most of the grit right toward her father, who was sitting on a chair on the beach reading a magazine. Morgan sat next to him, fiddling with his digital camera.

"Trina, stop it. If you want my attention, please ask for

it in a mature way, not by kicking sand in my face," Marcus said.

Trina plopped down next to him.

"Those kids next door are going to have a bonfire tonight," she said.

"Are they?" Marcus said. He looked over at the crowd of kids Trina had been trying to infiltrate all weekend. The same blond boy who had stuck out his tongue at Simon appeared to be their leader. He was directing the others to collect driftwood and stack it in a big pile above the water line.

"Can I go? Please?"

"Have you been invited?"

"It's not like that. I can just go."

Marcus inspected the group again.

"They look older than you," Marcus said. "And I haven't seen an adult with them all day. Will any parents be at this bonfire?"

"I don't know," Trina said. "Can't I go? They're going to bring a boom box so we can dance—"

"You're too young for that, honey," Marcus said, shaking his head. "You know that."

"You'd let April do it," Trina said, "if she was here."

"She's almost thirteen," Marcus said.

"Excuse me," Morgan said, "I've just remembered that I have something to do in the camper." He quickly walked over the beach toward the cottage.

"Young lady," Marcus said, "you've whined to the point that Dr. Morgan left. You should be ashamed. If you're going to pout, go into the house. I've been trying to read this one article all weekend."

Morgan returned, toting what looked like a dinner plate on a stick with a handle.

"What's that?" Trina asked, her troubles momentarily forgotten.

"Metal detector. Want to know how it works?"

"Yes!" she said.

"You fit your elbow into the armrest here and hold on with the handgrip. Here's the control box, where the electronics are. These knobs will set the detector to locate various metals. You can set it for gold, which is very specific, or relics, which will make the detector beep for almost anything that's nonferrous, including gold, silver, copper, lead, aluminum, zinc, and nickel. The disc at the bottom is the search coil. It transmits the pulses of the magnetic fields of whatever objects it detects to the control box."

"Wow," Trina said. "Can I hold it?"

"Sure. Make sure that you wave it over the sand in a very even motion."

"Are we going now?" she said.

"What?"

"Are we going now—to look for gold, I mean?"

"Honey," her father began, "I don't think Dr. Morgan meant—"

Morgan shushed him with a hand motion.

"Sure," he said. "Why not? But we're not going to find gold, honey. Maybe some other interesting things. Let's walk down to the beach to that little inlet and see what we can find."

She looked at her father for permission, and he nodded. Trina and Morgan walked down the beach to the inlet, passing the kids building their bonfire. A few of the kids looked at them curiously.

"It's a metal detector," Trina said to them loftily as she and Morgan walked by.

Marcus couldn't help but smile as he watched Trina and Morgan fade into the distance, Trina carefully moving the detector side to side, while Morgan helped her support its weight.

"What a pair," he said to himself before he went back to his article.

WHEN SIMON RETURNED TO the cottage from the pier, he found Julia on the deck reading his Nero Wolfe book.

"Hey, there," she said. "Did you have a productive morning?"

"Yes and no," he said. "Remember those magazines I told you about? The ones in the wall of the bathroom at the pier? I sneaked one away."

"Why on earth—"

Simon took the magazine out of his jacket pocket and showed it to her.

"I thought when you said they were nasty, you meant pornographic," she said.

"This is pornography," Simon said. "It's political pornography."

"Liberation," Julia read off the masthead of the magazine. "What is it? I never heard of it."

"It was a so-called journal published in Asheville, North Carolina, during the 1930s," Simon said. "It was a pro-Nazi publication. Its most famous excess was to print a fake speech by Benjamin Franklin supposedly given to the Constitutional Convention. It became known as "Franklin's Prophecy." The Germans used it for propaganda. You can still find it on Neo-Nazi sites on the Internet."

"Is it in this issue?"

"No. I just picked up the first issue I found. The wall was packed full of them."

"What was Franklin's Prophecy?"

"We don't need to go into all the details, but it was anti-Semitic in the extreme."

Simon didn't want to talk about *Liberation* with anyone, anywhere, anytime. He wished he hadn't found the damn magazine. He certainly didn't want to ask Dale Pearlie's permission to retrieve the rags from inside the wall of the pier bathroom, pack them all up, take them back to Raleigh, and catalog them for the Kenan College Library. But preservation of primary sources, no matter how detestable the material, was his duty as a scholar, and he was stuck with the job.

On February 3, 1934, *Liberation* published a speech supposedly given by Benjamin Franklin to the Constitutional Convention. The source for the speech was given to be a diary kept by Charles Cotesworth Pinckney, South Carolina's delegation to the Convention. The speech was a forgery, probably the invention of William Dudley Pelley, the head of an American Nazi group, who published *Liberation,* which sold a million copies in its heyday. The last two sentences of the "speech" were: "The Jews are a danger to this land, and if they are allowed to enter, they will imperil our institutions. They should be excluded from the Constitution." The "speech" was picked up by *Der Weltdienst, Der Volksbund,* and *Der Sturmer,* and circulated all over the world. The noted historian Charles Beard read the "speech" in an American bank newsletter, of all things, and set about investigating it with a professional historian's dedication.

Beard searched for Pinckney's diary everywhere. After eighteen months of exhaustive research in the National Archives, the Library of Congress, and the Franklin Institute, he concluded that the diary never existed, and there was no evidence that Franklin ever made such a speech. Besides, its content was entirely at odds with Franklin's well-known principles of tolerance, especially in religious matters.

In 1776, at the Continental Congress, Franklin suggested that the nation's new seal depict Moses parting the Red Sea. The archives of Congregation Mikveh Israel in Philadelphia contain a subscription paper dated April 30, 1798, signed by Franklin and forty-four other citizens of all faiths who made a contribution toward relieving the debt incurred by the congregation in building a synagogue.

William Dudley Pelley was run out of North Carolina in 1940. He was convicted of espionage in Indiana in 1942 and sent to prison. Pelley died in 1965, but his brainchild, Franklin's Prophecy, lives on in the dark side of cyberspace.

"I cannot comprehend why someone would read this stuff," Julia said, skimming the issue she still held. "How could anyone believe it?"

"Benjamin Franklin said it himself in *Poor Richard's Almanack.* 'The truth stands on two legs, whereas a lie stands only on one.' "

"What are you going to do?"

"Ask Dale Pearlie if I can dig the magazines out of the bathroom wall. Take them home to the Kenan College Library to be cataloged. Repulsive as they are, they could be important research materials. Besides, I don't want some kid to find them in the bathroom."

"Why were they in the wall in the first place?"

"They were used for insulation when the pier was built, I expect. Who knows where they came from originally? On a more cheerful note, I got some new information from Inez."

He gave Julia the old map and newspaper Inez gave him. She unfolded them carefully while Simon took the issue of *Liberation* into his bedroom and locked it in his briefcase.

"Now," Simon said, joining her again, "tell me about your morning."

Julia described the incident with Leland Pearlie and his shotgun.

"He scared the girls," Julia said. "And Marianne and me, too. Marianne said she'd never seen him act like that before. Simon, something strange is going on here."

"I know," Simon said. "And I believe it's all related to Carl Chavis's death." He took the map and newspaper from Julia. "I'm going to add these to my pitiful collection of evidence and see if I can't come up with some logical explanation for Carl's murder."

Julia followed him inside and watched him arrange the documents and photographs on the dining room table.

"*Pitiful* is an inadequate word to describe your so-called evidence," Julia said. "I'm afraid you're wasting your time."

"Want to help?"

"I can't right now. I promised the girls I'd help them build a sand castle."

Carl Chavis's murder was a vicious crime. Simon couldn't abandon his effort to solve it until he was sure he had done his best. So he concentrated on his documents, reading every word and inspecting every inch of every map and photograph carefully.

As Julia had so helpfully pointed out to him, his "evidence" was scant to say the least. He had a group photograph of Carl, Dale Senior, Nick Monahan, Henry Pearlie, and Colonel Watkins taken in the spring of 1942 by Inez Pearlie. Of course, they weren't the only five people around Pearlie Beach who could have had a hand in the murder, even if he excluded weekend beach traffic, but they were Chavis's close friends, whom he might have told about any discovery. That would make them at least material witnesses in any modern police inquiry. He had a shipwreck map pinpointing all the Confederate wrecks in the area, but he didn't know what might have been recoverable from those wrecks in 1942, if anything. He had a newspaper clipping about Chavis's disappearance, along with the issue of the paper that contained that article, which might offer some insight into what was happening in the area around the time of the murder. He had the medical examiner's report on Chavis's body. He had four books on shipwrecks and World War II culled from Marcus's paperback collection and the results of Morgan's Internet search, all of which confirmed his opinion that there was no known Confederate gold treasure anywhere near Pearlie Beach. He had already noted that a private individual could have been carrying enough gold to be worth a fortune today. Such a person could have drowned in a wreck or tossed his money overboard to prevent its being captured by Yankees. That could have happened anywhere off the coast, not just where ships were wrecked. And he had a 1942 tourist map of Pearlie Beach, then just a small sand island with a few buildings on it: the Pavilion, a half dozen cottages, the Pearlie home, and the ferry landing. He had made notes of the conversations he'd had with Watkins, Inez, and Henry, which covered exactly seven pages of a yellow legal pad.

Simon carefully examined the tourist map. Dale Pearlie Senior had taken an old navigation map, showing the depths and waterways of the area in 1942, and superimposed a drawing of the tourist features of the beach. It verified what Simon had already been told, that the sound and the inlets around it were much deeper in 1942.

Simon gently unfolded the old *Wilmington Star* Inez had given him, being very careful not to tear it along the creases where it had been folded for fifty years. He loved to read old newspapers. He would have enjoyed reading this one even if Carl Chavis hadn't disappeared two days before its publication date, which was Wednesday, May 13, 1942.

As always at the coast, the weather was page one news. On May 13, 1942, the temperature was expected to reach a high of 77 degrees, humidity was at 42 percent, sunrise was at 6:32 A.M., sunset at 6:56 P.M, and the new moon had begun to wax the previous Sunday. It would have been very dark at night, with no moonlight and a coastal blackout to boot.

The paragraph on Carl Chavis's disappearance had been clipped from "Wings over Wilmington," a feature column about the army air base, which dominated the life of

Wilmington during the war. The base pumped over a million and a half dollars into the economy of Wilmington every month. That didn't include what was contributed by oil terminals, shipyards, and other harbor properties. All those jobs and wages meant people looking for something to do on the weekend. The authorities counted five thousand people on Carolina Beach one weekend. No wonder Dale Pearlie Senior had a map drawn so that they would find their way to Pearlie Beach and his Pavilion.

Henry Pearlie must have made an excellent living on the black market. The newspaper was plastered with ads for automobile tire branding services, tire reliners, blowout patches, and patching kits. All rubber was diverted to the war effort, so it was impossible to buy new tires. New car and truck sales had been prohibited since the previous January. Everyone except doctors got just two gallons of gas a week. Fishermen, whether amateur or professional, had to get daily permits from the coast guard, a process that involved fingerprints, interviews, and citizenship verification. Sugar, butter, meat, cinnamon, allspice, and ice were rationed.

Naturally, though, the booming Wilmington community demanded entertainment. *When the Daltons Rode,* starring Randolph Scott and Kay Francis, was playing at the Manor Theatre. Blue and green low-wattage lights let local baseball teams compete at the city stadium without contributing to the loom, the background light that threatened shipping.

Considering that the Battle of the Atlantic was raging off the Carolina Coast, the newspaper mentioned very little local war news. Simon supposed it was heavily censored. In one tiny paragraph there was a mention of an incident the previous weekend, when the townspeople of Varnumtown heard gunfire and explosions and sent out boats to rescue the survivors of a torpedoed tanker. An editorial cautioned readers not to discuss the war, weather, or agricultural conditions, or to criticize the government, or to take photographs.

Simon had left his laptop computer at home to avoid working, but he missed it now, although it would be difficult to do any research. He didn't bother to have an Internet account in his own name; he could plug into Kenan College's computer network from his office or his library carrel and have access to all kinds of expensive services, including Lexis-Nexis, North Carolina Archives, and library collections all over the country. Morgan had his laptop with him, but Simon knew he didn't subscribe to any of the services he needed. He could call the Kenan College Library, but he doubted he could find someone who could help him on a holiday weekend. He did know someone else he could call, though. Simon checked his watch. This was about the time of day Otis smoked his second of three cigarettes for the day.

Otis answered his office phone on the first ring. "Gates here," he said.

"Getting your paperwork done?" Simon asked. He could hear Jessye Norman singing spirituals in the background.

"I've lowered the stack a couple of feet or so. Started from the bottom. Amazing how much you can throw out once you've left it for a while."

"Not busy now, are you?"

"What do you want?"

"For you to look up something for me in the state birth and death records."

"Nothing else?"

"Like what?"

"You know, the sort of thing one man would tell another."

"I hope you haven't been waiting with bated breath for me and Julia to get it on."

"I'm an old married man. I have to get my excitement vicariously."

"Pay attention. I want to see what's on record about a Nick Monahan's death in 1942 down here at the coast. He disappeared in an airplane scouting for Nazi submarines, so there should be a petition to declare him dead."

"You know, I'm not supposed to do this kind of thing," Otis said, but Simon could hear the click of his fingers on his keyboard.

"All amateur sleuths have a faithful friend in the police department to look up stuff for them. You should be honored."

"Got it," Otis said. "Monahan's widow filed a petition to have him declared dead in 1949, and the petition was granted. Want me to access it for you?"

"Please."

More keyboard clicks.

"The petition states that Monahan took off in his seaplane to patrol the coast south of Wilmington on May 11, 1942, and never returned. No trace of him or the plane was ever found."

"That was a Monday, the same day Chavis disappeared."

"Chavis was your corpse in a diving suit?"

"How did you know that?"

"Julia told me all about it when she checked in this morning. Could be just a coincidence. There was a war on."

WHEN JULIA CAME BACK from the beach, Simon told her what he had learned from Otis.

"If you think Chavis's death and Monahan's disappearance were related, you must have a theory about what happened," she said.

"I could speculate that Nick Monahan spotted a wreck from the air and told Chavis about it. With the help of his buddies and his equipment, Chavis retrieved the gold. They fought over it. Chavis got killed. Monahan conveniently disappeared. Dale Pearlie Senior and Timothy Watkins got rich."

"What about Henry Pearlie? Where does he fit in? He's poor as grits without gravy."

"True. If he had any money, he'd have a better truck."

"And if Watkins and Pearlie found the gold, why are their children out searching Pearlie Beach for it?"

"That's easy. They don't know their fathers found it. If you were Colonel Watkins, would you tell Woody anything?"

"You've made all this up. You couldn't hang a dog with it."

"I'm a scholar. I can make the facts fit any scenario I want."

"It's not funny to speculate that these guys committed murder."

"I know that; I wouldn't say anything to anyone but

you. And if I'm wrong, why are Leland and Nance Pearlie boating around at night with mapping equipment? Why is the Reverend Clare Monahan here? Did she engineer her appointment on this particular weekend? Had someone told her about Chavis's body being found? And why were she and Woody spending time together diving? Did she find something in her grandfather's papers besides photographs? Why didn't Colonel Watkins say he recognized Nick Monahan in the photograph I showed him? Why did Dale change his mind so suddenly about me investigating Carl's death? Why did Leland threaten you and Marianne and the girls this morning?"

"I don't know."

"I think the answer to Chavis's murder is right here," Simon said, tapping on the pile of papers with a forefinger. "I feel it in my gut."

"Your famous instincts," Morgan said as he slid open the door and came into the room, followed by Trina, full of news.

"We found teeth," she shouted, jumping up and down. "Look!"

She opened her hand and showed them a nasty old set of dentures, discolored and caked with sand.

"Yuck," Julia said. "Where on earth did you find those?"

"We've been metal detecting!" Trina said. "And we found a bunch of other stuff, too!"

"Anything valuable?" Simon asked.

"No gold, if that's what you're wondering," said Morgan. "Lots of spare change, a bottle opener, beer and soda tab tops, stuff like that."

"We threw all that away," Trina said. "But I want to keep the teeth. And the money."

"You can keep the teeth until we leave, honey," Marianne said, coming into the cottage followed by Marcus, Isobel, and Dolly. "Leave it on that shelf up there, where Dolly can't get it. Then please wash your hands well."

Trina carefully placed the dentures on a high bookshelf and skipped away to the bathroom.

"You might be interested to know," Morgan said to Simon, "that Trina and I weren't the only ones out treasure-hunting on the beach. We ran into those two friends of Woody's, the guys from the bar. They had a brand-new metal detector, still had the tags on it."

"Darryl and Mike? Did they find anything?"

"Same as us. They had a plastic trash bag full of junk." Morgan laughed. "They seemed mighty frustrated. Is there any turkey left? I'm starving."

"We promised the kids hamburgers," Marcus said, following Morgan. "So I guess we're off to the pier."

"I've stopped by there already," Simon said. "Henry says he's not cooking today."

"I could eat a burger, definitely," Morgan said.

"Me, too," Julia said.

THE CLEGGS BUCKLED THEIR girls into their van and went ahead. Morgan, Simon, and Julia followed behind in Julia's car, stopping at the Pearlie Beach Emporium to let Morgan pick up a pack of Lucky Strikes.

Darlene Pearlie was alone in the store, marking sale prices on a shelf of souvenirs. The snack isle and drink coolers were almost empty.

"Where's Leland?" Simon asked Darlene.

"That's a sore subject," Darlene said. "He and Nance

have been out on the *Black Pearl* almost twenty-four hours a day this weekend. They won't tell me what's going on. Well, I know what Leland's doing, he's avoiding the work of shutting this place down for the winter. Leaving it all to me. I don't understand Nance, though. He's responsible. He takes after my side."

"I think we saw them last night," Julia said. "We had stopped by the old ferry landing to watch the boats come into the sound."

"That's them. Leland said they wanted to get in on the last of the fishing. Fishing! As if they haven't fished practically every day of their whole lives."

"They had a mapping rig on board," Simon said.

"One of Leland's expensive toys," Darlene said. "He messed with it all last fall, looking for salvage he could sell. If he spent half as much energy at work we'd be rich."

Morgan heard that part of the conversation as he came up to the cash register with his cigarettes.

"Did Leland salvage anything interesting?" he asked.

"Not unless you think rusty anchors and car parts are interesting," Darlene said. "I thought he had gotten bored with all that. Now he's out playing around again. And dragged Nance into it."

Back in Julia's car, Morgan lit a cigarette and dangled it out the window. Julia carefully backed around two bicycles whose owners had dropped them in the middle of the parking lot and got back on the road leading off the island.

"You don't suppose," she said, "that Leland and Nance Pearlie really are looking for Carl Chavis's gold? I was sort of kidding when I said that yesterday."

"I think that's just what they're doing," Simon said.

Morgan finished his cigarette and threw it out the window.

"What I wonder," he said, "is if they know something we don't."

7

One look at the menu at the Shrimp Shack changed the adults' minds about ordering hamburgers. The menu's three photocopied pages, illustrated with children's drawings of shells and seabirds, featured just about every kind and combination of seafood the Carolina Coast could offer, and eastern-style pork barbecue to boot.

"We'll do the best we can," the harried waitress said. "It's just me out here and my husband in the kitchen. Our daughter went on a skiing trip with her college friends instead of working this weekend, we close after dinner tomorrow night for the season, and we're running low on food. We haven't got any soft-shell crabs, deviled crab, or baby back ribs, I can tell you all that right now."

Julia and Marianne ordered shrimpburgers, Simon and Marcus wanted oysterburgers with onion rings, and the girls ordered cheeseburgers and hot dogs with fries. Morgan requested a combination seafood platter with stuffed clams, crab cakes, and fried scallops.

"You're going to die young," Simon said.

"You're welcome to live forever," Morgan said. "Just you keep your paws off my hushpuppies."

Overhead fans in the restaurant turned languidly, but the glass casement windows were shut tight over the screens that kept the restaurant open to the outdoors in the summer. Little choppy waves disturbed the water in the sound outside, where boats bobbed in their moorings.

"I think I'd better winterproof the cottage before we leave on Sunday," Marcus said. "I don't think we'll be coming back until spring."

Simon and Marcus took the girls to the windows to see the traffic on the sound while they waited for their lunch. As Simon idly watched, he noticed that several boats were slowly cruising up and down the inland waterway in an odd crisscross fashion, as if their owners were looking for something. Surely they weren't treasure-hunting. Shortly one boat passed close to the restaurant window. He clearly saw two men on it bent intently over a gray sonar screen, so intently the boat almost collided with two dinghies tied together, floating near the dock next door to the restaurant. The dinghies were manned, he would swear in court, by Woody's two pals from the Do Drop Inn. Each man leaned over the side of his boat, peering inside a wooden packing crate held under the surface of the water, scanning the floor of the sound.

"Daddy," Trina said, pulling on her father's arm, "what are those men doing?"

"They're searching for something underwater, honey," Marcus said. "Those crates have glass bottoms."

"What are they looking for?"

"I don't know, honey, but trust me, they're wasting their time."

Marcus caught Simon's eye as he turned away from the window. "See what you've started?" he said.

"Don't blame me," Simon said.

"The story about your gold coins hasn't even hit the newspapers yet. I'm glad I won't be here next week. Chief Keck and Mayor Pearlie will have their work cut out for them."

As Simon turned to look out the window again, he noticed a private dining room at the back of the restaurant. Its door was half open. Inside, Dale Pearlie and Anita Watkins, the colonel's wife, were having lunch together. They were talking animatedly, and drinking wine with their meal. Not just a glass, either. A bottle sat on the table.

"How about that?" he said to Marcus, indicating the couple with a nod.

"Huh? Oh, that's nothing," Marcus said. "They've known each other for years. Grew up together."

Their lunch arrived, so they went back to the table. Simon's fried oyster sandwich melted in his mouth. It was so good he was distracted enough to let Julia steal some of his onion rings.

The adults, for once not needing to rush off, waited patiently for the girls to finish eating, topping off their glasses of sweet iced tea. Making conversation, Simon told them about his discovery of the issues of *Liberation* magazine in the walls of the pier.

"I know I'm not perfect, and I probably have some prejudices I could work on, but I cannot understand the kind of bigotry expressed in that magazine," Julia said. "Where does it come from?"

"It's biology, pure and simple," Morgan said. "It's good survival strategy for animals to fear other animals. Lessens one's chance of being eaten."

"It doesn't follow," Marianne said. "Humans are all one species. Why should they be afraid of each other?"

"Humans vary tremendously by culture and physiognomy, and most of us haven't evolved enough to distinguish between differences that are harmful and those that aren't. We suspect the guy that seems different, accept those who seem similar, even though it's the guy who looks like us who may be planning to rob us blind. It requires a lot of mental effort to overcome instinct, and you know we humans only use about ten percent of our brains."

"That's not encouraging," Julia said.

"It's not correct, either," Marcus said. "Human beings are bigoted for entirely psychological reasons. It's a self-esteem issue. If things have gone badly for a person in life, its easy to look outside oneself and blame another group for it."

"You're both wrong," Simon said. "Prejudice stems from economics."

"I didn't know you were a Marxist," Marianne said.

"I don't have to be Marxist to accept the reality of the pocketbook," Simon said. "In order to discriminate against a group of people, you have to believe they are inferior. Then you can exploit them, usually as cheap labor. Who in their right mind wanted to work in the cotton fields of the South for nothing? You had to bring in slaves to do it. The ideology of a prejudice develops to make you feel better about whatever nasty thing you've done to other human beings. It works the other way, too. If you're jealous of a particular group's wealth, you think of some way to justify your prejudice against them so you can take their stuff. When the Nazis purged German society of the Jews, they got to steal all their property."

The Clegg girls were restless. Isobel hung on to her mother, tugging at her clothes.

"Just a minute," Marianne said to her. "We're talking."

"Why do you think so many southerners today want to believe the Civil War wasn't about slavery?" Simon asked.

"Here we go again," Morgan said.

"They seem to think they have to justify the Civil War to be loyal southerners. Defending slavery is not acceptable today, so they have to find another reason why it was okay for the South to rebel against the United States. The truth is that the planter class, which comprised about two percent of the population of the South, controlled the governments of all the southern states. They owned the big plantations and most of the slaves, which made them unbelievably wealthy. To protect that wealth, the South seceded, and thousands of ordinary southerners died to defend the plantation economy, which was doomed anyway. What a waste."

"Keep your voice down," Marcus said, "or they might throw us out of here."

"I once had a teacher who told me that the Civil War wasn't about slavery," Julia said. "And I had one who told me Othello wasn't black, too."

"Once southerners realize we can be proud of the South without idealizing the Civil War," Simon said, "maybe we can quit making knee-jerk gestures like flying the Confederate battle flag over the North Carolina capitol on Robert E. Lee's birthday."

"I see a letter to the editor of the *Raleigh News and Observer* in your future," Julia said.

"He's already written several," Morgan said.

Dolly hauled herself up into her father's lap and took his face in both of her hands, turning it toward her.

"We're bored! We're ready to go!" she said.

AFTER LUNCH JULIA AND Simon offered to wrangle the girls so Marianne and Marcus could browse at an antiques store nearby. Always on the lookout for artifacts, Morgan joined them. Recently, in a shop in Blowing Rock, he had found an 1823 hand-colored map of North Carolina from *Fielding Lucas's General Atlas,* one of the most desirable nineteenth-century maps of the state, for just twenty-five dollars. Encouraged by this success, he now craved a famous map of the Southeast from *London* magazine, circa 1765, that marked period towns, Indian tribes, and forts. He was sure he could find one if he just looked hard enough.

"Don't buy the girls anything," Marianne said to Simon. "Marcus gave them each five dollars to spend. That's the limit."

"Don't say that," Simon said. "That's no fun for me."

"Seriously, you spoil them. That's not the way to get them to like you. You have to spend time with them."

"I want to do both," Simon said. "Spend time with them and buy them stuff."

"I feel strongly about this."

"Okay, okay. I won't buy them anything."

Simon, Julia, and the three girls went into the Olive Shell, Anita Watkins's shell shop next door to the antiques store. A matronly lady with blue hair and reading glasses balanced on the end of her nose manned the cash register.

"Good afternoon," she said, positively beaming at the

girls. "What pretty children. Can I help you find anything?"

"We're just looking," Julia said.

Everything in Anita's shop was made from shells, or driftwood, or coral, or sand dollars, or some other material scavenged from the sea. Large bins full of loose shells lined one wall: cockles, jingles, olives, scallops, and whelks. A few rare Scotch bonnets lay in state in a locked glass case next to the cash register. Shell jewelry, shell picture frames, shell boxes, shell collages, mosaic pictures made from shells, shell napkin holders, shell ashtrays, shell animals, and more filled the store's shelves. To see it you'd think every mollusk in the ocean was naked.

Julia collected tacky salt and pepper shakers as souvenirs. Here were some of the finest examples of the art she had ever seen. She was especially taken with a set made from coquina shells; the saltshaker was a pink mermaid; the pepper shaker was a blue Neptune hefting a tiny driftwood triton. The ceramic base was inscribed, PEARLIE BEACH. Priced at just $10.99, the shakers were a worthy addition to her collection.

Simon was at the cash register buying shell necklaces for the three girls. Trina already wore hers, a purple string of tiny scallops that hung below the waist of her jeans. Isobel had an identical pink one draped twice around her neck. Dolly selected a strand of spiky orange coral beads with a plastic Little Mermaid of Disney fame suspended from it. Simon and the girls went outside to admire their purchases in the sunshine when Julia got to the cash register.

"Your daughters are just so sweet," the lady said.

"Pardon me?" Julia said.

"Your girls. And your husband is so nice. When I said

that your girls were beautiful, he said that was because they looked just like you."

Julia was speechless.

"And he said you were trying really hard to have another baby, and that he hoped it would be a girl, too,"

Julia decided it would be easier not to say anything.

"There aren't a lot of men in the world like him," the clerk said.

"You're right about that," Julia said.

The girls dragged them into Marty's Beach Shop next door. All the summer merchandise was marked down, so Simon bought them each "jellies," plastic shoes in pastel colors embedded with sequins and glitter, and plastic backpacks to match. Trina's matched set was, of course, purple. The girls put their new shoes and packs on immediately, leaving Simon and Julia holding three pairs of dirty Keds and a frayed Girl Scout fanny pack.

When the little group rendezvoused at the cars, Marianne took the sneakers from them without a word.

"There's no point in speaking to you about this, is there?" she said to Simon.

"None at all," Simon said.

"These guys have to go home and take a nap," Marcus said.

Resigned, Dolly and Isobel climbed into the van, but Trina hung back.

"I don't take naps," she said.

"Julia and I are going on another field trip," Simon said. "Want to come?"

"Yes, please!"

Marianne caught Julia's expression.

"I don't think so, hon. You'd better come home with us."

"It's okay, really," Simon said. "We'd enjoy it."

"Oh, sure," Julia said, "why not? Come on."

THEY DROVE SLOWLY ALONG NC 17 looking for the turnoff to the dirt road that led to Nick Monahan's seaplane dock. The road sign was hidden by a decrepit tobacco barn, so they passed it the first time and had to double back. The road was deeply rutted, but the squashed weeds in the ruts were still green, indicating that it had been traveled recently. A stand of loblolly pines hid their view of the sound until they drove up almost to the edge of the water. Nick Monahan's battered dock and seaplane hangar still stood. It was a large two-story structure, gray with age and leaning a little to the south.

Trina hopped out of the car and ran toward the hangar. Simon leaned out the window and hollered at her, "Don't go in there without us!"

Julia took him by the arm to keep him in the car.

"You know," she said, "if you want to have a serious relationship, it's not good strategy to tell a stranger that you're trying to get me pregnant, then invite a ten-year-old along when we might have enough privacy to talk."

Simon smiled his quick and easy smile at her. To her surprise, she felt a tug at her heart.

"Heaven forbid that we have a serious conversation about us," he said. "I just want to pester you until you surrender."

"Speaking of pestering, why didn't Morgan come with us? His enthusiasm for our detective work seems to have dimmed."

"He's decided there's no Confederate gold to be

found," Simon said, "and he's not interested in murder."

"Hey, guys, come on!" Trina called. She was jumping up and down on one leg near the entrance to the hangar. "I want to see what's inside!"

The first story of the hangar was essentially a covered dock, deep enough for a big boat, or a seaplane. A five-foot-wide deck surrounded the space. A rusty iron ring, where the plane would have been secured, was bolted to the deck. A small crane, used to lift the plane out of the water for maintenance, had fallen over, dangling into the water. One rusty bolt kept it just barely attached to the dock.

"You wait right here," Julia said, holding on to Trina's hand at the doorway to the hangar. Simon tested the deck, walking carefully around it. He stomped on it hard.

"It seems solid enough. There's a second floor, and a metal roof on top of that, so the wood's been protected."

Julia and Trina ventured into the building.

An open trapdoor with a new metal ladder extending to the deck gave access to the second floor. "Can we go up there?" Trina asked.

"I don't think it's a good idea," Julia said. "There are holes all over. I'm sure it's unsafe. I can't imagine why anyone would have put a ladder there."

"This is so cool," Trina said. "But why did we come here?"

"I just wanted to see it," Simon said. "I think better when I can look at what I am thinking about."

"What are you thinking about?"

"How close this is to where Carl Chavis's body was found. And"—he pointed to the west—"I'm wondering if we can see Henry Pearlie's old fishing camp from the shoreline."

The three of them pushed through a squat stand of live oak and yaupon holly to reach the western edge of the inlet. They came out of the brush onto a mud flat about twenty feet wide. Bubbles popped on the surface of the mud, so Trina dropped to her knees and began to dig energetically for mud snails with a stick. A few old pilings from a forgotten structure stuck ten feet into the air at the waterline. An orange-throated cormorant perched contentedly on one, silhouetted against the blue sky, his wings stretched out to dry. Simon had his binoculars, as usual, and he stood for a long time looking across the inlet.

"Well?" Julia said.

"I think I see it," he said, handing the binoculars to Julia. "It's kind of far back from the shore, but Inez did say the inlet silted up to the point that Henry couldn't dock boats there anymore."

"Let's get in the car and see if we can find it," Julia said. "There has to be a road."

Trina gently returned the two snails and one quahog she had unearthed to the mud.

When the three of them emerged from the scrub they found the Reverend Clare Monahan standing by the edge of the water next to the hangar. She was wearing a wet suit and holding a pair of goggles. A snorkel and flippers were at her feet.

"Well, hello there," Simon said.

"Hi, yourself," she answered. "What are you-all doing here?"

Simon quickly rested his hand on Trina's shoulder and squeezed it to keep her from speaking.

"We're just looking around," Simon said. "I hope you don't mind."

"Ms. Monahan's grandfather owned this property and the seaplane," Julia said to Trina.

"I don't mind," Clare said. "Besides, my family hasn't owned it in years. It's part of a wetlands buffer zone now, and the hangar's just been left to fall down. I wanted to spend some time here because I never met my grandfather, and it makes me feel like I know him a little."

"Going to do some snorkeling?" Julia asked.

"I had a silly idea I might find some mementos here, inside the hangar or in the sound," Clare said. "Something my grandfather might have used."

"Like what?" Trina said.

"Oh, I don't know, an oil can, or an airplane spark plug, something like that. If I find anything, I'll bring it by the cottage and show it to you."

Woody Watkins's Explorer was parked next to Julia's car, but Woody was nowhere to be seen. Clare must have borrowed the car from him. Driving away, Simon watched her in Julia's rearview mirror as she walked into the water.

"I don't care how warm it is," he said, "November is a cold damn time to be in this water, even in a wet suit."

SIMON AND JULIA FOUND the road to Henry Pearlie's fish camp by pure instinct. It was so overgrown that Julia parked her BMW at the entrance and they walked in.

The small one-story building had once been painted blue. The metal roof was dark brown with rust. There were holes in it big enough for Trina to squeeze through. Simon peered through a broken window.

"There's no going in here," he said. "It's a mess. Probably full of mice and spiders."

A collapsing dock led from the back of the camp into a marsh overgrown with cordgrass. Their feet sank into the marsh muck, and a pungent smell rose from it. The dock petered out several feet before the marsh met the shoreline.

A rusted metal flat-bottomed boat lay upside down next to the camp. Trina kicked it and a hollow sound rang out. Quickly Simon picked her up and hoisted her a couple of feet into the air, in case anything crawled out.

"Careful, hon, that's just the kind of place snakes would love to hide in."

"Nobody's used this place in years," Julia said.

She shaded her eyes and looked toward Nick Monahan's hangar.

"I can't see anything. All this growth is in the way."

"If the shoreline was, say, ten feet closer in 1942, and there was no vegetation around the dock, I'll bet you could see that hangar," Simon said. "There would have been less growth around Monahan's dock then, too, because he would have kept it clear so he could maneuver his plane safely."

They carefully picked their way back over the unused road to Julia's car. Another car, a black Miata, was parked behind theirs. Dee Anna Frink came out of the underbrush, straight out of an Abercrombie and Fitch catalog. She wore khaki cargo pants, hiking boots, and a wide-brimmed hat, and carried a notebook and binoculars that looked more powerful than Simon's.

"Hey," she said, opening the door to the Miata. "I wondered whose car that was. What are you guys doing? Looking for gold?"

"We were just exploring," Simon said. "How about you?"

"Can't talk right now," she said, tossing her stuff into the passenger side of her car, climbing in, and turning the ignition switch. "I'm late getting back to the office. I'm on my lunch hour."

Dee Anna shifted the little car into first and pulled away, giving them a friendly wave as she went.

"She doesn't strike me as the type to spend her lunch hour in the boonies," Julia said.

AS THEY APPROACHED THE bridge over the sound on their way home, Simon saw one of the boats he had noticed from the restaurant window pull into the marina.

"I can't stand it," he said to Julia. "I've got to talk to those guys. Pull over, will you?"

Julia drove into the marina, passing the main building, a huge structure that stored boats for the winter, stacked up on six floors like a parking garage. She parked at the slip where the motorboat Simon saw had just docked. She and Trina strolled over to a nearby slip to admire a sixty-foot Hatteras yacht moored there while Simon approached the two men on board the motorboat.

"Hi, there," Simon said. "Any luck?"

"What do you mean?" the older of the two men said.

Simon didn't beat around the bush.

"I'm Dr. Simon Shaw," he said, stretching out his hand. "I'm one of the guys who found some Confederate gold coins earlier this the week. From the looks of you, I'd guess you're looking for more?"

"It seemed like a good idea last night, after we'd had a couple of beers." The older man laughed, shaking Simon's hand. "My son here heard about the gold coins at

Leland Pearlie's store. We thought it would be fun to check out the sound. I got sonar. You know, for locating fish."

"Find anything?"

"Do you realize how much junk is at the bottom of this sound?" the younger man asked. "I had no idea. No way sonar could distinguish between a box of gold and the other crap lying around on the bottom of the inland waterway. It makes the county dump look like a park."

"Tell me," the older man said to Simon, "you're the expert. Do you think there's more gold out there?"

If the two men didn't know Chavis had been murdered, Simon preferred not to tell them.

"I don't think so," Simon said, "I really don't. I've researched the question very thoroughly. I think Chavis found someone's pocket money, that's all, and drowned because of the limits of his equipment."

"One thing's for sure," the younger man said, throwing an empty pop bottle onto the deck of the boat in frustration, "If there was treasure out there somewhere, I don't think anyone could find it unless they knew exactly where to look."

"Have you got a mapping system on this boat?" Simon asked.

"Lord, no," the older man said. "That costs a bundle. I don't even have GPS navigation. I've spent summers and weekends here all my life and I don't take this boat anywhere I don't know by heart. My name's John Wells, by the way, and this is my son, Jack."

"I need to get to work," Jack said. "My shift starts in an hour."

After squeezing his father's shoulder, Jack disembarked from the boat and walked toward the parking area.

"He's a pharmacist," the elder Wells said. "The work pays great, but his hours are awful."

"You've got sonar, you say?"

"Yeah, just a handheld machine. Want to see how it works? My dock is across the sound, and I'm on my way there now. We can look for sunken treasure on the way," he said, laughing.

"Sure," Simon said. "I'd like that."

Julia and Trina agreed to go back to the cottage by car, and Simon climbed onto Wells's boat. It was an older wooden boat, beautifully maintained, with polished chrome and brass fixtures and red leather upholstery. A white canvas cover shaded the interior.

"What a beautiful boat," Simon said.

"It's a 1961 Chris-Craft Continental, eighteen-footer," Wells said. "My Dad bought it when he retired. I've kept it up all these years. It's got the original outboard motor, gauges, and fixtures. I did have to recover the seats and cushions about ten years ago."

They motored slowly under the Pearlie Beach bridge.

"I hate that bridge," Wells said, "but the old draw-bridge was so unreliable. I didn't mind if the tourists had to wait for hours when it broke down, but it was inconvenient if you needed an ambulance or a fire engine on the island."

This was the first time Simon had been on the water directly under the bridge, and he saw why the bridge contributed to the silting up of the sound. The big pillars caught sand and trapped it around their bases. Every year the channels between the pillars got narrower, until the Army Corps of Engineers dredged them out again. Runoff from development contributed to the problem, not just at Pearlie Beach, but up and down the entire length of the Intercoastal Waterway. Hurricanes and storms wore away the beaches, depositing sand on the other side of the island, too.

When they got into the sound, Wells showed Simon his sonar equipment. It was just a black box with a small screen and a three-inch cylinder attached to it with a cable. He threw the cylinder overboard and adjusted the knobs on the screen. The bottom of the sound leapt into relief on the screen. The bumps and peaks were totally unidentifiable to Simon.

"This is great for fishing," Wells said. "After some experience you get so you can see the dropoffs, old stumps, brush piles, and junk, and guess where the fish will be." A flash of dark gray crossed the screen. "There's one now," Wells said.

Wells hauled up the sonar cylinder and stowed it away while Simon steered the boat toward the sound side of Pearlie Beach. Wells took the tiller away from him to dock at a short pier jutting out from the deck of a late fifties era mint-green cottage. It was the kind of beach house Simon liked; small, weathered, and circled by a big screened-in porch. Two bunk beds sat in a corner of the porch.

"No air-conditioning," Wells said. "In the summer we sleep outside."

SIMON WALKED ACROSS THE street from Wells's place to the Cleggs' cottage. On the deck Julia and Trina were curled up together in the hammock. Julia was reading *The Doorbell Rang,* and Trina was wrapped up in a Nancy Drew mystery.

Simon left them there and went inside. The first thing he

saw was Morgan, standing at the sink wearing rubber gloves, scrubbing at a small disc with a wire brush. Simon's heart skipped a beat. Morgan saw his expression and smiled.

"It's not what you think," he said. "It's just a button. I bought a tin box full of buttons at the antiques store for five dollars. I think some of them are quite old."

"I guess I've got gold on the brain," Simon said. "Did you notice all those boats out on the sound with sonar rigs?"

"Yeah," Morgan said. "And you'll never guess what we saw on the drive back here. A glass-bottomed tourist boat out of Wilmington, but with no tourists on board. So help me, five people were lying flat on the deck, faces to the glass. Definitely not rocket scientists."

"There's something alluring about gold," Simon said. "Haven't you ever seen that television commercial for gold ingots and coins? I find myself wanting to order up a bar."

"I can truthfully say I have never had that urge," Morgan said, holding up the disc he had been cleaning, now gleaming brightly. "I prefer the state retirement fund. Look at this. It's a seventeenth-century brass button. I swear I love antiques shops."

"Seventeenth century? Isn't that the sixteen hundreds?" Trina asked, popping up next to them.

"Right," Morgan said, showing her the button. "Here's the head of Charles II, clear as day. This came off the tunic of one of North Carolina's first colonists. Want it?"

"Yes, please," Trina said, and ran off to show the gift to her parents.

"THE HEART OF EBENEZER Scrooge himself would melt at this sight," Marcus said.

"This means Christmas to the kids more than anything else we do," Marianne said, hoisting Dolly to her shoulders so the little girl could watch the Christmas boat parade over the guardrails of the Pearlie Beach bridge.

The holiday flotilla had assembled at Fort Caswell on Oak Island, near the mouth of the Cape Fear River. The boats started cruising west on the Intercoastal Waterway just as dusk fell, and would dock at Sunset Beach on the South Carolina border by late evening. A motley collection of vessels made up the parade, each decorated for Christmas.

Red, green, and gold lights spelled out MERRY CHRISTMAS on the hull of a big Hatteras yacht. As it slid under the bridge, speakers fore and aft blared out "Jingle Bells." A tall sailboat went by next, its mast transformed into a holiday candle. Old-fashioned fat red lights wrapped around the full length of the mast, while yellow strings of tiny blinking lights arranged in the shape of a flame clustered at its tip. The flame of the candle flickered as the boat sailed serenely onward, shadowed by its wavering reflection in the dark water. Then a coast guard fireboat motored by, holding a huge, fully decorated Christmas tree in the stern. Santa Claus himself operated the deck water gun, shooting a huge arc of water, colored by the Christmas tree lights, out over the sound. When he saw the children on the bridge, he dipped into a sack and threw a handful of candy toward them. His jolly "Ho, ho, ho" was barely audible, blown away by the wind.

The girls ran to pick up the candy that had fallen at their feet. Officer Joe Pearlie appeared and grabbed at Isobel, who was stretching for a Tootsie Roll pop.

"This is not a safe place to be standing," Joe said.

"There's no traffic, and the verge is three feet wide," Marcus said. "And I was holding Isobel's hand; she wasn't going anywhere."

"There's a town ordinance," Joe said. "No spectating from the bridge." He gestured to the other groups watching him and raised his voice. "No loitering on the bridge."

"It's the Christmas parade," a woman said. "We always watch it from here."

"I'm sure the town council passed the ordinance for a good reason, ma'am," Joe said.

"We certainly don't want to break the law," Marianne said. "Let's go, girls," she said. "We can finish watching from Captain Nance's docks."

Grudgingly the small groups of people moved off the bridge.

Simon tilted his beer back to drain it.

"Is that a beer bottle?" Joe Pearlie asked.

"Why, yes," Simon said. "Let me guess, I'm breaking the law?"

"No drinking on public property," Joe said.

"Sorry," Simon said, throwing the bottle into the trash can.

"I'll let it go this time, Dr. Shaw," Joe said, hitching his pants up over his belly.

"What a jerk," Julia said under her breath as they followed the Cleggs off the bridge and onto the docks of Captain Nance's seafood market.

"I don't understand how Chief Keck could hire someone so clueless, even if his name is Pearlie," Simon said.

The refugees from the bridge gathered on the docks of the seafood market to watch the conclusion of the parade. The last sailboat in the procession was a black sloop with a simple cross outlined in small white lights on its mainsail and the lit outline of a dove perched on the tip of its mast. It was a stunning sight, so lovely that no one spoke a word, even the children. They watched until it sailed around a curve in the shoreline, emptying the sound. It was quite dark now; the stars shone brightly in the deep darkness, as if replacing the lights of the boats.

"I don't want to leave," Julia said. "It's so peaceful."

"You go on ahead," Simon said to the Cleggs. "We'll walk back."

Simon and Julia sat quietly on the dock, dangling their feet over the edge, watching the night sky and listening to a flock of black-headed laughing gulls chattering at each other. Simon slipped his arm around Julia just as she lay her head on his shoulder.

"The light's off," Julia said suddenly.

"What light?" Simon asked.

"The halogen light at Nance's. I was trying to figure out why the night was so dark and the stars so bright when I realized it."

"I expect Nance turned it off on purpose," Simon said. "So everyone could see the lights of the parade better."

The sound of a large engine ignition startled them both, and then the far end of the dock was flooded with light from the deck of a boat moored there. The light illuminated the side of the boat and the two of them saw its name—it was the *Black Pearl.*

"It's Nance's boat—going out at night again!"

"Stay quiet," Simon said. "They must not see us."

Simon watched the boat through his ever-present binoculars as it moved out into the sound, turning toward Lockwood's Folly Inlet. The deck lights went out, and the navigation lights weren't lit.

"They're running in the dark again," Simon said. "Very dangerous. Where is Joe Pearlie when you need him?"

"I thought I saw Leland on the deck carrying a shotgun," Julia said.

"That's him. And Nance is on the flybridge, driving."

Julia's fingers closed tightly on Simon's forearm.

"Where do you think they're going?"

"Let's find out," Simon said.

"How?"

"We'll borrow one of the motorboats Nance rents. There's one tied up over there. I'll see if the key is in the ignition."

"Wait for me."

Julia rushed back to her car, unlocked it, and took two items from the glove compartment. She hurried back to the boat. Simon had started the big outboard motor and was idling it, waiting for her. She stepped carefully into the boat, rocking it very slightly.

"What did you get from your car?" he said.

Wordlessly she lifted her jacket and showed him her gun in its holster clipped to her belt.

"Excellent, Watson," Simon said. "Your service revolver. You didn't bring a torch, by any chance, did you?"

Julia drew a heavy police-issue flashlight out of her jacket pocket.

"Do you think we can navigate by flashlight?" she said.

"Sure, as long as we can hear their engine ahead of us."

Simon slipped the boat's mooring line off the wooden stanchion that held it and turned the boat toward Lockwood's Folly Inlet.

"The game," Simon said, "is afoot!"

8

AT FIRST THEY FOLLOWED THE *BLACK PEARL* EASILY. A BOW-mounted spotlight on the boat periodically flashed on for a few seconds at a time, orienting the Pearlies as well as their pursuers. The noise of the big boat's twin diesel engines drowned out the sound of their own motor. Simon and Julia couldn't talk, but occasionally she looked back at him from her seat in the front of the boat and smiled at him as he steered the motorboat with his hand on the tiller of the outboard motor. He knew he should have second thoughts about pursuing the Pearlies. It could be dangerous. After all, years ago Carl Chavis had been murdered by someone who wanted the gold he had found. Simon now assumed that Chavis had found a treasure trove of some kind and that the Pearlies were searching for it. Why else were they cruising the sound at night, armed, without using their navigation lights? Perhaps the two of them had already found the gold, alerted by some clue that had surfaced with Chavis's body that Simon hadn't recognized. He and Julia should have gone straight to the nearest phone and called Chief Keck, but the urge to follow the Pearlies was just too powerful to resist.

The spotlight on the *Black Pearl* described a fast, wide arc, then flicked off. The Pearlies turned to port to journey up Lockwood's Folly Inlet. Simon shoved the tiller to his right, following them. He couldn't see the shoreline clearly, but he knew that Nick Monahan's seaplane hangar was on the bank to the east of them, and within a few minutes they would pass Henry Pearlie's deserted fish camp on the west bank. Simon visualized the Cape Fear shipwreck map hanging on the wall back at the cottage. There was no known Civil War shipwreck in this inlet; it was too shallow for one to go undiscovered. Maybe Chavis's gold coins didn't come from a wreck, as he had already speculated.

Simon let his imagination run free. The Confederate Treasury, one hundred thousand dollars in gold ingots, was lent to the rebel nation by France. Jefferson Davis had given France his personal word that the gold would be returned, whatever the outcome of the war. After Lee surrendered at Appomattox, the gold, together with a half million dollars more from the vaults of Virginia's banks, was packed into two wagons in Richmond. Under armed guard it was sent south to Savannah to meet a French ship. On May 24, 1865, in Georgia, the wagons disappeared and the gold vanished. It had never been traced to anyone's satisfaction. Simon always thought the Confederate soldiers had stolen the treasury and split it up among themselves. Had one of the soldiers hidden his share here, then died without revealing its whereabouts? Or, in a completely different scenario, had a wealthy southern family submerged a casket of valuables in the inlet, planning to return and retrieve it? Again, everyone who knew where the valuables were would have had to keep that secret for their entire lives. It didn't seem feasible.

Then again, Chavis or his murderer might have hidden the gold in the inlet. Apparently the Pearlies knew, or figured out, its location, which meant that Dale Pearlie, Sr., must have been involved in the murder. That would explain where he got the money to rebuild Pearlie Beach in 1954 after Hurricane Hazel's rampage. Maybe some of the gold was still hidden in the waters of the inlet. If the secret of its location died with Dale Senior, the discovery of Chavis's body might have stimulated Leland and Nance to search for it before anyone else did.

Suddenly the outboard motor gasped, hiccuped, and made an awful rasping noise that sounded like stripping gears. Instantly Simon cut the engine off, swearing under his breath. Julia crawled toward him from the bow.

"What happened?" she said.

"I have no idea," Simon said.

Deprived of direction, their boat began to drift. At least the tide was coming in, so they'd continue moving up the inlet. It was so dark Simon couldn't tell if they were out in the middle of the water or close to shore.

"Better put on your flashlight," Simon said to Julia.

She did, cupping her hands around it to keep the light to a minimum. The sound of the *Black Pearl*'s diesel engine drifted away from them as distance opened between the two boats.

"I doubt they can see us," Simon said. "I need all that light."

Julia moved closer to him and exposed the entire beam of the flashlight. Simon tilted the outboard motor out of the water. Entangled in the screw was a thick white cord with a plastic milk jug tied to one end. The milk jug floated on the water, marking the location of whatever was tied to the other end of the cord underwater.

"What's that?" Julia said.

Simon leaned out over the stern of the boat to untangle the line from the screw. He couldn't reach it easily, and the boat bobbed unsteadily whenever he shifted his weight. Whatever was on the end of the line dragged taut on the screw, making it hard to disentangle. He pulled on the line to create some slack, and a crab pot broke the surface. He hauled it into the boat. Freezing cold water sloshed in with it. The crab pot was a heavy iron cage the size of a milk crate, with an inverted funnel leading from the outside of the cage to the interior. Lured by scraps of fish, crabs crawled inside, but couldn't get out. This pot had two captives dining on fish heads inside, oblivious to their fate. They briefly examined Simon and Julia, their eye stalks rotating toward them, before going back to their dinner.

"Enjoy it while you can," Simon said to them. "You'll be dunking in seafood sauce yourself tomorrow night, I'll bet."

Simon stretched way out over the stern toward the propeller of the upturned outboard, while Julia dragged in the milk jug.

"I can't get it untangled," Simon said. "I think I'm going to have to cut the line."

Stymied by the mess, and after almost falling into the cold water, Simon cut the line with his pocketknife. Finally he was able to free the screw. He was left holding on to two ropes, one with a crab pot fastened to it and one tied to a milk jug float.

"Now what?" Julia said. "We've vandalized someone's property."

Simon lifted the cage and inspected the crabs.

"Good," he said. "No eggs on either of them. Let's tie the two ends together and throw the whole thing back."

Simon tied a bowline knot in one end of the line, looped the other end through it, tied it into another bowline, and tossed the entire rig back into the water.

"I wish I could see the expression on that crabber's face when he pulls in that pot tomorrow," Simon said. "He'll never know why there's a knot in his line."

Simon powered up the outboard. After a brief stutter, it started. Simon turned the tiller to steer the boat up the inlet with the tide. Julia was still in the stern of the boat with him and had flicked off her flashlight.

"I hope we can catch up with the Pearlies," Simon said.

"How could we not? The inlet's too narrow for us to miss them, coming or going. Should I move up to the bow and use the flashlight again?" Julia said.

"Yeah," Simon said. "We're far enough behind them so they can't see us."

"Ouch!" Julia said. "Damn!"

Before Simon could ask her what had happened, their boat hit the shore with a sickening crunch. A tree branch whipped over the boat directly at him, prompting him to throw up his left arm to protect his face. The branch stung his forearm viciously.

"Are you okay?" he asked Julia.

"I was almost impaled by a tree branch," she said, "and I'm smothering in Spanish moss, but I'm okay. It's so dark! I can't see a thing."

Simon put the outboard engine in neutral while the two of them got reoriented. Julia moved carefully to the bow of the boat.

Simon pulled a dead branch from the tangle of brush hanging over them and used it to push the boat free of the shore.

Julia leaned over the bow of the motorboat, shining her flashlight out over the water ahead of them. The small pool of light in the vast darkness was worthless for any purpose other than avoiding a collision dead ahead.

"I hope the batteries last," she said.

Slowly they motored up the inlet, both of them straining to hear the sound of the Pearlies' boat.

Suddenly Julia extinguished her flashlight and turned toward him, drawing her hand across her throat. Simon instantly shut off the outboard engine. The *Black Pearl* loomed ahead of them, moving very slowly. The big boat's spotlight came on, allowing Simon and Julia to see where they were.

The *Black Pearl* maneuvered around a long, high dock leading to a shoreline edged in live oak and marsh grasses. Partly hidden by the brush was a garage-sized green metal storage shed. They watched as the Pearlies moored their boat, extinguished the spotlight, and climbed onto the dock. By the light of Nance's flashlight Simon saw that both men were carrying shotguns. The two men went into the storage shed, and a light came on inside.

Julia crawled back toward the bow of their boat. Simon had completely killed the engine, and they were drifting toward the dock themselves.

"This is the place!" Julia whispered.

"What place?"

"This is where Leland frightened Marianne and the girls and me while we were crabbing this afternoon."

"We're most of the way up the inlet, then," Simon said.

"What are we going to do? Call Chief Keck?"

"Did you bring your cell phone?"

Julia patted her jacket pockets. "No, damn it! I left it in my car."

"If we leave, by the time we locate Chief Keck and get back here, they could be long gone, with whatever they're hiding in that shed."

"What can we do? They've got guns."

"So do you. Besides, I don't plan to confront them. Let's watch and see what happens. Unless you want to go on home."

"No, I really don't. I want to stay."

Their boat hit a piling hard, then drifted under the dock. The joists were several feet over their heads. Both of them grabbed on to the rung of a ladder that reached from the deck of the dock down to the water.

"Ouch!" Julia said.

"You okay?"

"Just bumped my head a little. I guess we should tie up?"

"Yeah. If we stay quiet here underneath the dock, they'll never see us when they come back, and we can follow them home."

"I hope Marianne and Marcus don't worry about us."

Simon grinned at her. "They'll just think we're shacked up somewhere."

"Throw me the rope."

"Always changing the subject."

Simon tossed Julia the mooring rope and she tied it

securely to the ladder. The boat bobbed and wobbled in the water. The two huddled together in the stern.

"I'm freezing," Julia said. "It's hard to believe that this afternoon I was out on this dock crabbing in shirtsleeves."

"Here," Simon said, pulling up his sweatshirt. "Put your hands in here."

Julia wrapped her arms around him, inside his sweatshirt.

"Better?" he asked.

"Yes," she said, "but I can think of someplace even warmer." She pushed her hands under his shirt against his warm skin.

"Better for you, maybe, but your hands are extremely cold," Simon said. "I demand reciprocity." She didn't object when he placed his own hands under her jacket and shirt against her skin. He kissed her. His mouth and lips were very warm, and she kissed him back. They paused a few minutes later, and both laughed quietly when their breath steamed, as if from passion rather than cold.

"You know," Julia said. "David Morgan is right. We don't date rather well."

"Perhaps we shouldn't date more?"

"Maybe so."

"If things work out, we could move on to not dating seriously."

They huddled together again, and Simon felt her nipples harden under his touch.

"Don't get cocky," Julia said, reading his thoughts. "How do you know it's not the cold?"

"It certainly could be," Simon said. "Except for the core of my body, which is, as I'm sure you realize, hot with desire, I'm absolutely freezing."

"What do you think Leland and Nance are doing in that shed? Surely they're not going to stay there all night?"

"I've been thinking," Simon said.

"Don't want to hear it."

"I could slip up to the storage shed and look inside."

"Don't be crazy. If they see you, who knows what they might do?"

"My curiosity is killing me."

"Of course it is. But your instinct for self-preservation should be stronger."

"I'm going up there." Simon reached for the ladder and pulled himself onto it.

"Don't do that!" Julia grabbed at him but missed.

"I'll be careful. First sign that they're leaving that shed, I'll hide behind it. If they do leave before I get back, stay quiet; they'll never see you."

Julia handed him her gun, butt first. "Take this."

"I don't need it."

"They're not carrying shotguns to develop their biceps. Do you know how to use a gun?"

"I grew up in Boone, North Carolina. I teethed on a twenty-gauge shotgun."

"Fool."

Simon, who really knew almost nothing about handguns and thought even less of them, had last fired an uncle's shotgun in his teens. But he took Julia's stubby .38 Police Special from her. He wanted to find out what was in that storage building, and he didn't want to waste time arguing about it.

"The safety's on," Julia said. "Don't forget to release it if you decide to shoot someone."

"Okay." Simon stuck the gun in his belt and started to

climb the ladder. Julia flicked on the flashlight so he could see to ascend. A movement in the deck joists over their heads startled them both, stopping Simon halfway up the ladder.

"What's that?" Julia asked, aiming her flashlight toward the sound. A long, writhing shape dropped out of the floorboards into the boat at her feet. It was an enormous snake. It coiled on the bottom of the boat and raised its head, its eyes fixed on her.

"Oh, God!" Julia managed not to scream. She scrambled back in the stern as far as she could, hunkering down next to the outboard motor.

"Don't move!" Simon called out to her.

Julia froze and put her hand to her mouth as if to stifle a scream. The beam of flashlight crossed her face. The movement of the light stimulated the snake to slither toward her and coil again, not eighteen inches from her feet.

Simon had climbed back down the ladder and held the boat steady with a foot, one arm still hooked around a rung. The incoming tide rocked the boat.

The rocking boat agitated the snake even more, and its tail began to vibrate. It coiled more tightly and raised its head high, staring at Julia. Its mouth gaped wide open.

"Shine the flashlight on him. Julia, listen to me, shine the flashlight directly on him so I can get a shot," Simon said.

The beam of light showed a brown snake nearly five feet long, with dark crossbands patterning its back. Its head was triangular.

Simon fired three shots in quick succession. The snake jerked a foot into the air, then collapsed like a rope dropped on the ground. It didn't move again.

"Oh, God," Julia said. She put her head down on the gunwales of the boat.

Simon scrambled the length of the boat and sat down beside her, taking her in his arms. She was shaking violently. He stroked her hair until she took a deep breath and collected herself.

"I hate snakes," she said.

Simon reached down and lifted up the snake. "It's a cottonmouth," he said.

"They're poisonous, right?" Julia said.

"Very."

"Good shooting."

"I was highly motivated."

Simon threw the carcass over the side of the boat.

"Maybe the Pearlies didn't hear the shots," Julia said. "The dock and the water could have muffled them."

"Let's not wait to find out," he said. "I'm through with detecting for one night. We'll find our way back home and tell Chief Keck what we've seen, and he can take it from there."

"Can we get back by ourselves?"

"Sure. We just cross the inlet, sail south hugging the shore, when we get to the sound we turn right, and we'll see the streetlights on the Pearlie Beach bridge after a couple of miles. We'll tie up at Nance's, then we'll walk home and have a mug of very hot coffee with an inch of bourbon in it. Nothing to it."

"Simon."

"Hmm?"

"The boat's sinking."

"What?"

"The boat's sinking. You shot holes in the bottom of the boat."

"Damnation! Got anything to bail with?"

"It appears we didn't bring a bucket."

The boat filled quickly with dark water, corkscrewing up from the three bullet holes in the bottom. Helpless, Simon and Julia perched on the ladder, watching the boat sink.

"You realize," Julia said, "we stole that boat."

"Did not. Borrowed it, subject to rental."

"We stole it."

"Maybe my homeowners policy will cover it. If I pay for the damage, they won't press charges, will they?"

"We need to find Chief Keck and tell him everything right away. How do we get out of here?"

Simon's arms ached from hanging off the ladder, and he was colder than ever.

"Let's sneak past the shed and get to the road. You remember the way, don't you? Then we can hitch a ride."

"Who's going to give us a lift at this hour?"

"Stop arguing with me, woman, and let's get out of here before the Pearlies find us."

As Simon started up the ladder, the bright light of a powerful flashlight blinded him.

"I thought I heard something!" Nance Pearlie said. He leaned over the ladder and peered at them. "Dr. Shaw, Miss McGloughlin, I really wish you hadn't followed us. Come on up here."

Julia and Simon went up the ladder and stood on the dock. Except for the fact that he was glad to be standing on something that didn't rock, Simon would have liked to be anywhere else. He rubbed his eyes to clear his vision of the dark globs caused by Nance's flashlight. Nance held the big flashlight in one hand and had his shotgun casually cradled in the crook of his other arm. He did not look happy with them.

"Daddy! Come here! Looks like we were followed."

Leland Pearlie joined his son. He also had a shotgun, but he grasped his firmly in both hands and pointed it right at them.

"What do you two think you're doing? How did you get here?" Leland asked.

"We, ah, borrowed one of your rental boats," Julia said.

Nance glanced over the side of the dock.

"Where is it?"

"It sank," Simon said. "A snake dropped into the boat, and I shot it, and the bullet holes . . . I'll pay for it, of course."

"You've got a gun?" Nance asked. "I knew I heard shots. Hand it over."

Simon gave him Julia's gun.

"I work for the Raleigh Police Department—" Julia began.

"Do the police in Raleigh often steal boats?" Nance asked.

"We're sorry about that," Simon said. "We got carried away."

"I think you'd better explain," Leland said.

As Simon explained, Leland and Nance began to smile, wider and wider, until they were both laughing out loud. They broke open their shotguns and laughed some more, wiping tears from their eyes. Simon was glad they found his story so funny. He hoped that meant they were going to let him and Julia live.

"Lord, that's wild!" Nance said. "I thought you didn't buy into this lost Confederate treasure theory!"

"I figured you knew something I didn't know."

"You were right," Leland said. "We did find a treasure. Want to see it?"

"Please!" Simon said.

As the four of them walked toward the storage shed, Simon forgot about whatever danger they might be in and anticipated seeing something remarkable. On the way to the shed Julia took his hand and squeezed it, hard. She was excited, too.

They reached the door of the shed and Nance threw it open triumphantly. Simon and Julia went in first. To Simon's surprise, he saw only piles of black logs.

"Old utility poles?" he said.

"This is your treasure?" Julia said.

Nance and Leland were both smiling broadly.

"Come over here," Leland said, "and see what those utility poles look like when they've been milled."

At the back of the shed was a stack of milled timber. When Simon saw it, he understood what the Pearlies had found. It was a treasure. He ran his hand over a rich yellow pine plank cut from an ancient tree.

"I've heard about this, of course," Simon said, "but I've never seen any before. It's beautiful."

"What is it?" Julia asked.

"Riverwood," Simon said.

"What?"

"In the nineteenth century when American forests were

being harvested, logs were floated down every river in the country to get to sawmills on the coast, some on rafts, some on barges, some lashed together. The demand was huge. North American old growth forests were nearly gone by the 1900s. Heart pine was commercially extinct in North Carolina by 1910. Most of it was made into shingles, of all things. Anyway, lots of that timber sank to the bottoms of the rivers. Maybe twenty percent, millions of board feet, is submerged in rivers all over the country. Now it's being salvaged."

"We don't know how this shipment got into this little inlet, and we don't care," Leland said. "I expect a raft blew out of the Cape Fear River during a storm and sank here."

"Look at this," Simon said to Julia, showing her the fine grain of one plank. "Wood hasn't grown like this in one hundred and fifty years. Modern commercial wood is grown very quickly. Its growth rings are wide, and it's usually cut after about twenty-five years. This wood has a tight, delicate graining. And it's rock-hard."

"Some of these trees were hundreds of years old when they were harvested," Nance said. "We can sell the wood for fine furniture, paneling, hand-carving, modeling. You don't see grain patterns like this anymore. It's irreplaceable."

Simon leaned over and sniffed the plank. It still smelled of aromatic pine.

"Look over here," Leland said, showing him a giant black log cut in cross-section.

"It's cypress," Simon said, running his finger along countless growth rings. "How many rings does it have?"

"I quit counting after eight hundred," Leland said. "That was one old tree. Those there are axe marks. That tree was chopped down in the early 1800s, before loggers switched to saws."

"It must be worth a fortune," Julia said.

"It is. Now it's got to be kiln-dried, and milled, and marketed, and all that, but we can sell it for four-fifty a board foot," Nance said. "As long as nobody steals it from us first."

"So you guys have been standing guard over it?" Simon said.

"Day and night," Leland said. "After you-all found Carl's corpse and those gold Confederate coins, we were worried that some fool treasure-hunter would find this timber. We don't have our salvage permit from the state yet. We can't get a crane in here and bring it all up until we do."

"We had to file an environmental impact statement to get a permit," Leland said. "Do you believe it? Damn tree-huggers. The riverbottom will be more natural after we bring up those logs than it was before."

"I don't trust Woody Watkins and those two worthless friends of his," Nance said. "They've been combing this area for Confederate gold. While we're wrestling with the government, they could come in here some night, find this wood, and steal it from us."

"All this trouble will be worth it," Leland said, "and not just because of the money. I can't wait to see the look on Darlene's face when I tell her. She gave me so much grief when I bought that sonar equipment."

"Daddy," Nance said, "you go on home. I'll stay here tonight."

"You stayed last night."

"That doesn't matter. If you sleep on that old cot in this

cold, your arthritis will seize up on you and you won't be able to move in the morning. Besides, if the *Black Pearl* isn't tied up at my dock tomorrow morning, folks will get curious."

"That's true enough."

"Nance," Simon said, "about your motorboat . . ."

Nance shrugged. "Don't worry about it," he said. "I got insurance. I'll let you know if it doesn't cover everything. It won't be much."

Simon cleared his throat. "Leland?" he said.

"Yeah?"

"Can Julia and I get a lift back to Pearlie Beach with you?"

THE CABIN OF THE *Black Pearl* was fitted for fishing, not for luxury. Simon and Julia huddled in gray surplus army blankets on metal folding chairs. A metal table was bolted to one wall of the cabin. There was no other furniture, unless you could count the giant ice chest on another wall. Simon had seen the contents when Leland opened it to get him a Coke and Julia a diet Pepsi. Beer, plastic bags of bait, and cans of soda floated around together in water and ice. On a fishing trip, lunch and freshly caught fish would be added indiscriminately to the mix. Rods, reels, nets, floats, and tackle boxes cluttered up the rest of the cabin.

"Do we have to tell everyone what happened tonight?" Julia said.

"Definitely not. I have no intention of letting Marcus and Morgan know about this. They would never let me forget it, and they have enough on me already."

"So what do we say?"

"We met the Pearlies at the dock and they offered to take us for a short cruise. That's my story and I'm sticking to it."

Leland tied up at Captain Nance's dock, throwing thick mooring lines over two stanchions, fore and aft. Whenever he looked at the two of them he grinned. Then he gave them a ride back to the Clegg cottage in his ancient Suburban.

"Answer a question for me, Leland," Simon said in the car. "How did your dad rebuild Pearlie Beach after Hurricane Hazel?"

"Borrowed the money from the bank," Leland said. "He kept it quiet, though. Everyone around here would have been shocked. Paying interest is a sin, you know."

"The other night, after you and Nance talked to Dale, he discouraged me from investigating Carl Chavis's murder. Was that because of the riverwood?"

"Yeah. We didn't want anyone poking around Lockwood's Folly Inlet for any reason. And I'm sorry I scared Mrs. Clegg when I found her and the kids crabbing there. It's just that the wood doesn't belong to us until we get that salvage permit. It's made us paranoid, I guess."

A block away from the Cleggs', someone had been hard at work decorating his beach house for Christmas. Strings of lights outlined the porch and deck. Santa, his reindeer, and a sleighful of presents poised atop the roof, ready for takeoff. Red-suited elves toiled below under a palmetto. A softly lit nativity scene gave meaning to it all.

"He's retired," Leland said, by way of explanation.

"When I get to where I can't work anymore, shoot me," Simon said.

Leland pulled up to the Cleggs' door. "I won't tell anyone about what happened tonight, if you don't," he said.

"You read our minds," Julia said.

"Listen," Leland said, "we're going to cut a few slabs off that cypress in cross-section for ourselves, to make tables. Would you each like a slice? Make a nice souvenir."

"Yes, please," Julia said. "I'd love it."

"Definitely," Simon said. "And thank you for not shooting us and asking questions later."

The light was on in Morgan's camper, but they didn't stop by to see him. Inside the cabin, Marcus was the only person up, watching *The McLaughlin Group* on PBS.

"Hello, children," he said. "Where have you been? I called the Pearlie Beach Motel, and they said no couple matching your description had been in tonight."

"You did no such thing," Julia said. "We accepted a ride on the *Black Pearl* from Leland Pearlie."

"How was it?"

"Cold," Simon said. "Dark." He was already pouring two mugs of coffee from the thermos of decaf on the counter. Julia searched the cabinets for bourbon.

"The booze is in the cabinet over the refrigerator," Marcus said. "Fix me one, too."

SEDATED BY HIS MUG of coffee and bourbon and worn out from his excursion up Lockwood's Folly Inlet, Simon wrapped himself in a quilt and an afghan and fell instantly asleep on top of his bed. He wasn't even dreaming when Julia shook him awake, as it turned out, not thirty minutes later.

"Don't," he said. "Go away."

"Wake up," she said. "It's important. Something weird is going on next door."

"Sure," he said, rolling over and closing his eyes again.

Julia ripped the covers off him and dragged on his arm.

"All right, all right!" Simon sat on the edge of his bed and rubbed his eyes open. "This had better be good," he said.

Julia was fully, and warmly, dressed. She was wearing a heavy jacket, knit hat, and gloves.

"What's with you?" he said. "You look like you're going coon hunting!"

"I never went to sleep. When I was in the bathroom brushing my teeth I saw all this activity next door, so I went out on the porch to see what was happening. It was cold, so I borrowed some clothes from the storage closet. Then I got so suspicious I had to wake you up. I think Woody and Dee Anna are up to something."

"Haven't we done enough for one night?"

"Please, just look. You'll agree with me, I know it."

Simon wrapped his quilt around him and trailed it behind him as he went to the window. He was wearing flannel boxer shorts and a sweatshirt. This was the first time Julia had seen his legs, and they passed muster. He definitely had thighs and calves.

Simon looked out his window at the Watkins house. What he saw made him rub his eyes again and move closer to the glass.

Woody's Explorer was parked on the cement pad outside the house. Woody and Dee Anna were packing it for some kind of expedition. Woody wore a wet suit, canvas shoes, and a fleece jacket. Dee Anna wore jeans and a hooded East Carolina University sweatshirt. They loaded a crate into the back of the Explorer, then lifted Woody's surfboard to the car's roof rack, securing it with elastic straps. They didn't say a word to each other. Once or twice Woody looked up at his house, where lights were still on in the living room and the colonel's study.

"They're going surfing, at midnight?" Simon said.

"See what I mean?"

"Yeah," Simon said, chewing his lip.

"We should follow them, don't you think?"

Obviously Woody wasn't a suspect in Carl Chavis's murder. He was too young. His father wasn't, though. Absent any other clues, Colonel Watkins's wealth suggested he might be a major player in the mystery surrounding Chavis's murder. His home, his clothes, his wife's jewelry, his big house, his valuable paintings, and his museum-quality collections surely should have been out of the reach of a retired army officer. Simon had not yet heard a reasonable explanation for his wealth. Watkins had lived in Pearlie Beach for years, his wife her entire life, yet no one knew where his money came from.

If—and it was a big *if*—Watkins had a hand in Chavis's murder and profited richly from it, where did Woody fit into the picture? From their confrontation in the bar it was clear to Simon that Woody was actively looking for more Confederate gold coins. Even though chasing the Pearlies up Lockwood's Folly Inlet had turned into a wild goose chase, maybe Simon's original hypothesis was correct, substituting different characters. Assume Dale Pearlie Sr., Nick Monahan, and Colonel Watkins all knew where Chavis's gold was. The first two men were dead. Perhaps Watkins had let slip some clues to his wayward son. Perhaps Woody and Clare, who had recently sorted through her grandfather's papers, got in touch and shared what information they had. When Chavis's corpse was found, this made their search more urgent, and Clare engineered a week at Pearlie Beach as chaplain. Dee Anna, of course, would be Woody's eager accomplice in any adventure. The three of them had been canvassing Pearlie Beach all weekend. They must not have all the information they needed, or they would have gone straight to the gold. It was more likely that they just had partial clues, and that Woody was following up on one now.

Simon borrowed a heavy wool sweater and a hat from the Cleggs' closet. The sweater hung down to his thighs and he had to roll up the sleeves. He wasn't sensitive about it; it kept more of him warm that way.

"We look like criminals ourselves," Julia said, as they slipped out of the cottage, careful not to wake anyone.

The Explorer pulled out of the Watkins driveway and headed west. Beach View Road ran the length of the island straight as a Roman highway, so Simon and Julia felt safe following at a discreet distance with the car's headlights off. They trailed Woody and Dee Anna all the way to the western end of the island, near Shallotte Inlet, where Woody pulled into the parking lot of the turtle sanctuary. Julia pulled off the road a quarter of a mile away, waiting for Woody and Dee Anna to unpack their stuff and climb the stairs over the dunes.

"This is where we looked for those wrecks with Trina, isn't it?" Julia asked.

"Yes," Simon said. "The *Bendigo* and the *Iron Age*."

"Woody and Dee Anna are out of sight. Let's go see what they're doing."

Simon and Julia hiked toward the sanctuary parking

area, but stopped short of it, opting to climb over the dune instead of using the stairs, just in case Woody and Dee Anna were on their way back to their car. They slipped and slid in the sand trying to climb the dune, finally dropping to their hands and knees to crawl to the top.

"Ouch!" Julia said.

"Watch out for sandspurs," Simon said. "They really hurt."

"Thanks for the warning," Julia said, carefully removing several tiny offenders from the spot where they were embedded in her wrist.

On the top of the dune they lay flat and peered toward the shoreline. Daytime warmth had seeped out of the sand, and it was very cold. For once Simon had forgotten to bring his binoculars. They could just make out Woody and Dee Anna moving around on the beach. Using a flashlight with a red beam, they searched the sand for something, bent almost double. Woody's surfboard and the crate sat nearby.

"What in heaven's name are they doing?" Julia said.

"They look like they're chasing sand fleas," Simon said. "And stashing them in the crate."

"Doesn't look like a treasure-hunt to me, unless gold coins can move."

"I can't stand it," Simon said. "Let's go find out what the hell they're doing."

The two of them slid down the dune on the beach side, catching at the tall, tough stalks of beach grass to steady themselves on their way down the six-foot slope.

Dee Anna saw them and waved them over.

"Hey!" she called out. "Come help us!"

Since the confrontation at the Do Drop Inn, Woody had

ignored Simon and Julia, barely acknowledging them when he had to. On this occasion he just glanced at them, nodded briefly, and bent back over the sand.

The beach all around them was crawling with tiny baby turtles, blindly making their way toward the water. Half-dollar-sized, with four flat flippers struggling to propel themselves, they clumsily scaled mountains of sand and deep abysses as they moved toward the sea, lured by the reflected light on the ocean. The red light from Dee Anna's flashlight wouldn't distract them from what moonshine there was on the water.

"We want to get them out past the breakers and give them a head start," Dee Anna said. "I've been watching this nest. It's hatched really late in the season."

So Simon and Julia chased baby sea turtles. The little ones were so soft and small in his hands Simon couldn't imagine how they could survive to grow up. They seemed so fragile. Once the crate was full of the wriggling green babies, Woody put his surfboard in the water. Simon held it steady, up to his knees in freezing water, while Woody tied the crate to the surfboard with an elastic cord. Then Woody pushed the board over the waves and swam out past the breakers until they could barely see him. There he scooped handfuls of turtles out of the crate and dropped them into the water.

"The water may be too cold for them to survive, anyhow," Dee Anna said. "Water temperatures below sixty-five degrees can paralyze them. They just freeze up and wash back to shore."

"The Gulf Stream is eighty miles away," Simon said. He couldn't imagine that any of the baby turtles would reach it.

"Sometimes the coast guard will take baby turtles out to the Gulf Stream and drop them off, but they didn't have a cutter available tonight. Too many sailors off for Thanksgiving. This was the last nest of the season. The turtle patrol spotted the mother coming ashore on August thirtieth. That's the latest date we have on record."

Simon had seen the turtle patrol at work last summer. Residents along the beaches called Pearlie Beach Realty when they found the signs that a nesting turtle had dragged herself over the sand to bury her eggs the night before. Turtle patrol volunteers, driving little dune buggies with a turtle flag flying, marked the nest for observation and protection. If it was below the high-tide mark, they'd carefully move the eggs so they wouldn't rot, reburying them in a safe spot. The process attracted a lot of attention from children on the beach and was great publicity for the conservation effort on the barrier islands.

"Woody is an animal-lover?" Julia asked.

"Woody doesn't give a damn about turtles. He does this because I ask him to. I'm the director of the Pearlie Beach Coastal Wildlife Project. We keep track of all the endangered species on the island."

"Is that why we saw you near Henry Pearlie's fish camp yesterday with binoculars and a notebook?" Simon said.

"I was counting the nests in a small egret heronry near there. The chicks and adults have left by now, so I could get real close without disturbing any birds."

Simon and Julia drove back to the cottage. Woody's Explorer followed them, but turned off on a side street toward Dee Anna's apartment.

"Another wild goose chase," Simon said. "I'm considering changing professions. How do you think I would make out as a fantasy writer? I'm very good at concocting wild stories out of thin air."

"We can be coauthors. My imagination is just as vivid as yours. Do you think Woody and Dee Anna believed our story about being out for a drive and just happening to run into them?"

"Would you?" Simon said.

LIGHT BLAZED FROM EVERY room in the Clegg cottage. Marianne ran down the steps to the car before it came to a full stop, grabbing on to the passenger-side door handle while the car was still moving. Morgan followed her, gently prying her hands from the door so Julia could pull under the cottage.

"Tell me she's with you!" Marianne said.

"Who?" Julia asked.

"Trina! Didn't she go with you?"

"No," Simon said. "What's happened?"

"She's missing," Marianne said. She sat down on the lower step and put her head in her hands.

"We hoped she'd gone off on some adventure with you two," Morgan said.

Julia sat down next to Marianne and put her arms around her.

"I know she's all right," Marianne said. "She's too smart to get into trouble. Isn't she?"

"Of course she's all right," Julia said. "Tell us what happened."

"I heard Isobel crying. She has nightmares sometimes, especially here at the beach. While I was comforting her, I noticed that Trina wasn't on the top bunk. I thought maybe she was in the bathroom, or in the living room reading. After I looked everywhere and realized that you two were gone, I hoped she'd gone with you somewhere."

"We would have left you a note," Simon said.

"Of course you would have," Marianne said. "Where could she be? It's so dark and cold! She wouldn't go down to the beach, would she?"

"Marcus went to the police department," Morgan said. "But I had a thought. She was playing all day with those obnoxious kids down the street."

"She wanted to go back outside after dinner," Marianne said. "The kids were going to build a bonfire. I wouldn't let her go."

"The window in her room is open," Morgan said. "And I know where the alpha male from that little pack of kids lives."

"Let's go," Simon said.

"I'll stay here with Marianne," Julia said.

SIMON KNOCKED ON THE door of a huge new beach house several blocks away. Built of brick and lavishly trimmed with wood, it had a landscaped lawn and a three-car garage. Simon couldn't understand why anyone would build a house at the beach that looked like it belonged in an upscale subdivision in Raleigh. What was the point? He preferred the traditional beach house, like the Cleggs' cottage, outfitted with just the bare necessities for going coastal: a few rocking chairs, a hammock, a grill, a clothesline with swimsuits hanging from it, an outdoor shower, a beach umbrella, and roomfuls of friends. This place possessed none of those essentials that Simon could see.

A man wearing a bathrobe and penny loafers answered the door, gesturing for them to come inside. The house was furnished as if a truck from a reproduction furniture gallery had backed up and unloaded a few showrooms into it. There was nothing personal or original about the decor. Simon half expected to see price tags still hanging off the nondescript prints on the entryway wall.

"Who are you?" the man asked. "What do you want?"

Morgan told them the story in his pithy, academic style. The father called his son out from his bedroom. The boy, rubbing sleep from his eyes, wore pajama bottoms and a Carolina Hurricanes sweatshirt.

"These gentlemen tell me that a little girl is missing. Her name is Trina Clegg."

"I don't know where she is," the boy said. "Why would I? She's a geek."

"See?" the father said. "He doesn't know anything."

"We think she climbed out of her window to join you and your friends at a bonfire on the beach," Simon said.

"A bonfire? I told you not to build a fire!" the father said.

The boy shrugged, unconcerned.

"If anything happens to her," Morgan said, "it'll be the police here next."

That impressed the father, who glared at his son.

"Oh, she's okay," the boy said. "I thought she'd be home by now."

"Where is she?" Simon said.

"Down at the other end of the island," he said. "We went on a snipe hunt."

231

"SHOULDN'T WE CALL MARIANNE? Or the police?" Morgan said as he switched on the ignition of his truck.

"I don't think so," Simon said. "We don't know anything for sure yet."

"I can't imagine anything bad happening to Trina. She's such a neat kid."

"Don't think about it," Simon said. "Just get to the eastern end of the island. That's where they left her."

Hurricane Fran had grazed Pearlie Beach in 1996, destroying two cottages and tearing up a mile of road at the east end of the island, leaving a steep drop to the beach. The town council wisely decided not to try to rebuild. The road was blocked with cement "jersey" barricades and the little cliff shored up with huge sandbags to prevent erosion.

Morgan shifted into four-wheel drive as the damaged road became rough, and switched on the yellow fog lights mounted on the roof of his truck, brightly illuminating the way ahead. Simon vowed never to tease him about his utility truck package again.

"There she is," Simon said.

Trina was draped over a barricade, her legs hidden from view, with her head in her arms.

"Thank God," Morgan said. "I'll call Marianne."

Simon was out of the truck before Morgan had finished his sentence.

"Hey, sweetie," he said as he reached her. "Are you all right?"

Trina raised her head. Her face was crumpled and tear-stained. She clutched an empty pillowcase in one hand. Simon put his arms around her and, feeling how cold she was, took off his jacket and draped it around her.

"I wasn't scared," Trina said, "and I could have walked home, but . . ."—her faced scrunched up and she blinked back tears—"my foot's stuck."

Her foot was stuck indeed. Trina's left leg had slipped between the barricade and a sandbag. Simon tugged on her leg gently, and she cried out.

"It hurts," she said. "Do you think it's broken?"

Morgan joined them.

"She's pinned here," Simon said.

These were not your average sandbags, but were big as feed sacks and soaked with water. Simon and Morgan couldn't budge the one that trapped Trina, at least not without risk of collapsing the entire stack.

"I guess we'll need to call the fire department," Simon said. "I hate for her to be out here any longer than necessary." Simon had gone looking for Trina without changing out of his wet jeans and was so cold himself he was trembling. Amazing what the temperature differential could be between day and night.

Trina panicked. "Please don't call the fire department," she said. She tightened her grip on Simon and grabbed Morgan, too. "Please don't!"

"We've got to get you home, hon," Simon said.

"If you call the firemen or the police, everyone will know about the snipe hunt," Trina said. "I'd rather die!"

Simon paused in the face of preadolescent humiliation.

Morgan scratched his head. "You know, I've wanted to test the winch on my truck ever since I got it," he said. "Give me five minutes."

He went to his truck and unwrapped a heavy wire cable from the winch mounted under the front bumper. A large hook dangled from the end of it. The cement barricade had metal eyes embedded in it so it could be lifted into place with a crane. With Simon's help Morgan hooked the metal cable securely into one of the eyes. Simon moved behind Trina and held on to her. Morgan fired up his motor and turned on the winch. It made an impressive mechanical noise and began to wind up the cable. The barricade immediately pulled away from the sandbags just enough for Simon to lift Trina out of her trap.

"There you go," Simon said. "Safe and sound."

Morgan drove while Simon held Trina in his lap on the way home.

"I wasn't a bit scared," Trina said. "And I didn't believe those guys. I knew there were no such things as snipe. I was just going along with them for the heck of it. I could have gotten home fine and gotten back in bed without Mom and Dad even knowing it, if I hadn't hurt my leg."

Marcus and Marianne were waiting for them when they got back to the cottage. Marcus lifted Trina out of the truck. She wrapped her arms and legs around him and lay her head on his shoulder, bursting into tears.

"Thank you," Marianne said to Simon and Morgan.

SIMON, MORGAN, AND JULIA scrunched into Morgan's camper to give Trina some privacy with her parents before Simon and Julia went upstairs. Morgan hung over the edge of the bunk over the cab to talk to the two of them, squeezed onto the little built-in sofa. Simon wrapped his cold legs up in Morgan's smelly sleeping bag.

"Okay," Julia said, "so explain to me. What is a snipe hunt?"

"Where were you raised, girl?" Morgan asked.

"Richmond, Virginia."

"That explains a lot."

"A snipe hunt," Simon said, "is an exercise wherein the cool crowd takes advantage of the clueless. It's an old southern rite of passage, usually happens during the preadolescent years."

"Mostly at camp," Morgan said. "Sometimes the juvenile period is extended into the freshman year in college, for males, especially those males in fraternities."

"What happens is," Simon said, "a group selects an innocent victim and invites him or her to join them on a snipe hunt. The victim gets to hold the sack, which is represented as a coveted position. The entire group goes out with flashlights at night to a deserted area that snipe are known to frequent. The snipe holder is instructed on how to hold the sack, in Trina's case a pillowcase, and how to call the snipe."

" 'Here, snipe, snipe, here, snipe,' is the usual chant," Morgan said. "But there are variations."

"The rest of the group go into the brush and darkness to become snipe herders. The victim calls snipe, shaking the bag, until the victim realizes that he or she has been completely deserted out in the country somewhere. Of course the victim has been highly suspicious of the exercise all along, but wants so badly to be a member of the group that he or she will endure almost any humiliation. Then, of course, the victim has to find the way home alone, which can take hours, depending on where he or she has been abandoned."

"That's awful," Julia said. "That's about the worst thing

I have ever heard of children doing to another child. I'm glad I was never taken on one."

"You wouldn't be," Simon said. "You were one of the cool kids."

"How do you know that?"

"It's written all over you."

"I was not."

"Now, Dr. Morgan here and I, we were geeks. I was small and kept my nose in a book. The perfect candidate for snipe sack holder."

"I was fat and collected stamps," Morgan said. "When I was at camp, I was abandoned about two miles from my cabin, barefooted and in pajamas. I was extremely scared. But then I realized that I was right on the lake, and all I had to do was follow the shore until I got to the camp. It seemed to take all night. What happened to you?"

"Actually, I never experienced a snipe hunt. I did get tied up and thrown in the Dumpster outside my junior high because I told the captain of the football team to take a long walk off a short pier for some reason or other. I beat on the side of Dumpster with my feet until the janitor finally heard me about three hours later."

"I'm exhausted," Julia said, stretching her arms above her head. "Think we can go inside now?"

FOR THE SECOND TIME that night Simon collapsed onto his bed. He felt a bit like the victim of a snipe hunt himself. Here he kept telling anyone who would listen that there was no gold near Pearlie Beach anymore and that Carl Chavis's murderer would never be found, but still he chased after any so-called clue that appeared, embarrassing himself completely in the process. At least he hadn't made a fool of himself alone. Julia had been his willing accomplice. He sincerely hoped that the two of them could get away from this weekend without too many people knowing what fools they had been. He resolved again to give up investigating Chavis's murder. There was no urgent need to solve it, anyway. The man had been dead for so many years his own mother had forgotten him, the gold, if there ever was any, was long gone, and the murderer's trail was ice-cold.

9

SIMON WOKE UP JUST A FEW HOURS LATER. IT TOOK HIM SOME time to regain full consciousness, for his brain to process the information that something unusual was happening outside his window. Then the meaning of the flashing blue and white lights, the low voices, and the radio static connected. The police were next door at the Watkins home. He got up and looked out the window. Two Pearlie Beach police cars and a Brunswick County sheriff's vehicle were parked in a semicircle around the big beach house. It was still dark, and though floodlights lit up the exterior of the house, Simon couldn't tell what had happened. He did see Joe Pearlie circling the house, methodically creating a perimeter with yellow tape. Every few feet he stopped and drove a stake into the ground, then stapled the tape to it. He fumbled with the stakes, tape, and stapler, dropping one of them every few feet as he plowed through the sand.

Simon had slept in his clothes. He tucked his shirt into his jeans and slapped some water on his face in the bathroom before going into the cottage living room. Marcus was up, answering a knock at the kitchen door. Chief Keck stood there. Despite the early hour, he was fully and immaculately uniformed.

"I'm sorry to wake you," Keck said.

"What's happened?" Marcus asked.

"Colonel Watkins is dead. Fell off the widow's walk," Keck said. "Is Ms. McGlouglin here, I hope?"

"Right here," Julia said, coming out of her room. She had fallen asleep in her clothes, too. She still wore the jeans and flannel jacket she had borrowed from the Cleggs' closet last night.

"Are you sworn?" Keck asked.

"Yes," Julia said.

"Do you have your firearm?"

"Yes, in the glove compartment of my car."

"I need you," Keck said.

"I'm coming," Julia said. "I need two minutes in the bathroom."

"What's going on?" Marcus said.

"Just being careful," Keck said. "I want to secure the accident scene, and I don't have enough officers. The Brunswick County sheriff lent me two deputies, but I don't know how long I can keep them."

Julia and Chief Keck left the house together. Simon could hear Julia's car door open and slam shut as she retrieved her gun. Automatically Simon started a pot of coffee. Then he and Marcus went outside onto the porch to see what was happening.

Julia, wearing a Pearlie Beach police ballcap and an orange vest with a big gold star on it, stood watch outside the yellow tape at the side of the Watkins home facing the Clegg cottage. It seemed too lighthearted a gesture to wave to her, so Simon just raised his hand. She nodded back at him. Joe Pearlie was at the front door of the house, while a deputy stood watch at the back, facing the beach. Simon didn't see another soul. The body had to be on the ground at the other side of the house, facing the vacant lot. The Watkins house stood on pilings, like the Clegg cottage, so the distance from the widow's walk to the ground was four stories, quite a fall.

Back inside, Simon watched the coffee drip, excruciatingly slowly, it seemed to him, as Marcus paced around the room. They spoke in low voices to prevent waking anyone else up.

"Damn!" Marcus said. "As if enough hasn't happened already this weekend."

"How's Trina?" Simon asked him.

"She's okay," Marcus said. "Sound asleep. I'm worried that her ankle might be broken. It's black and blue and very swollen."

"Poor child."

"Growing up is more painful for some children than for others, it seems," Marcus said.

"I'm going to take a cup of coffee to Julia," Simon said.

"Take some to everyone, and I'll make a new pot," Marcus said. "There's a box of Krispy Kreme doughnuts in the pantry. Take those, too. Find out what's going on if you can."

Outside, day was just dawning. The cold light coming from the east fell at a low angle on the pilings and beach grass, casting long shadows over the sand. Indian summer had departed Pearlie Beach, and Simon shivered in his sweatshirt.

Julia's gun was clipped to the waistband of her jeans,

and her shirt was hiked up around it so she could reach it easily. Her auburn hair was pulled back through the hole in the back of her Pearlie Beach police ballcap. Simon thought she looked wonderful.

"Have I ever told you? I'm very attracted to powerful women," Simon said to her. "Especially those bearing arms."

"How much sleep did we get?" Julia asked, sipping from the mug of coffee with lots of sugar that Simon had brought her with one hand, and scarfing a doughnut with the other.

"Maybe four hours," Simon said.

"I feel like I have a layer of sand under my skin all over my body," she said, "including under my eyelids. Is Trina all right?"

"Marcus thinks her ankle might be broken."

"Poor girl."

Julia took another slurp of coffee. "Chief Keck thinks Colonel Watkins was murdered," she said. "But he didn't have time to give me any details."

Simon sincerely hoped Chief Keck was mistaken. He preferred homicides to happen in the distant past, so distant that their solution became an academic problem, like Carl Chavis's murder.

Simon carried the coffee and doughnuts around to the front of the Watkins home. Joe stood solemnly at attention with his arms crossed, wearing cop sunglasses that hid his eyes, even though it was barely light. He wasn't aware that the bottom button of his shirt had popped open, leaving a bit of belly poking out.

"I'm not sure you should be out here," Joe said. "This is the scene of a crime, you know."

"Lighten up," Simon said. "I'm one of the good guys. Have a cup of coffee and a doughnut."

"Well," Joe said, "I guess it's okay." He didn't have coffee, but took two doughnuts.

Keck came around the side of the house and joined them. He passed on the doughnuts, but drank a mug of coffee, black, in one gulp, then refilled his mug.

"Thank you," Keck said. "Remind me to give you a free ticket for the Holland grill the town raffles off every Fourth of July."

"Julia says you think Watkins was murdered?" Simon said.

"The circumstances are suspicious," Keck said, "and I'm not taking any chances. I've called in the SBI. The homicide unit from Wilmington will be here in thirty minutes. We've never had a murder on Pearlie Beach before, and I know my limits. The SBI has the equipment and the experience to handle a murder investigation. Convictions are all about science these days, and I don't want to hear some slimy defense lawyer argue in court that my department contaminated a crime scene."

"Who found the body?"

"A guy on his way to the beach to fish called the office, complaining about a dog—Wolfie, of course—growling and whining at him when he cut through the vacant lot on the way to the beach. He was concerned the dog might be ill or injured," Keck said. "Joe and I found the colonel squashed on the pavement, with his wife and son sound asleep in their beds. When we woke them up, Anita starts screaming, and Woody is furious we won't let him call an undertaker. He insists the old man just fell off the roof. I called Dale Pearlie—he and Anita have been friends for years—and Ms. Monahan, the lady preacher. They calmed Anita down. There's a sheriff's deputy inside keeping them all in one room until the search warrant arrives. Anita gave us permission to look around the house, but Woody objected, rather strenuously, I might add. I'd rather the SBI conducted the search anyway."

"And you think it's murder because?"

"The railing around the widow's walk is too high to fall over easily and there are obvious signs of a struggle. There are four empty beer bottles up there, but they represent two different brands of beer. So either the colonel switched beer brands in the middle of the evening, or he had a visitor. Since you're here," Keck said, draining his coffee and handing the empty mug to Joe, "I need your opinion about something. Come with me."

Simon knew right away that Keck wanted him to look at the body. He didn't want to, but what could he say? That one corpse a week was his limit?

They went around the house. Watkins's body was screened from the street by a white tent with POLICE stamped all over it in big block letters. The tent was new; the plastic bag that had contained it, ripped open, was crumpled beside it. Inside, Watkins's corpse lay on its stomach, splayed out like a cartoon character fallen off a cliff. Simon hesitated, drawing in a breath.

"I don't relish inspecting dead people, either," Keck said. "Pretend you're an actor in an episode of *Law and Order.* That's what I do."

Simon pretended, and it helped. It also helped that Watkins had shed little blood. Keck crouched down, careful to stay some distance away from the body, and shone his flashlight at an angle, into the partially clenched hand of the corpse.

"I think you can see it from here," Keck said. "There."

Simon flattened himself into the sand and peered into the palm of Watkins's hand. A small gold disc rested there.

"I don't believe it," Simon said. "It's a gold piece."

"I know you can't see it real clear," Keck said. "Once the SBI gets here they can bag it and we can look at it closer."

"I don't believe it," Simon said. What was going on? He had just talked himself out of investigating Chavis's murder after making a fool of himself chasing red herrings all night, only to have a modern-day murder associated with gold Confederate coins happen right next door.

"Do you think this might be related to Carl Chavis's murder?" he asked Keck.

"It's not my job to think anything at this point," Keck said. "I need to keep my mind open until all the evidence is in. But I don't believe that the colonel just fell off the widow's walk. And if that coin matches the ones you found on Chavis's body, well, that's one hell of a coincidence. I'm going to be real interested to see if there are two sets of fingerprints on those beer bottles or not. If there are two sets, I think he was murdered."

TWO DARK BLUE VEHICLES emblazoned with the seal of the state of North Carolina pulled up in front of the Watkins house. One was a sedan and one a big van with FORENSIC UNIT stamped on the side. The SBI had arrived. Right on their tail was the coroner's black station wagon.

"This should wake up the neighborhood," Keck said, moving to greet the SBI agents and the coroner. Simon, not sure what he should do, retreated to sit on the steps of the Clegg deck, just a few feet away from Julia's post. Two suits and two uniformed officers got out of the SBI car and four technicians in jumpsuits exited the van, opening the rear doors and removing metal cases of equipment. The suits, a man and a woman, talked at length to Keck, then went into the Watkins house with him. The uniformed officers relieved Julia and the Brunswick County deputy sheriffs, who got into their patrol car and drove off. Julia joined Simon on the steps. She had surrendered her orange vest, but was still wearing her Pearlie Beach police cap: "Keck gave it to me," she said, flicking the brim with her finger. "As a souvenir."

Simon watched the coroner and the SBI technicians go around the side of the house where Watkins's corpse lay, hauling their equipment with them.

"What exactly are they doing?" Simon asked her.

"You don't want to know what the coroner's doing. The first thing the technicians will do is videotape, photograph, and sketch the body. Then they'll search the area around the house, photographing and bagging anything, and I mean anything, that looks suspicious. Then they'll go in the house and do the same thing, starting with the widow's walk and working their way down. The suits will interview Anita and Woody, and then they'll canvass the neighbors."

"That's us. Did you hear anything last night?"

"Nothing. I was dead to the world."

"Me, too. I wonder when it happened."

"It's hard to say. I don't remember that side of the

house being lit at all while we were up, and it was so dark last night. I guess he could have been lying out there while we were still driving around. The coroner should be able to estimate the time of death."

"How long will all this take?"

"Hours. They're not in any hurry."

MORGAN STOOD ON THE deck smoking, blue smoke mingling with his frosty breath. When he saw Julia and Simon he crushed his cigarette into his empty coffee mug and followed them inside.

Marcus and Marianne were packing.

"We're going back to Raleigh this morning," Marianne said. "Trina's ankle might be broken, and if we went to the Brunswick County Hospital Emergency Room we'd be there all day. I'd just as soon take her to our own doctor."

"And we don't want the girls to know about Colonel Watkins," Marcus said. "That it might be murder, I mean. A fatal accident's disturbing enough, but murder is just plain scary. We'd like to get them away before they know what's happened."

"I'll stay behind," Simon said, "and clean up and shut down the cottage. Anything you forget I'll bring to you tomorrow."

"I'll stay, too, of course," Morgan said.

"Thanks. Stay as long as you like," Marcus said. "No need for you to leave. Don't worry too much about cleaning up. I'm going to have to come back another weekend to winterize the place anyway."

TRINA SAT PROPPED UP in her parents' bed, absorbed in the *Merck Medical Manual, Home Edition.* Her foot, packed between two bags of ice, was elevated on a pillow.

"Hi, there," Simon said. "How are you doing?"

Trina looked up from her reading. Her brow was furrowed from concentration, and her frizzy hair stuck out from her head in several directions.

"I don't think it's broken," she said. "It says here that when the foot rolls out, its usually a sprain. When it rolls in, the ankle breaks. I remember it bent out when I slipped. Plus I can move it pretty well. I'm pretty sure it's a sprain."

"Can I see?" Simon said.

Trina moved the ice bags and blanket off her foot. The lump on her ankle was the size of a golf ball, and the area around it was bruised black and red.

"That must hurt like crazy," Simon said.

"Mom gave me some aspirin and a teaspoon of bourbon whenever I woke up during the night. It says here that sometimes a sprain takes longer to heal than a break. I'll probably have to have a cast. They come in colors now. I hope they have purple."

Simon leaned over and kissed her on the forehead. "I'm so sorry, sweetie," he said. "What an ordeal you had."

"It's okay," she said. "Like Daddy said, I'll chalk it up to experience. But thank you, and thank Dr. Morgan, too, for getting me out without calling the fire department. Then everyone on the beach would have known how stupid I am."

Trina stifled a couple of tears that welled from her eyes, and rubbed her nose.

"Forget it," Simon said. "Someday those kids will eat your dust."

Trina didn't look convinced, so Simon changed the subject. "You guys are going to go home early, I hear," he said.

"You and Julia get to finish the turkey."

"Julia?"

"Mom said she was going to stay here with you," Trina said.

NYLON CLOTHESLINES WERE STRUNG on the pilings underneath the cottage between the parking area and the Watkins home, handy for wet bathing suits and towels. This morning Marianne had hung up all the bedspreads in the house on them, hiding the ugly scene next door from her girls. The old-fashioned chenille rectangles in faded green, blue, and yellow billowed in the wind. Dolly and Isobel were half asleep still when Marianne buckled them into the van. Marcus carried Trina down the stairs. Julia had brushed her hair and wound it into a neat bun. Trina had recovered enough to enjoy the attention and gave them all a regal wave as her father tucked her into the van amid pillows and blankets.

"Remember," Morgan said to her, "as soon as you can walk, call me and I'll give you a special private tour of the paleontology section of the new museum."

"Don't worry about anything here," Simon said as Marianne and Marcus got into the van.

"I'm sorry about your vacation," Marcus said.

"Think nothing of it," Simon said. "This makes finals week look restful."

After the Cleggs drove away, Morgan went back into the cottage for a coffee refill. Ostensibly Simon and Julia stayed behind to take down the bedspreads, but really hoping to find out what was going on next door. Keck saw them and walked over.

"What's happening?" Julia asked. "Anything you can tell us? Are there two sets of prints on the beer bottles?"

"Even better," Keck said. "Watkins's prints were all over the Michelobs. The two bottles of Bud were wiped completely clean."

"Sounds like his visitor killed him," Simon said.

Keck shrugged. "It does to me, too," he said. "But the SBI is a reserved bunch. They won't jump to conclusions. By the way," he said, pulling a notebook out of his pocket, "I understand you had a big night last night. I believe its time for you to meet Agent Locklear and give us a statement."

Agent Locklear was a middle-aged woman with a brown pageboy haircut. She wore the female version of an agent's uniform, a navy blue pantsuit with a white shirt, a man's watch, and a gold wedding band. Diamond earrings and expert makeup offset the masculinity of her clothing.

Simon and Julia offered them the hospitality of the Cleggs' porch. Once they were settled in four weathered rocking chairs, Simon and Julia told them everything. And Simon threw in a few extras: the argument he had heard between Woody and his father about money; Clare and her scuba diving trip at her grandfather's seaplane hangar; and the confrontation at the Do Drop Inn. Locklear nodded occasionally while she listened, rarely looking at them, and took lots of notes even as she recorded their statements on a Sony cassette recorder. Keck smiled when he heard about Leland's and Nance's escapade.

"I knew those boys were up to something," he said. "I

figured, knowing them as I do, it was harmless."

"Okay," Agent Locklear said. "This is the important part. Can you remember what time it was when you got back to the cottage from your trip up the inlet?"

"*The McLaughlin Group* was on," Simon said.

"Okay. Between ten and ten-thirty P.M.," Locklear said. "Can you remember anything about the Watkins house when you got back? Were there lights on? Could you hear music, television, anything?"

"I don't really remember," Simon said. "I was tired. We had a drink and I went straight to bed."

"Ms. McGloughlin," Locklear said, "at what point did you see Woody Watkins and Dee Anna Frink packing up the Explorer?"

"I'm not sure," Julia said. "I was brushing my teeth and noticed them from the bathroom window. About eleven, maybe."

Locklear referred to her notes. "Then you went out on the porch for a while, and then decided to wake up Dr. Shaw. Got any idea what time?"

"Maybe eleven-thirty."

"Do either of you remember what else might have been happening at the Watkins house?"

"The lights were on in the living room and the colonel's study," Simon said, "but I didn't see anyone else other than Woody and Dee Anna."

Agent Locklear consulted her notes again, then looked up at them, not even attempting to suppress a broad smile.

"At this point, you pursued Woody Watkins and Dee Anna Frink, believing them to be about to dig up a treasure chest full of Confederate gold?"

"Yeah," Simon said. "That's right."

"But they didn't dig up a chest of gold?"

"Unfortunately, no."

"You came back to the cottage after helping them"—here Locklear smiled again—"rescue a batch of baby turtles?"

"You've got it," Simon said.

"You returned to the cottage, which you found in an uproar over Trina Clegg's disappearance," Locklear said. "What time?"

"Twelve-thirty," Julia said. "I looked at my watch."

"And the Watkins house?"

"Dark," Simon said. "Completely dark."

"No one ever came out to find out what all the fuss was about?"

"No," Julia said. "I stayed at the house with Marianne until Simon and Dr. Morgan got back with Trina, at one forty-five. I must have looked at my watch every five minutes while they were gone."

"Then you talked in Dr. Morgan's camper for . . . ?"

"About half an hour," Simon said.

"Until after two o'clock," Locklear said. "Did you hear or see anything unusual next door?"

"Nothing," Simon said.

"One more thing," Locklear said. "Could you tell over here when Colonel Watkins was using his telescope up on the widow's walk?"

"His house is two stories taller than this one," Simon said. "We couldn't see him. I did once see the reflection of the telescope lens."

"So there's no way that last night you could have noticed if and when he was up there?"

"No," Simon said.

"Thanks," Locklear said, "I'll need to talk to Dr. David Morgan now. Then the Cleggs."

Keck cleared his throat. "I let the Cleggs go home," he said. "Trina needed medical attention, and their parents didn't want the little ones to see the crime scene."

"That's okay," Locklear said. "We can get the Raleigh office to take their statement next week. And you two," she said to Simon and Julia, "we'll transcribe your statements and fax them to Raleigh. You'll need to go down to our office there and proofread them and sign them next week."

Simon couldn't stand the suspense. "Agent Locklear?" he said. "Have you removed the coin from Watkins's body yet?"

"Not yet," she said. "But when we do, I'll bring it over here for you and Dr. Morgan to authenticate. But I'll tell you right now," she said, "some mythical Confederate gold treasure had nothing to do with this man's death."

Keck compressed his lips, started to say something, then stopped.

"I've been in this business for twenty years," Locklear said, "and I have never seen yet a murder that was about anything other than sex or money. Modern day sex or money. You'll see, that's what this one is about, too. That gold coin will prove to be a pure coincidence."

FROM THEIR VANTAGE POINT on the porch of the cottage, Simon and Julia could see and hear everything that went on next door. Simon even had his binoculars with him, but he had not yet been so shameless as to use them.

"This is really awful of us," Julia said, peering through the screen at the scene next door.

Anita came out of her house. Her face was distorted and streaked with tears, and she clung to Dale Pearlie's arm. With his free hand Dale was hanging on to Wolfie's leash. The dog looked as miserable as a dog could. He moped along behind Dale, with his tail between his legs. Dale helped Anita and the dog into his car. Chief Keck came up to speak to them. Dale closed the car door just as Keck reached them, as if refusing Keck permission to speak to Anita.

"Was it really necessary to have her fingerprinted?" Dale asked Chief Keck.

"Yes, it was," Keck said. "Standard procedure."

"I think it was uncalled for," Dale said. "Watkins fell off his roof. He'd been drinking."

"You don't want any suspicion to attach to Anita, do you? Look at it this way: If it looks like Watkins's death wasn't an accident, we can identify a stranger's prints by excluding hers."

"I'm going to take Anita to my place," Dale said, somewhat mollified. "At least until the SBI is out of there."

"She needs to be available for further questioning," Keck said.

"She will be," Dale said.

Keck watched them drive away.

Woody Watkins stomped out of the house next, furious. If he'd had a shotgun with him, he'd be loaded for bear. He took his fury out on Joe Pearlie, screaming at him to leave his post at the door of the house. Joe stood his ground. Then Woody turned toward the Clegg cottage and saw Simon and Julia sitting there. He shook his fist at them, then walked quickly toward the steps to their porch.

"Oh, hell," Julia said. "Let's go inside."

"No," Simon said. "Let him get it out of his system."

Woody took the steps two at a time. Out of the corner of his eye Simon saw that Keck was following him, breaking into a run. Simon silently opened the porch door for Woody, who shoved past and turned on him.

"You!" Woody said, poking his index finger very close to Simon's face. "You and your friends started all this! Just because my father owned a Confederate gold coin you think he's been murdered, too! He could have gotten that coin anywhere. He has two safe-deposit boxes at the bank full of old stuff."

Simon pushed Woody's hand out of his face. "I didn't find Chavis's body," he said. "The dredge brought it up."

"Your father's death would be suspicious without the gold coin," Keck said, arriving right behind Woody. "It has nothing to do with Professor Shaw. Go home. You've had a rough morning."

For a second it seemed that Woody might challenge them both, but instead he stalked back to his house with his clenched fists at his side, running into Joe Pearlie again on the way.

"Get your fat butt out of my way!" he said to Joe, who immediately flushed to his hairline. He didn't do or say anything, just stepped out of Woody's path.

Without another word Woody got into his Explorer and drove off, gears grinding and tires spewing sand as he went.

They were so intent on Woody's exit they didn't notice Clare Monahan until she knocked on the screen door. Clare was pale, with dark circles under her eyes. She seemed thinner than usual, as if she had lost weight overnight. Simon thought she seemed more distressed than she should be over her morning with the Watkins family, no matter how uncomfortable it might have been.

"I need to talk to you," she said to Keck. As Simon and Julia moved to leave them alone, she stopped them.

"You should hear this, too," she said. "And Dr. Morgan." Simon opened the door to the cottage and called Morgan, who came out onto the porch looking annoyed, until he saw Clare.

"Yesterday I was diving over at the hangar my grandfather used to own," Clare said. I was looking for souvenirs. I found more than I wanted to."

Keck made no sign that he had heard of her search before.

Clare took a piece of wood, smoothed by the ocean, out of her pocket. Two rusty rivets held about a half inch of rusty metal to the handle.

"It's a knife handle," she said needlessly. "The blade's been broken off."

Keck inspected the knife carefully, turning it over in his hands.

"Ms. Monahan," he said, "there is no way this could be linked to Carl Chavis's murder. It's true that there was a knife blade in Chavis's body, but it can't be connected to this handle. How many broken knives have been thrown away into the sound over the years? Hundreds, probably, maybe thousands."

"I just felt you should know," she said. "I'm so glad to give it to you. I wanted to anyway, but ever since Dale woke me up this morning and asked me to sit with Anita, it's been burning a hole in my pocket."

"Where exactly did you find it?" Simon asked.

"Right inside the hangar, actually. You know, it's basically just a covered dock. I dived in, moved my flashlight around a bit, and there it was."

"Chief Keck is right," Morgan said. "No way this means your grandfather is involved in Chavis's murder."

"I have the strangest feeling it does," Clare said. "And I'm not usually superstitious."

AN UNMARKED GRAY VAN pulled up to the Watkins house. Two solemn men in jumpsuits unloaded a gurney and rolled it around the side of the house to pick up the colonel's body. Everyone on the crowded Clegg porch was completely silent until Agent Locklear joined them.

"We're done here," she said to Keck. "After the corpse is removed, you can release the house to the Watkinses."

She handed a clear plastic bag containing a gold disc to Keck, who showed it to Morgan. He inspected it very carefully.

"It's a gold Dahlonega dollar, definitely," Morgan said. "Just like the ones we found on Chavis's body."

"Would you be willing to swear to that in an affidavit?" Keck said.

"Sure," Morgan said. "Of course, I'd like to examine all the coins in my lab first." He gave the coin back to Locklear.

"I doubt anything like that will be necessary," she said.

"Did you get some prints off it?" Keck asked her.

"Too smudged," she said. "Do you want to join us at the office in Wilmington? We'll be holding a case conference at three o'clock to go over the evidence."

"I'll be there," Keck said.

"Let me take you home," Morgan said to Clare.

"Thanks," she said, "I would appreciate that."

"Would you guys like to see the scene of the crime?" Keck asked Simon and Julia, "Before Woody and Anita come home?"

"Sure," Simon said.

"Not me," Julia said. "I'm beat. I'm staying right here in this rocking chair."

The staircase on the outside of the house rose four steep flights up to the widow's walk. Simon's chest burned by the time he had climbed to the top. Even Keck was breathing hard. The widow's walk was about ten feet square, fenced by a railing four feet high. The railing served as the backrest for a bench that also enclosed the space. Simon didn't see how anyone could fall accidentally off the widow's walk, unless they were standing on the bench for some reason.

The area was black with the graphite used to find fingerprints; otherwise the space was clear.

"They've taken everything away," Keck said. "But there was a struggle up here. Watkins's telescope was smashed on the floor. Glass from the lens was scattered everywhere, but there wasn't any blood. The beer bottles had rolled under the bench and several bench cushions had fallen on the deck."

"He put up a fight."

"Yeah, poor old guy."

"No suspects yet?"

"No. And everyone on Pearlie Beach would know he was up here last night. He spent hours with that telescope, especially when there was no moon."

"Like last night," Simon said.

The view from the widow's walk was spectacular in

daytime, too. The dune below was a high wide mound of pure sand, protecting everything landward from wind, waves, and storm. It was thick with hardy plants, the sea oats and beach grass that could survive the desertlike conditions of the beach. Without them the dune would blow away.

Past the dune the beach stretched fifty feet to the sea, the expanse broken occasionally by a tidal pool or a hillock of grass or a driftwood log. Birds hopped along the boundary between the beach and the frothy white breakers, feeding on tiny crustaceans. The bright blue sea stretched beyond the beach forever, blending into the sky so that it appeared to reach all the way to the sun. A few tiny ships and an orange marker buoy bobbed on the horizon. The ageless sight was somehow soothing, reminding Simon that the world was old and wise, whatever foolishness occupied a man during his brief time in it.

WHEN SIMON AND KECK got to the bottom of the stairs, Joe Pearlie was removing the yellow crime scene tape from the perimeter of the Watkins house. He wound it carefully around one hand, making sure it was straight and unwrinkled. Simon wondered how many years would go by until the Pearlie Beach Police Department needed to use it again.

All trace of the SBI was gone. The little knot of spectators who had gathered across the street from the house scattered, walking away, talking solemnly together in groups of two or three. Just as Keck reached his car to leave, a white Ford Taurus station wagon with the logo of a Wilmington television station on it pulled up in front of the Watkins house. A young man got out, brushing an expensive suit and checking his hair in the car's side mirror. His cameraman unloaded equipment from the trunk.

"I hate the first amendment," Keck said.

Simon joined Julia on the Cleggs' porch, where they watched Keck handle the newsman. His technique was masterful. Keck took the newsman by the arm, talking expansively to him, gesturing all the while. Then Keck led him around the house to show him where Watkins's body was found, modestly waving the reporter off when videotaping started, refusing to be on camera. When they were done, he slammed the door of the station wagon and waved a friendly good-bye.

Once they left, Keck abandoned his cheerful demeanor, joining Simon and Julia.

"There'll be a report on Watkins's death on the news tonight," he said. "They don't know it might be a murder. I figure that will come out just about the time the media gets wind of Chavis's murder and his gold stash. All hell will break loose around here, oh, about Wednesday, I predict. This island will be swarming with treasure hunters and reporters. I'd rather have a hurricane blow in."

"Surely it won't be that bad," Simon said.

"That's easy for you to say," Keck said. "You-all will be back in Raleigh. I want to warn you," he continued, "I plan to refer all questions of an historical nature to you, Dr. Shaw."

Simon groaned.

"Don't pay any attention to him," Julia said. "He loves publicity."

"The SBI isn't interested in any relationship between Carl Chavis's murder and Watkins's death," Keck said.

"Agent Locklear is sure that either Woody killed his father for his money, or that Dale and Anita killed him."

"Dale and Anita?" Simon said, shocked.

"They were high school sweethearts, but they broke up when Dale went to college. Dale married Joe's mother, and Anita married the colonel. He was rich, and she was a former Miss Brunswick County. It was the biggest wedding anyone around here has ever seen. Then Dale got divorced, and the colonel got old. Rumor has it Dale and Anita have been spending time at the Seahorse Motel on the other side of Wilmington. You can bet that the SBI will be concentrating on them as suspects. When I explained about Chavis's murder and the gold coins to the investigators, their eyes just glazed over. I'm stubborn, though. I think a possible relationship between the Chavis and Watkins murders still bears thinking about. You are still thinking about it, aren't you, Dr. Shaw?"

"I'm always thinking," Simon said.

10

Julia and Simon were alone together, but they were too exhausted to care. Julia went straight to her room to nap. Simon sat down on one of the sofas in the living room and let his head hang over the back, rolling his neck back and forth to work the tension out. He didn't plan to collapse, but he could feel the adrenaline quickly leaking out of his system. A blurred blotch in his left eye, a migraine aura, warned him of impending pain. He got up and got a cold Coke from the refrigerator. In the bathroom he shook a handful of pills into his hand and swallowed them whole. His empty stomach rolled when the pills landed, so he drank half his Coke. He undressed, ran the water in the shower as hot as he could stand, and sat under it with the cold Coke can pressed to his temple.

Simon was in an unfamiliar situation. Never in his life had he failed at any intellectual exercise he undertook, until now. He simply could not get his mind around the puzzle of Chavis's and Watkins's murders. Everything that had happened since Chavis's corpse had been discovered—

the research he had done, the people he had interviewed, the documents he had collected, and the evidence gathered in Watkins's murder—was jumbled up in his mind until it resembled the attic at his grandfather's general store. No matter how he arranged and rearranged the facts, he couldn't make sense of it. He was too frustrated to care any longer about looking foolish. He wanted answers.

After twenty minutes in the shower, Simon's medications kicked in, so he went to bed, falling instantly asleep. He dreamed about a snipe hunt. He stood on a cold beach, holding an empty pillowcase, calling the snipe to come to him, while his tormenters ran away, abandoning him. He didn't recognize the faces of the other players, but he had a feeling they were all named Pearlie. The dream played over and over again, like a video on automatic rewind and replay. When Simon awoke, his brain scrubbed clean by codeine and serotonin, a fresh thought about the murders had surged into his consciousness.

He found Julia in the kitchen making herself a turkey sandwich.

"Feel better?" she asked.

"Much," Simon said. "Did you sleep? What time is it?"

"I just woke up a few minutes ago. It's about four-thirty. What a day . . . or has it been two days?"

She spoke with her mouth full of turkey sandwich. Simon made himself one with dark meat, salt, lots of mayonnaise, and white bread.

"Where's Morgan?" Simon asked.

"Gone out," she said. "He just left. He said Clare needed cheering up, so he was going to drive her up to some ancient Indian crossroads near Wilson, then they're going to stop at Mitchell's on the way home for barbecue."

"And," she continued, "Chief Keck called. From Wilmington. He was there brainstorming with the SBI detective in charge of the case. Watkins's death has been officially classified as a homicide."

"Did Keck find out what Anita's and Woody's alibis were?"

"Woody swears he spent most of the night at Dee Anna's and came home about four in the morning. All the exterior lights were out, so he didn't see his father's body. Anita was at a Chamber of Commerce dinner, after which she and Dale went out for a drink. She got back home about ten-thirty, hollered up at Watkins from the stairs inside the house, he answered that he was stargazing, so she went to bed."

"She didn't hear anything?"

"She wears earplugs at night.

"Did Keck say when Watkins died?"

"They don't know for sure. Roughly between midnight and two. The autopsy will narrow it down. They've sent the corpse to Chapel Hill and are hoping to get the results early next week."

"Watkins was murdered while we were driving around the island looking for Trina and talking in Morgan's camper."

"Yes. Chief Keck also gave the SBI investigator all your notes about Chavis's murder and the gold coins and everything. She just doesn't think it's relevant."

"Great."

"Look at it from her perspective," Julia said. "She's following standard law enforcement procedure, derived from experience. Most victims are murdered by their nearest and dearest, either because of sex or money. That makes Woody and Anita first-class suspects. The SBI will work that angle to death before they try something more unusual. It's a matter of statistics. You might be intrigued by a colorful notion about gold coins and decades-old murders, but you wouldn't go to Las Vegas with it."

Simon made himself another sandwich, then sat down on a sofa with his notes.

"No one can say you're not persistent," Julia said. "Some might say stubborn or even obsessed."

"I know," Simon said. "I can't let go. What if these two murders are related? The only thing linking them is a gold coin, but like Chief Keck said, that's a mighty big coincidence. And if the two murders are related, could someone else be in danger?"

"I hadn't thought of that."

"Inez and Henry come to mind."

Julia was wearing her black knit pants again today, with a heavy green sweater and hiking socks. She turned up the propane stove, then sat down next to Simon and curled her feet up under her.

"If the SBI is wrong, then one of the people in this photograph might hold the key to both murders and be in danger," Simon said.

"That photograph is a very tenuous link to what happened in 1942."

"Agreed. But this was Dale Pearlie, Sr.'s birthday party, attended by his closest friends, who we can assume, in this small environment, were Chavis's closest friends. I'm not saying that one of them killed him, but it certainly wasn't healthy to be in this photograph."

Julia straightened up suddenly. "You're right, they're

dead—I mean, not all of them, but the ones that are . . ."

"Not a natural death among them. Chavis murdered, Nick Monahan crashed on the same day, Dale Pearlie, Sr., died in an accident, and now Watkins's been murdered."

"Who's left? Just Henry? He can't be Chavis's murderer. He's dirt poor. Do you think he's in danger?"

"Maybe. But remember, Inez took this picture, so she was there, too. She could know something important about Chavis's murder and just not know she knows it."

"Have you forgotten that we made fools of ourselves jumping to conclusions like that yesterday?"

"No, I haven't. But I'm a glutton for punishment. And"—here Simon turned the photo around so Julia could see it—"there was someone else in this photograph."

Julia jabbed her index finger onto the arm of the young African-American woman in the picture, the maid whose face was hidden.

"The waitress!"

"Let's go see Inez," Simon said.

INEZ ANSWERED THE DOOR with her finger to her lips.

"Shh," she said. "We just got Anita to sleep. Let's talk outside."

The three of them stood on the stoop outside Inez's house. Wolfie, tethered to a railing, lay at their feet with his head on his paws. He didn't stir, just looked at them morosely. Simon showed Inez the picture again.

"Of course, that's Viola," Inez said. "She worked for us some during the war. Her daddy sharecropped for Henry's daddy and then Henry. She's younger than me, you know.

I'd guess she was about fourteen then. Why do you ask?"

"Inez," Simon said. "Have you talked to Chief Keck today?"

"Why, no."

"I don't want to frighten you, but I think you shouldn't be alone for a few days. We don't know yet whether the colonel's death was related to Chavis's. You could be a material witness."

"Whatever you say," Inez said, "but I don't believe it."

"One more thing," Simon said. "What kind of investigation did the military police do of Chavis's death? Did they question anyone? Or did they just assume he drowned?"

"Honey, that was so long ago, I can't remember. Wait a minute." Inez screwed up her face, thinking. "I do remember Dale Senior saying the military police asked him when was the last time he saw Carl."

"What did he say?" Julia said.

"He saw him at the Pavilion the Sunday before. Dale and I had that day off, as usual, but Dale went over there to fuss at Henry for flying the Confederate flag again. Dale said Carl was there talking about how he had leave the next day and was going to go diving. Of course, that was when he disappeared."

"And Nick Monahan vanished on the same day," Simon said.

"But the two weren't related," Inez said. "In fact, now that you've jogged my memory, I remember the seaplane flying over the island that day. Nick died scouting for German submarines."

"How many other people would have been at the Pavilion that night?" Simon asked.

"Oh, it was packed, I'm sure. Always was on the weekend. Servicemen and factory workers from Wilmington."

"Did the police speak to Henry?" Julia asked.

"I suppose so," Inez said. "But I don't know for sure."

Inez pulled her sweater around herself. "I don't mean to be unfriendly," she said, "but it's chilly, and I need to be where I can hear Anita if she calls for me."

"Of course," Simon said.

Simon and Julia sat in Julia's Beemer outside Inez's house, brainstorming.

"If the Pavilion was full that Sunday, anyone could have heard Carl talk about going diving and his treasure-hunting ideas and followed him," Julia said. "He could have been murdered by someone who lives in Albuquerque or Chicago now."

"I don't think so," Simon said. "That gold coin in Watkins's hand shows a definite local link."

"Then you must believe that there is a Confederate gold treasure here, still, and that someone killed Watkins because of it."

"No, not really."

"You're not making any sense," Julia said. "You can't have it both ways. Either Watkins's murder is linked with Chavis's because of the gold, or it's completely unrelated."

"Bear with me," Simon said. "Could you drop me off at the cottage, then go talk to Viola? I want to review some things, then maybe walk down to the pier and see if Henry's there. I've got more questions for him."

VIOLA'S LITTLE HOUSE WAS an old single-wide trailer home with a clapboard addition and a big screened-in porch built from a kit. It was located in a working-class subdivision across the bridge from Pearlie Beach and several streets off Pearlie Beach Road and its congested tourist strip. All the rest of the houses were like Viola's, trailers added on to over the years. A long time ago the street had been paved with gravel, now sinking deep into the sand underneath. Julia's tires churned up sand as she drove. She could hear it making a gritty, pinging sound as it flew up under her car.

Viola's home was painted lavender with white trim and lavish latticework hiding where the added-on bits came together. Her raked gravel yard contained a decorative windmill with arms turning in the breeze, a flock of ceramic seagulls, and several bird feeders. The screened porch was wild with overgrown ferns, begonias, and other potted plants brought in from the cold. Stunning orchids hung from the rafters in pots filled with pebbles. A long roll of heavy plastic lay on the floor. Doubtless Viola planned to seal off the porch for the winter to greenhouse the plants. Behind the house was a beautifully tended plot of herbs, collards, lettuces, and other greens Julia couldn't identify, all thriving in the sandy soil.

Viola opened the door before Julia had a chance to knock. A heavenly aroma wafted out, and she breathed it in deeply.

"You're cooking something wonderful," Julia said.

"Come in, honey," Viola said. "Come into the kitchen—I've got to tend my fried chicken." Her face glistened with steam and grease; Julia followed Viola through a sitting room furnished with a blue velvet suite protected by plastic slipcovers into the kitchen, which, along with a bathroom, occupied most of the original trailer.

Viola had two stoves—a cast-iron woodburner and an electric range—a big new Kenmore refrigerator, and an old, stocky Frigidaire freezer. A bushel basket of freshly picked collards sat on the linoleum floor. Two trays of hot biscuits cooled on the top of the cast-iron stove. Pans loaded with frying chicken cooked on every eye of the electric range.

"I'm cooking for the church supper tomorrow," Viola said. "Now, what can I do for you, young lady?"

"You know about Colonel Watkins?" Julia asked.

"I heard," Viola said. "Is it true he was murdered?"

"Yeah. The SBI is investigating. What Simon and I wonder is if it's connected to Carl Chavis's murder."

"How could that be?"

"Watkins was clutching a gold coin identical to the ones that Chavis had."

Viola shrugged disinterestedly. Neither murder had anything to do with her. She began to pack the collard leaves into a giant stockpot. She saw Julia's expression and chuckled.

"Don't worry, honey, I won't cook them until after you're gone."

"I like to eat collards," Julia said, "miles away from where they were cooked. Like, from a can."

"I understand. My momma used to say a pot of good collard greens cooking smelled like the feet of angels."

"Inez Pearlie said you were working at the Pavilion the Sunday before Carl disappeared. Did the military police interview you?"

Viola stopped packing collards and smiled, the wet wrinkles in her face laughing at Julia.

"Of course not, honey, I was just the colored girl who

worked in the kitchen. I do remember that night, though. Henry and Dale Senior had a huge fight while I was cleaning up the kitchen that night."

"What were they fighting about?"

"Dale Senior was furious that Henry was flying the Confederate flag off the Pavilion. Said it was a disgrace to fly any flag except the Stars and Stripes, especially during wartime. Then he went outside and drug it down. I never expected to hear two white men argue about such a thing in my life, and I've never forgotten it."

"Did you see Carl that day?"

"That evening. He came in the kitchen late looking for leftover fried chicken and ham biscuits, just like I'm cooking now. But Henry had already taken the leftovers to his fish camp to sell the next day. So Carl went over there."

"To Henry's camp? To eat?"

"No, honey, I made him an egg and bacon sandwich at the Pavilion. He went over to Henry's to rent a boat. So that he could get to diving right away in the morning."

SIMON WAS NOT STUDYING documents or doing anything remotely resembling detecting when Julia called. He sat outside in a deck chair, with his hands behind his head and his eyes closed, face tilted toward the sun. When Julia told him what Viola had said, he nodded to himself. He needed just one more piece of information.

"Can you stay with Viola?" he asked Julia.

"I guess so," she said. "Do you think she's in danger? And Henry?"

"Could be," Simon said. "I'm going to the pier to find Henry and ask him some questions. He may know more than he realizes, too. You stay with Viola. I'll call you in a half hour to check in."

IT SEEMED LIKE A year since he had last walked down the beach. Just three days ago he and Julia had sunned themselves, bare-legged, watching the Clegg girls play in their bright bathing suits. Today the sea was a cold metal gray, the waves broke roughly on the beach, and the sun was shrouded in clouds. He had to lean a little bit into the wind and pull his jacket collar around his face. Ahead of him the pier rose into view. Its thick, tall pillars stood like trees sprouting from the sand.

Simon went up the back stairs and entered through the back door. The pier was deserted. Henry was in the grill, standing on a stepstool, cleaning out cabinets.

"We're closed," Henry said. "Out of food. Come back March fifteenth next year." His old man's laugh was a cackle from deep inside his chest, then he coughed.

Simon hoisted himself onto the counter. His legs swung, so he rested them on a rung of a barstool.

"Weather's turned cold," he said.

"That happens in the winter," Henry said. "Every year since I've been born."

"You heard about Colonel Watkins's death?"

"Yeah, I heard." Henry pulled a bag of flour out of the back of a cabinet and inspected the contents. "Mealy worms," he said, and tossed it into a garbage can at his feet.

"They're saying it's murder," Simon said.

"Who would want to murder him? He was just drunk and fell, I expect."

"The railing on the widow's walk is too high to fall over."

"Maybe he was trying to fly." Henry pulled out a box of instant hot chocolate from the cabinet.

"Expiration date, February 1992. Don't think I can get away with that," he said. The box of hot chocolate followed the flour into the garbage can. Henry stretched, and Simon could almost hear him creak.

"You know how old I am?" he asked Simon.

"Eighty?"

"So old I owe Moses a quarter!"

Simon couldn't help laughing.

"It's better than the alternative," Henry said.

"Listen," Simon said, "I was in the bathroom outside the pier here the other day, and I accidentally pulled back a piece of paneling near the sink."

"Yeah," Henry said, "there's a loose nail there."

"I pounded it back in. But I noticed there were some magazines stuffed into the wall."

"After the pier was built, everyone complained that the bathroom was cold. One guy told me his stream smoked when he peed. People these days don't know what cold is. I can remember pulling in crab pots in December when I didn't dare piss off the side of the boat for fear my member'd freeze. Anyway, I brought a stack of magazines from home and stuffed the walls with them. Old newspapers and magazines are the best insulation there is."

"They're your magazines?"

"Yeah."

"Tell me something," Simon said. "What did Carl Chavis see at your fish camp that night that made you need to kill him?"

Henry stood up erect, leaning back and resting his hands on his hips. "What trash are you talking?"

"You were the last person to see him alive," Simon said. "Viola remembers he was on his way to rent a boat from you the Sunday night before he disappeared."

"So? What if he did?"

"What did he see that you had to kill him?"

Henry kicked the garbage can, hard. It rolled out into the middle of the room, spilling its contents.

"I didn't kill nobody," he said. "Who the hell are you, to come here and stick your nose into our business?"

"Was it a German submarine?"

"You people are smart," Henry said. "I always heard it."

"Well, was it a submarine?"

"It was the U-66. She came into my inlet a couple of times to stock up on fresh food. I fixed it with a German agent in Wilmington."

"How much did they pay you?"

"I didn't do it for the money. I agreed with Hitler. Still do, about a lot of things."

"The Confederate flag was a signal?"

"Yeah. When Carl showed up that night, there that Nazi sub was, tied up at my camp. Those German sailors were sitting on my dock wolfing down Viola's fried chicken and ham biscuits just as fast as they could. It was real funny to see them."

"Carl didn't think it was funny."

"No, he didn't, damn fool. He hid in the woods until the sub sailed off, pretty near dawn. He was mad as hell, going to call the military police. I couldn't make him see reason, calm him down."

"So you killed him."

"Had no choice. Otherwise I'd have been hung."

"You dressed him in his diving suit . . ."

"Couldn't get the knife blade out. It got caught up on his ribs. Put him in the dinghy and rowed the body into the sound, weighted him down, sank him, and sank the boat over him. I about drowned, doing all that and swimming back to shore."

"Where'd the gold coins come from?"

"That was hard—giving those coins up. Got them from a man who needed new tires so he could visit his sick momma in Burnsville. Filled his tank with gas a couple of times, too. I put the coins with Carl so that when his body was found everyone would think his killing had something to do with him finding treasure. I never thought he wouldn't be found for so long."

"Those gold coins distracted us, all right, even fifty years later."

"People are blinded by money; it's like the Bible said, it's the root of all evil."

"What about Nick Monahan?"

"After I got rid of Carl's body, I walked back to my camp. I saw across the inlet that the light was on at Nick's place. Sometimes he slept on the second floor of his hangar so that he could get an early start patrolling for submarines."

The old man laughed at the irony of it, then dug around in his pockets, unearthing a squashed packet of cigarettes. He lit one, sitting down in a chair and inhaling deeply.

"I knew he hadn't seen the sub," Henry said, "or the place would of been crawling with soldiers already, but I feared he might have seen me leaving with Carl. So I swum over to the hangar, siphoned off about half of the gas out of the airplane. I knew he wouldn't know it because his gas gauge hadn't worked in a long time. He couldn't get the parts because of the war. I tossed the knife hilt into the water while I was there."

"When Monahan ran out of gas, the plane crashed."

"Yeah. He must have been pretty far out to sea, on account of no wreckage or nothing ever washed up on the beach."

"Did you kill Dale Senior, too?"

"Watch your mouth. Dale was blood kin to me. He died in that accident. I'll never forgive myself for getting to that marina too late to help him."

"Killing Colonel Watkins was your big mistake. Otherwise you might have gotten away with it."

"Yeah, I had forgotten I had give him one of those coins in trade for that Nazi football I showed you."

"I was at his house for drinks Wednesday night," Simon said. "I showed him that group picture of you-all, and photographs of the coins we found on Chavis's body. He didn't say a word."

"He called and told me about it. He wanted to give me a chance to explain myself first, for old times' sake. He asked me over to his place last night, because his wife and kid were gone."

"You couldn't explain."

"No, I couldn't, not to his satisfaction. He'd had a couple of beers. We fought, and he hit his head on the edge of the bench. After that it was easy to heave him over the rail of the widder's walk, although I pulled my back. I wiped the beer bottles and everything else I touched clean, but I didn't dare hang around to search his corpse for that gold coin. There was so much commotion next door I was afraid someone would see me. I was lucky to get down those outside stairs and get away."

Simon jumped down off the counter and reached for the old black rotary telephone on the counter next to the cash register.

"I expect Chief Keck's back from Wilmington by now," Simon said. "Let's give him a call, shall we?"

"You don't think I'm going to let you do that." The old man squashed his cigarette directly into the counter. The Formica sizzled and smoked.

"You don't have a choice," Simon said.

"Don't I? I may be old enough to fart dust, but I can still deal with the likes of you, college boy."

Henry reached behind him and, before Simon could connect the old man's actions with its consequences, lifted a spear gun off its rack behind him. The long bright metal tube was loaded; a three-pronged spear point, like a trident, was pointed right at Simon's belly. Simon was so taken by surprise he didn't move, and in the blink of an eye Henry had cocked the gun.

"Thought I was too old to put up a fight, didn't you?" Henry said.

Then the phone rang.

"Don't move," Henry said.

"That will be Julia, looking for me," Simon said.

"Baloney," Henry said. "It's someone wanting to know if we're open."

"Give it up, Henry. Let me call Chief Keck."

"I'll call Donnie Lee, all right, and tell him about this terrible accident you had."

Instinctively Simon pressed his back against the counter, hard, as if he could melt through it and disappear out the back door. The phone stopped ringing.

"I was showing you this spear gun, see, and damned if it didn't go off. I am going to be the sorriest old man in Brunswick County afterwards. No one is going to cry harder at your funeral than me."

"You won't get away with it."

"Won't I? If you're dead, who's going to explain all this to anyone? I may only have finished the eighth grade, but I know no one is going to send an eighty-four-year-old man to prison for an accident. Too bad you won't be alive to see me shake and cry at the inquest. Folks will feel sorrier for me than for you."

"Chief Keck and Julia McGloughlin know everything—"

"If Donnie Lee Keck knew I had murdered anyone, he'd be here this minute buckling me into a pair of handcuffs. You're the only person on the face of this earth who knows."

JULIA WAITED IMPATIENTLY FOR Simon's phone call, fidgeting on the sofa in Viola's tiny living room. Viola had fixed them both tall glasses of sweet iced tea garnished with fresh mint. She sat on a chair opposite Julia, rubbing her feet.

"I'm thinking," Viola said, "of having my feet fixed." Viola took off her slippers, revealing a pair of awful bunions. "My feet hurt me so bad all the time. I had planned to go my whole life without letting anyone cut on me, but two years ago I had my uterus removed, and honey, I never felt better."

"Does your phone work?" Julia asked her.

"Of course it does. Medicare won't pay for it, though."

"The phone?"

"No, honey, fixing my bunions. But Gaye and Mack said they'd cover it. They're doing real good—they bought me a brand-new car for my birthday. It would be nice to wear real shoes again. Honey, you're as restless as water on a griddle. Why don't you just call him yourself?"

Fifty minutes had passed since Julia had left the cottage. She lifted the receiver of Viola's white portable telephone and called the Clegg cottage. There was no answer. Viola went back into her kitchen, barefooted, singing "Oh Happy Day" to herself as she checked on her frying chicken.

"Viola!" Julia called into the kitchen. "What's the number at the pier?"

Viola answered her, and Julia dialed. She let the phone ring ten times. There was no answer. She almost threw the phone down onto its cradle. "Damn that man," she said.

"Damn them all, honey," Viola said, coming into the living room, wiping her hands on her apron. "It won't do no good. God made them the way they are."

"Where is he and what is he doing?"

"You can leave here, honey, no one's going to hurt me," Viola said. "I told you the whole story."

"You're a witness to whatever happened to Carl Chavis in 1942, just like Colonel Watkins was. I can't leave you alone."

Julia looked up the number of the police department and called it. Joe Pearlie answered the phone.

"Is Chief Keck back?" Julia asked. "Or Officer Galloway?"

"Not yet," Joe said. Julia could swear she heard him chewing something. "I expect them back anytime. Something I can help you with, Ms. McGloughlin?"

"Would you look out your window and see if there are any cars parked at the pier?"

"I just see Henry's pickup," Joe said. "Is something going on I should know about?"

Joe would be worthless in a crisis, Julia thought.

"No, Joe, just ask Chief Keck to call me at Viola's as soon as he gets in."

Julia hung up the phone and then lifted the receiver again, dialing the pier. The phone rang and rang. If Henry, or Simon, or the two of them were there, for God's sake why didn't one of them answer the phone? Julia was frightened. She was conscious of every breath she took and her hands and feet were cold. There was something wrong here. She looked at her watch. It would take her fifteen, maybe twenty minutes to get to the pier herself. She lifted the receiver of the phone again.

THE PHONE RANG AGAIN insistently, then stopped. Simon's back was still pressed up against the counter. He had folded his arms across his chest, to block the barbed spear that was pointed at him from just a few feet away. Henry was smiling triumphantly at him. He was enjoying this. Simon tried to control his fear and think. That was easier said than done. Perspiration had broken out all over his body, and his heart was pounding. His head was pounding along with it.

"You can't accomplish anything by killing me, Henry," Simon said. "Chief Keck, or Julia, or someone will figure it out."

"Maybe, maybe not. Let's see, what part of you will bleed the most? The heart's not an easy target. Belly, maybe?"

Simon's stomach contracted.

"Of course, I've got more than one of these spears." He tapped the gun. "If the first one doesn't do you, another one will. But then it wouldn't look like an accident, would it? I got to get it just right."

The door crashed open. Joe Pearlie blundered in, his handgun drawn. He was bright red, sweat glistened on his forehead, and he was breathing hard from his run across the street from the police station to the pier.

"Damn!" Henry said. "What are you doing here, boy?"

"Put that spear gun away, Uncle Henry. Now!"

"Thank you," Simon said quietly.

"Listen, boy, you don't know what you're doing," Henry said to Joe. "This is bigger than you and me."

"Ms. McGloughlin said you had something to do with these murders," Joe said. "You put that spear gun down right now."

Henry turned his head slightly toward his young relative, while keeping one eye and the spear gun on Simon.

"Joe," he said, "do you know what will happen if you arrest me? Pearlie Beach and the entire Pearlie family will be ruined. Everything your grandfather and father have worked for all these years."

"Henry killed Carl Chavis, Nick Monahan, and Colonel Watkins," Simon said. "He was a German collaborator during the war. He provisioned U-boats at his fish camp."

"That not true, is it, Uncle Henry?" Joe lowered his gun a few inches, and he looked at his uncle with sorrow in his eyes.

"It don't matter now," Henry said. "The important thing is keeping it quiet. Who do you think will vacation at this beach once this hits the papers? The Pearlie name will be ruined. I'm sorry, boy, but it's too late now. The only thing to do," Henry said, gesturing the spear gun toward Simon, "is shut him up for good. He's the only one who knows."

"Except me," Joe said, raising his gun again.

"You going to shoot me, your kin? I don't believe it. Let me take care of him, and you and me will cover it up afterwards."

Joe reluctantly holstered his gun, averting his eyes from Simon.

Simon sucked in his breath and tensed his abdominal muscles instinctively, as if that would blunt the impact of the spear. He focused on keeping control of his mind, trying to think of what else he might do to save his life. He was at the point of prayer when Joe stepped in front of him, his big body shielding Simon completely.

"What . . . ? Henry said.

"You're right, Uncle Henry, I can't shoot you. But I'm not going to let you kill Professor Shaw. It's wrong. Everything you've done is wrong. You put down that spear gun now."

"You're a fool, boy."

"What happens to Pearlie Beach doesn't matter. What matters is that you pay for what you've done."

Joe was scared. A stream of sweat ran down from his hairline into the collar of his shirt. Stains quickly spread under his armpits and down the middle of his back. His hands were clenched, and he swayed a little.

Please don't faint, Simon pleaded silently. He couldn't

see Henry from behind Joe's big body, so he couldn't tell what the old man was doing.

"Move away, boy," Henry said. "Don't make me kill you."

"No," Joe said.

"I'll do it."

"No."

"Oh, hell," Henry said. Simon heard the spear gun clatter on the floor. "I can't shoot my own flesh and blood."

Joe's chest heaved as he drew in a big breath. Then he pulled his handcuffs off his belt.

"You're under arrest, Uncle Henry," Joe said.

WHEN JULIA BURST INTO the grill with her own gun drawn, Viola on her heels, she found Joe Pearlie calmly delivering the Miranda warning to his "uncle," who, when Joe had finished, spit on the floor at his feet. Joe picked up the spear gun, carefully uncocked it, and nudged Henry toward the door.

"In a bit, when you've collected yourself, Dr. Shaw, come on over to the station so I can get your statement," Joe said. "You, too, Ms. McGloughlin. Chief Keck should be back soon."

"We'll be there," Simon said.

"Move along, Uncle Henry," Joe said. The two of them walked out the door.

"Unreconstructed old goat," Viola said as Henry passed by her.

Simon folded his arms on the counter and rested his head on them for just a second, before straightening up.

"Are you okay?" Julia asked.

"I think I'd like to sit down for a minute," Simon said. "Would you look in the cooler and bring me a Coke, if there is one?"

Simon lifted a chair off a table and put it on the floor. He sat in it heavily.

Julia brought him a Coke. "Are you okay?" she asked again.

"I'm fine."

"You're very pale."

"I'm not surprised." Simon drained half of his Coke.

Julia took another chair off a table and sat down next to Simon. Simon finished his Coke in one gulp.

"Thanks," he said, "for sending the cavalry. Of course, I had the situation well under control. I had almost talked Henry out of skewering me when Joe walked in."

Simon's grin conveyed to Julia that he didn't expect her to take him seriously.

"What possessed you to confront Henry?"

"I thought he was too old to resist. Was that stupid, or what? He would have killed me, too, if Joe hadn't stopped him."

"Who knew Joe had it in him? But he was all I had. When I couldn't reach you at the cottage and you didn't call me, I phoned the pier. Then I called Joe, who told me Henry's truck was parked outside. I called the pier again, and when no one answered, I called Joe back and told him everything."

"Thank you," Simon said again. "Joe really came through, didn't he? I guess Chief Keck saw something in him we all missed, until now."

Viola stood, hands on her hips, and surveyed the grill room.

"What a mess," she said, and went for a broom to clean up the spilled contents of the garbage can.

"Ugh," she said, sweeping vigorously, "mealy bugs. I told that man over and over—keep the flour in the refrigerator and it'll stay fresh."

Julia held the dustpan for Viola while she swept the powdery mess into it.

"You know," Viola said when they had finished, "now that Henry's been arrested, I guess I'll be running this place. I'm telling you, there will be some changes made. Might as well take stock." She vanished into the back storeroom.

Simon's color had returned.

"Tell me," Julia said, "I can't stand it. Where's the gold?"

"There isn't any," Simon said, and told her why Carl Chavis, Nick Monahan, and Col. Timothy Watkins had been murdered.

"I am stunned," Julia said a few minutes later. "I never knew that Nazis ever actually set foot on the American mainland."

"There have always been rumors," Simon said. "Once a skin diver found a Holsum bread wrapper in a sunken German submarine off the coast of Florida. In Myrtle Beach, not far from here, a theater operator supposedly found a German newspaper on a seat after a Saturday movie matinee during the war. And Germans definitely landed farther north, on Long Island."

"I'm surprised the Nazis would take such a risk."

"They were hungry. They weren't supposed to return to Germany until all their torpedoes and ammunition were spent. Didn't matter if they ran low on food."

"How could a sub get up the inlet?"

"Those subs were small and gray and quiet, very difficult to see at twilight or at night. They only needed about fifteen feet of depth when cruising on the surface, and the sound and the inlet were much deeper then. Remember how dark it was the night we followed the Pearlies up Lockwood's Folly Inlet? There was a new moon, and lights were out because of the parade. There was no moon on the day Chavis died, and the inhabited parts of the coast were blacked out. I figure that on Sundays when the weather was right and the night was going to be dark, Henry would fly the Confederate flag all day to signal that the coast was clear. That night he could expect a German submarine to cruise into his fish camp for provisioning. Inez told us he didn't fly that flag every Sunday, just occasionally."

"Incredible."

"It was Trina's snipe hunt that made me see we were all on the wrong trail. We were chasing snipe, too: those gold coins. Talk about a red herring. Planting those Confederate coins with Chavis's body was a stroke of genius. Henry had gotten them in trade from a guy who was desperate for tires and gasoline.

"The entire weekend I assured everyone that there was no gold on this beach, probably never was," Simon continued, "and then I turned right around and behaved as though I thought there was. But nothing fit together right. So I finally asked myself, what if the gold had nothing to do with Chavis's death? What if the murderer's motive was completely different? I did what I should have done in the beginning, reconstructed Chavis's disappearance as best I could from what little evidence I had: the newspaper, those copies of *Liberation* magazine, survivors' memories. Viola's statement to you about Carl visiting Henry was the clincher."

"When the military police investigated Chavis's death, they didn't interview Viola," Julia said. "She wasn't holding anything back. No one ever asked her. I suppose it never occurred to her that Henry might have murdered Carl."

"I already knew that Henry was a cruel, insensitive man," Simon said. "I'd watched him refuse to give a crippled pelican scraps from a fish he was cleaning. When I found out those copies of *Liberation* belonged to him, I knew he was capable of treason, at least. He killed Watkins because that gold coin linked him with Chavis's death, and Monahan because he might have seen him with Chavis the night he murdered him. He is absolutely amoral. His only perceived obligations are to his blood relatives."

"Thank goodness Clare's not involved," Julia said. "I really like her."

"Clare's visit to Pearlie Beach is a coincidence," Simon said. "The only real one in this entire case."

"So where did Watkins's money come from?"

"I'm just guessing," Simon said. "Remember when he told us all about the 'souvenirs' he brought back from Germany, and the Nazi officers who would do anything to save themselves directly after the war? The Germans had plundered Europe—it wouldn't be an exaggeration to say high-ranking Nazis, especially the Gestapo, might have pockets full of diamonds. After Watkins's will is probated, I would love to see the contents of those safe-deposit boxes he was always talking about. And this is just a theory, but I wouldn't be surprised if Henry helped him fence some of that stuff. That might explain why Watkins didn't turn Henry in right away."

"I've got to go," Viola said, emerging from the storeroom. "My chicken is soaking in grease back at my house."

"I'll take you," Julia said. "Then Simon and I will go on to the police station."

"Why don't you two join me for supper after you're done?" Viola said. "There's plenty."

"Sure," Julia said.

"I'd love to, a little later," Simon said. "First I want to find Dale Pearlie and get his permission to burn some old magazines."